CODE TO EXTINCTION

CHRISTOPHER CARTWRIGHT

Copyright © 2017 by Christopher Cartwright

This book is protected under the copyright laws of the United States of America. Any reproduction or other unauthorized use of the material or artwork herein is prohibited. This book is a work of fiction. Names, characters, places, brands, media and incidents either are the product of the author's imagination or are used fictitiously. All rights reserved.

PROLOGUE

―――――○☙○―――――

Oymyakon, Eastern Siberia — 20 Years Ago

THEY BURIED HIS mother under a bruised sunset of purple, red and ochre.

It had taken the better part of a week to dig the grave. A task made strenuous and painstakingly slow by the ground's constant state of permafrost. Through a process of lighting a bonfire, letting it burn for hours and then shifting the coals to the side, they were able to dig, inch by inch into the soil until the hole was finally big enough to hold the crude hewn coffin. When it was all done, they all went inside his father's log hut, and he was left all alone.

Ilya Yezhov stared at the raised mound of soil and snow where his mother now lay. It seemed like the pitiful evidence of a wretched life. His solemn blue-gray eyes, almost silver in the shade of the horizon, remained dry, but his throat felt the unfamiliar thickness of grief choking him. She was the only one who'd ever been kind to him and he would miss her. Oymyakon was a hard place to live, and his family had been dominated by hard men.

It was one of the coldest permanently inhabited locations on Earth.

Nestled into the bend of the Indigirka River, the village of Oymyakon translated to the words, *non-freezing-water,* in reference to a section of the river warmed by thermal pools where the fish spent the winter. Despite the local thermal pools, the village endured an extreme subarctic climate, competing with the town of Verkhoyansk for the title of coldest inhabited place on Earth. In 1933, the town recorded a temperature of minus ninety degrees Fahrenheit, the lowest officially recorded temperature in the Northern Hemisphere. Locked between the Verkhoyasnk Range in the north and the Stanovoy Range in the south — both peaking at nearly ten thousand feet — Oymyakon remained covered in snow all year round. In summer, days lasted twenty-one hours, and in winter, they were less than three.

Jobs were in short supply, with most of the five hundred odd villagers subsisting on reindeer-herding, hunting and ice-fishing for survival. Ilya's father was an exception. He labored in a diamond mine in neighboring Yakutsk, staying there to work for up to two months at a time, before coming home for a week, as he had recently, to help bury their mother. Tomorrow morning, he would leave them again.

Besides the obvious issues of remoteness, the cold itself forced the village to be a simple place with few conveniences. Cars were hard to start with frozen axle grease and fuel tanks, unused pipes could freeze within five hours, and batteries lose life at an alarming speed. Block heaters were used when the vehicles were turned off to keep the engines from freezing permanently. Electronics, including GPS, fail at anything below minus 35 degrees Fahrenheit. Thick fur coats, and multiple layers were a must, even to step outside for a few minutes.

His eyes swept the snow-covered landscape. The Indigirka River ran in a gradually southeastern direction. Frozen solid, large chunks of ice nearly ten feet high met the edge of the river, where natural hot water springs warmed the water until it flowed at a trickle. White mountains rose nearly to an altitude of 3,600 feet on opposite sides of the river, causing cold air to pool in the valley below, with Oymyakon freezing at its center.

A road of ice ran parallel to the river, and a thick forest of pine continued from the road to the bottom third of the mountains on either side of the river. The trees were twisted and dwarfed as their roots were unable to penetrate the permafrost. On the outside, the entire place looked wicked and cruel in its stark emptiness. A world God had forgotten.

But that was just an illusion.

In summer, the taiga forest, densely populated with stunted spruces, firs, pines and larch, provided a floor of grass, moss and lichen, where berries and mushrooms grew and reindeer flourished. In the nearby rivers, fish were plentiful. Below the inhospitable surface, the land was well endowed with raw materials. The soil contained large reserves of oil, gas, coal, diamonds, gold, silver, tin, tungsten and many other valuable gemstones. The nearby region of Sakha where his father worked produced ninety-nine percent of all Russian diamonds and over twenty-five percent of the diamonds mined in the world.

One day, he smiled, he would be rich—but first he would need to live that long.

At the age of twelve, with a diet of fish and reindeer, he was barely able to meet subsistence for nine months of the year. Ilya's growth had been stunted. A fact worsened by his older brother, Demyan, who at the age of fourteen had already reached puberty and was well on his way to becoming a strong man like his father.

And like his father, Demyan was quick to enter a fight and even faster to end it. They were only two years apart, but Ilya had never won a battle. One day, he swore, he would catch up, and when that happened he would be the toughest man in Oymyakon—then he would teach his big brother a lesson he'd never forget.

"Ilya!" Demyan shouted. "Come inside before you freeze to death."

He smiled. Until that day, he would answer to his brother.

"Yes, Demyan."

"Yes, Demyan." Resolve burned in his hazel eyes. Until that day, he would answer to his brother.

Ilya glanced at the pitiful remains of his mother's life and turned to go inside. He promised himself that his life wouldn't end here, his body lying sadly buried in a pathetically shallow grave. No, he would make something of his life. He would be different. He would be a rich and powerful man, feared by everyone around him.

"Goodbye mother," he murmured, then he turned and left.

It was late in the winter. The sun was starting to make its presence known on the edge of the horizon for short periods each day, after nearly four months of nearly permanent darkness. At three a.m. the sun was still far from rising.

Demyan Yezhov listened as his father prepared to leave the house in silence. They'd said their goodbyes last night. His father was due to return to the diamond mines in Yakutsk. It was dangerous work, but the money it provided made it worth it. Their risk of starvation without the income it provided was much greater than the chances of a mine disaster.

Through dark eyes — almost black with gold flakes, he watched his father leave.

It would be the last time he'd see him for the next month. Ever since he could remember, he'd been secretly waking so he could watch him walk out the door. It was somehow stranger this time around, now that his mother was gone. Demyan was head of the house — although that was a strong word for the small ten by ten-foot log hut they called their home — and now they were on their own.

It wasn't lost on him that in the harsh environment of Oymyakon any failure on his part would easily lead to their starvation or freezing to death well before his father came home.

His father had grown up in the tough snow-filled lands, and accepted death with the rare equanimity of a man with a strong belief in a future already written—his boys would survive, or they wouldn't.

He grinned. *This one would survive, even if he had to kill a neighboring household to do it.* Demyan was less confident of his little brother's survival. The kid was a runt. Tenacious and filled with a raw underlying violence in his eyes. If he made it to adulthood, his little brother would end up becoming an underground mine manager, like his dad—in a position of power over a lot of weaker men. He'd probably end up hurting a lot of people in the process. Demyan held his breath as he thought about it. His brother would most likely end up hurting the hell out of him, if he lived that long.

But they'd both have to live that long. His mind returned to the task at hand.

He'd promised his little brother he'd take him fishing today, in the new lake. Previously unfished, it was said to be full. Despite their differences, he'd never really wanted to hurt his little brother. He knew the kid had taken their mother's death the worst out of the whole family. She was probably the only person who'd ever shown him any kindness.

Demyan made a mental note to try and change that, although the simple fact in their village was that life was not kind, and the sooner Ilya learned to live with that, the better. Still, he wanted to make his life a little easier, and they needed to eat, so if the fish were indeed plentiful, it would be worth it. Let him forget their miserable existence and tomorrow they could both learn the true hardship of survival in their desolate and unforgiving land.

The door opened again and the solid outline of his father entered the room. He picked up a second duffel bag, one he hadn't used before. It was bigger and appeared full. Normally, everything he needed while at the mine was stored on site, so his luggage from home was generally negligible.

Demyan watched his father reach the door, only to stop and look directly at his open eyes in the dark. "You're awake. Good. I need to talk to you."

"Yes, father?" Demyan asked, obediently.

"You're now in charge. Do your best to keep Ilya alive. If you get into trouble, ask for help, the rest of our community will help."

"Yes."

"Good man. Next year you will be big enough to work in the mines. Maybe all three of us can move to Yakutsk. Would you like that?"

"Yes." The mines were notoriously dangerous, inside men died nearly every day, but until he worked in the mines, they would live permanently on the edge of famine. Demyan could think of worse directions for his life to take.

"Good." His father moved toward Ilya who appeared to still be asleep, and kissed him on the forehead in an uncommon show of fatherly affection. "Goodbye, my son. Obey your brother and he will look after you."

Demyan watched as Ilya squeezed his eyes shut. It was probably for the best. Neither of them quite knew how to take their father like this. Perhaps the death of their mother had somehow softened him.

He watched as his father left in silence.

The goods truck came by and picked up his father on its way to Yakutsk. He waited a full ten minutes in silence. Then removed his sleeping bag, crossed the floor of the single small room and opened the door a crack to look out. He watched the truck leave the Oymyakon village in darkness. Demyan closed the door and woke his brother.

Ilya opened his blue-gray eyes. "Has he left?"

Demyan nodded. "I watched the truck leave." He looked at

his little brother. The kid was a runt, but despite his frequent beatings, he was filled with a natural ability and a tendency to fight, that ran in his family. For all his faults, he had to give it to the kid, he was brave and tough to the point of stupidity. "Are you sure you still want to go see it?"

"The mysterious lake?" Ilya sat up, now wide awake. "Of course."

"Good. Then get your stuff together. It's a long walk and you know we're not supposed to know about it."

Ilya slipped out of his sleeping bag.

He pulled up the two layers of thick snow-pants and slipped his arms into a fur coat. Like most people in his village, his heavy coat was long, reaching all the way to his midcalf. Below which he wore boots made of reindeer leather, with the fur still on. He grabbed his fur hat and then wrapped layers of knitted scarves around the lower part of his face. He then rolled his heavy fur coverings from his bed, and placed them inside his large rucksack. A hunter's cabin they would use for shelter was a few miles short of the lake. They could stay there overnight and then fish tomorrow.

Demyan had already planned it out, including packing a small bag of food and cooking equipment. At times like this, he wondered why he and his brother fought at all. They both shared the ruthless will and defiant bravado of his father, even if his big brother had the physical size to back it up. They both knew people weren't supposed to know or talk about the new lake, because of its close proximity to Boot Lake. But he and his brother wouldn't listen to such nonsense. The lake was thawing and there were fish, so they would go and see it.

The lake had formed below an old ice field, twenty miles to the south-east of Oymyakon's village. It was once used by the Alaska-Siberian air route as an airfield during World War II as a stepping stone to ferry American Lend-Lease aircraft to the Eastern Front. Now, part of the icy ground below had melted, making way for a large lake. The surface of which was still frozen solid, but below the ice, there was talk of a massive labyrinth of warm water, filled with fish.

The lake had appeared a few months ago, thawing during the start of winter as if by magic. Ilya had no superstitious doubt about where the lake had come from. It was clearly caused by a recent shift in the Earth which leaked hot water from deep thermal springs far below. His father had talked about these ancient moving plates on which the Earth rested like a house on its piers. It was how the hot springs formed near Oymyakon, and without them, their village would have perished years ago.

His mind turned to his father down the mine shafts. He'd once said that it was the movement of these plates that caused tremblors and mini-Earthquakes that were unable to be felt on the surface, but catastrophic to those down in the mines.

Oymyakon had plenty of such hot water pools. There was nothing mysterious about it. The thermal springs would spurt boiling water to the surface, thawing the ice, and making it warm enough for fish to survive all year round. If there was water, there would be fish, and he was hungry. Always hungry. So, he was excited to go to Lake Mysterious, as they had decided to call it.

It was midday by the time they reached the peak of a three-hundred-foot hill and stared down at the western edge of Boot Lake. The entire lake was approximately ten miles long from north to south and somewhere between two and five miles wide at varying parts, in such a way that it appeared to form the shape of a giant boot made of ice, superimposed on a sea of snow. The entire thing was angled downward, and a little askew. At the back of the field of ice were two smaller lakes that formed the shape of the heel. Two-thirds of the way up, an outcrop of dark igneous rock jutted out from the ice to form an island, almost in the shape of a boot buckle.

The rocky island jutted out of the ice in sheer walls of vertical stone, at least fifty feet high. On the top of which, were two man-made structures. One was an older building made of thick concrete with a heavy dome on top, from which multiple modern antennas protruded. To Ilya, the structure looked sinister, like some sort of old prison—a remnant of Stalin's Death Camps—although no one in his village or elsewhere had ever been able to tell him what the island had once been used for. He had no doubt the building was just the tip of the iceberg, and that a series of hollowed out stone tunnels, penetrated deeply into the stone below, where he had no doubt, many men had once lost their lives.

To its right was the second man-made structure. This one much more modern. Its construction was completed nearly two years ago, and it was supposedly used for the sole purpose of producing the world's largest geothermal power station.

In the distance behind it, right there in the middle of the lake, a cooling tower rose out of the sheet of ice, nearly seven hundred feet into the air and over a hundred feet long in a wide hyperboloid shape. They said the station was going to power all of eastern Siberia and most of the heavily populated west, too. But that was all some bullshit story. It had been running for two years and there still weren't even any powerlines running out from it. In fact, although steam rose from its crest, there was no sign of where the power could have possibly been going—yet still, like some sinister neighbor, the monster seemed alive, and continued to breathe dark clouds of steam into the skies.

The lake remained frozen all year round, but the fishing used to be good in summer. The mysterious lake was somewhere on the other side of it. It would take six or more hours to go around the boot-shaped lake, but they could cross it in under an hour— that was, if it were still possible.

Everyone knew that the story of it being an enormous nuclear power plant was just a cover, one of their mother Russia's many disinformation campaigns. Ilya just couldn't understand why they hadn't tried to hide it any better. There was no doubt in his mind what it was, and he was still a kid—it was a secret military installation.

A big fence went up right around the damned lake, too. A road was built around it and heavily patrolled during construction, but all of that had mostly ceased, since. After all, why bother? The location was secure enough in itself. No one could get there, except on foot, and those who could were too cold to do anything destructive. Ilya and Demyan stumbled their way down the hill and approached the lake's edge.

Ilya stopped at the fence.

A reindeer must have taken offense to the barbed wire fence, because there was now a small hole in it. Not big, but enough for the two of them to squeeze through.

"Do you want to take a shortcut?" he asked, out of bravado more than desire.

Demyan wasn't to be provoked into stupidity. "No. We'll go around. We're not supposed to even know about the mysterious new lake, let alone if it's guarded. We're better off not getting spotted before we even get there."

Ilya felt that he'd achieved one rung above his brother on the bravery ladder, but knew better than to mention it. Instead, the two of them followed the service trail as it wrapped its way around the shore of Boot Lake.

It took them until the late afternoon to reach the empty hunter's hut toward the southern end of the lake. They stayed there overnight and in the morning continued along the service trail, toward the far end of the lake.

Now on the eastern side of Boot Lake, Ilya glanced back at the old island in the middle of the sea of ice. There were no windows on the old stone prison, but somehow, he felt as though he was being watched. He'd been told since he was a kid to stay away from the place, because it was haunted by the ghosts of those who'd been imprisoned there during the reign of Stalin's Death

Camps. Ilya was old enough to know that haunted islands are nothing more than stories to frighten children, and yet he'd never heard of anyone ever going anywhere near it.

He turned to face his brother. "Do you think they can see us?"

"I doubt it. If they could, we'd probably already see one of their patrol cars on its way to intercept us." Demyan turned to the east. "Come on, the old airstrip and strange new lake isn't far now. I want to catch some fish and get back to the hut before we freeze to death."

Ilya nodded and followed him across the snow-covered hills to the east. He felt uneasy with his back to the strange island behind him, as though some sort of evil predator was watching him. He shook the fear off, but kept glancing over his shoulder as though he might catch something or someone.

Thirty minutes later, they reached the mysterious new lake.

It was approximately a mile wide by another three in length. There was very little to identify it as anything other than the remains of the old, World War II era, landing strip made out of thick ice.

Ilya just stared at it. "We've been had, haven't we?"

"I don't know," Demyan replied, his eyes sweeping the entire area for signs of ice thinning. His eyes stopped at a small section toward the southern end of the field, where the icy ground had dipped, and some parts had collapsed. His lips turned upward into a smile. "There! I'd say that's the remnants of the thin ice collapsing."

"You think there's a hot spring below?"

"Must be! But there's only one way to find out for certain. Let's go check it out."

Demyan stepped onto the ice.

His eyes swept the entire frozen lake. There were no cracks

or breaks in the surface ahead of him and no flowing water at its edge. He made a mental note to stay clear of the southern end, where the hard surface of the ice appeared to dip and a small patch of white ice spread over several feet—a sign the ice had recently thawed and then refrozen, making it highly unstable.

His boots tentatively crunched into the hard ice at the edge of the lake—often the most dangerous part to walk on any frozen lake. Ice near the shore is weakest. The shifting, expansion and buckling action of the lake or stream over the winter continually breaks and refreezes ice along the shoreline.

The surface underneath his feet was solid.

He took another step, followed by a number of small, slow steps toward the middle of the lake. After crossing thousands of frozen lakes and rivers he'd developed the intrinsic knowledge of what ice would hold his weight and what wouldn't. His senses were specifically attuned to such knowledge. A skill grown over his relatively short lifetime in the harsh, Siberian landscape. Despite his confidence, his nerves were on edge, as he strained to hear the sharp snapping of ice. His center of balance told him the ground wasn't moving even an inch.

A third of the way across the frozen lake, he stopped and dropped his rucksack on the ground.

"What do you think?" Ilya asked.

"I think there's only one way to find out if there are fish."

He withdrew an axe and started chipping away a six-inch-wide by eight-inch-long hole into the ice. It was a slow process, but he'd done that, too, a thousand times before.

The ice was thick, more than a foot in total.

Demyan could have kept going, but it would have meant widening the opening, and that would have increased their risk of falling through. He glanced at his little brother, whose face betrayed his eagerness and naïve willingness to take risks.

"Do you want me to try?" Ilya asked.

Demyan shook his head and picked up the axe. "Don't worry about it. We'll head farther toward the middle. The ice is always thinner as it approaches the center. Trust me, there'll be plenty of water in there."

"You think?"

"Yeah. Look at all those air bubbles. There's flowing water down there and that means fish."

They both glanced into the hole.

Water was easily visible just below the ice. It had a soft prism of red, yellow and blue. There was something unusual about that in itself. In ice, the absorption of light at the red end of the spectrum is six times greater than at the blue end. As a consequence, the ice surrounding every other opening he'd ever made for ice-fishing had always appeared blue.

Demyan was about to make a comment about the strange prism of color, but a swift movement from down below the surface of the ice, interrupted his thoughts. A large fish swam by, providing a dark silhouette from the light below.

"Whoa!" Ilya's grin was visible beneath his thick woven scarf. "Did you see that fish!"

Demyan smiled. "That's got to be a Hucho Taimen!"

He felt his heart race and forced himself to breathe slowly. A fish like that could be over two hundred pounds. Catching it would go a long way to providing for both of them throughout the last of the winter, into early spring.

Hucho Taimen were normally found in fresh water. They preferred cold flowing water over a stony or gravel bottom and never migrated to sea. It was extremely good luck to find one trapped in a lake.

"Come with me, quickly," Demyan said.

He picked up his rucksack and ran across the ice toward the middle of the lake, in the same direction the Taimen had swum—without stopping for one second to ask why the fish should cast a shadow on the underside of the ice.

Instead, he ran at full speed across the ice with the axe in his hand. As the ice thinned he began to be able to spot the dark outline of the massive fish, which formed a strange shadow in an otherwise light-filled lake. His chest was pounding as he sucked in the subzero air. Demyan swore out loud. If it took them a week to catch, they were going to drag the fish out of its frozen prison.

He stopped somewhere in the middle of the lake and immediately started slamming the head of the axe into the ice. It sent hundreds of shards of ice splintering out around them. Below the rapidly thinning ice, he noticed the fish turn around in one giant arc and swim toward the opening he was trying to create.

"Get the Mormyshka out! Quick!"

Beside him, Ilya worked quickly to set up the fishing line and lure, known as a Mormyshka. It was named after the Russian word, *mormysh,* which meant freshwater shrimp. It consisted of a metallic head made of tungsten with a small piece of gold given to them by their father and soldered onto the back of the tungsten, along with a hook. In the stagnant environment beneath the ice, fish would spot the sparkle of the gold and take a bite.

Demyan's axe finally pierced the bottom layer of ice, into the thawed water below. The monstrous fish, swung round again, curious and interested in the sudden change to its protected environment.

"Holy shit!" He turned to his brother. "He's coming back!"

Ilya fed the line through the small hole of the tungsten and handed it to him. "Here."

"Forget the Mormyshka, just pass me the hook. I'm going to snatch this monster the next time it comes around for another pass!"

Ilya handed him the fishhook. "Here."

Demyan drove the axe as hard as he could against the remaining sheet of ice at the bottom of the hole he'd dug. In his haste, he'd carved a much larger hole in the ice than he'd meant to. It was closer to ten or twelve inches wide by an equal length.

The fish snapped around, toward the opening. An ancient predator at the top of the food chain inside the confines of the frozen lake, the creature swam to the opening, unable to grasp the risk that it might not be the deadliest beast in existence.

The predator reached the surface of the opening Demyan had created. Its giant mouth opened, ready to feed on whatever it discovered, and Demyan ran the large fish hook through the side of its body, and pulled.

The Hucho Taimen weighed more than he expected. At least two hundred pounds. More than he could pull out of the hole without his brother's help. The problem was that it would place more weight on the precariously thin ice than it could take.

Demyan racked his brain, trying to come up with a solution before he lost the best catch of his life. Something that might just keep him and his brother from starving to death.

An instant later, the damned fish turned its head, as though no longer interested in whatever it had found in the outside world, and simply dipped back into the icy water and disappeared.

Demyan ran his gloved palms across his forehead and cursed loudly. They'd lost the fish, and by the looks of things, it wouldn't be coming back any time soon.

He and Ilya glanced down into the opening. Like the previous one he'd made, the ice appeared to reflect a prism of reds, yellows, and blues.

"What the hell is that?" Demyan asked.

Ilya carefully stepped closer. "I have no idea."

Demyan stared at the clear waters of the freezing world

beneath the ice. What stared back up at him, made him instantly forget about the loss of the fish.

An eerie glow distorted his vision. He blinked and he started to make out a series of shapes and colors he'd never seen before. Something moved from below the ice. It was too big to be a fish. Too fast to be anything human. It glowed with a radiant color of the morning sun, and then it was gone. In its place, the water was clear enough now, that Demyan could make sense of what he was seeing.

A strange city, filled with refractory metallic structures he'd never seen before, in books or anywhere else — like crystals set at unique angles and fractals, jutting out like a giant city of another world. A world filled with fractals and prismatic crystals.

Ilya took a deep breath. "What the hell is that?"

"Beats me." Demyan remained staring at the strange city, entranced, as though he'd just witnessed the opening of a gateway to another world. He swallowed hard. "But whatever it is, I'm certain we're not supposed to find out!"

He took a step back. There was nothing specifically to be frightened of from down beneath the ice — certainly nothing that could swim out of the freezing water and attack him — but he still felt the instinctive need to place some sort of distance between him and the opening. That ancient part of his brain that had developed out of necessity to predict danger, was acutely aware of his entire surroundings.

His pupils dilated, and his vision widened. His heart pounded and chest burned. Adrenalin surged through his body, giving him the superhuman strength required to fight or run from his predator.

Ilya kept his feet planted where they were on the edge of the opening in the ice. His eyes fixed on the strange city, and his lips curled in the tight smile of a man who knew he was witnessing the most extraordinary event of his life.

Demyan took his eyes off the opening and swept their surrounding landscape. The surface of ice remained solid throughout the lake. The edge met an area of at least a hundred feet of snow-covered hills, before a forest of stunted pine and spruce trees blocked his vision. Their environment was silent. He could hear the sound of his heart pounding in his ears, and his breath crystalized in front of him — before everything changed.

A beam of light shot up through the opening in the ice. It sent a glow hundreds of feet into the gray and somber sky. Simultaneously, an old air-raid siren started to wail.

His head snapped to the right, where half a mile away, a white military truck came charging out of the ground beyond the tree line.

Demyan yelled, "Run!"

Ilya turned and ran.

Behind him, the siren kept wailing. He kept running. He'd never seen that type of armored truck before, but he'd heard about it and his brother had previously mentioned that the occasional one had been spotted near Boot Lake. The VPK-3927 Volk was legendary in Russia. Designed as a tactical high-mobility multipurpose military armored vehicle, it was renowned as a legend among Russia's armored division.

But why was it even here?

One thing was certain, such a truck was unlikely to have a legitimate purpose for guarding a nuclear power station in the remote wilderness of Oymyakon. And it certainly wasn't approaching them for anything positive.

They headed toward the frozen bank of Boot Lake. It would be impossible to outpace their pursuers, but if they could reach it they might be able to cut across it.

It took ten minutes exactly to reach the barbed wire fence

along the eastern edge of the Boot Lake. Ilya glanced over his right shoulder. The massive VPK-3927 Volk, rounded the bend and drove straight toward them.

He hacked at the fence with his axe. It took a few strikes and part of the fence broke apart. He pulled at it with his hands, and the gap opened large enough for him to squeeze through. "Come on! Let's cross the lake."

Demyan looked over his shoulder. Their pursuers were driving hard in the snow-covered truck. There were no longer any other options. "All right."

Having squeezed through the narrow opening Ilya and his brother started to run across the frozen lake. It was only a little over a mile wide where they were crossing and nearly twenty for the truck to get around the lake following the service trail. If they could reach the opposite side before their pursuers, they could flee into the snow-covered forest, where it would be impossible for the truck to follow — they just had to reach the other side in time.

About half a mile across, Ilya allowed himself to glance back across the lake. The Volk was traveling fast, making good time around the lake, but there was no way it was going to reach the other side before either of them.

He grinned. His heart pounded and his chest burned, but he felt amazing. A certain euphoria was rising quickly, as he realized they were going to make it. They'd lost the fish, but they were going to live. Having gained nothing, he was now far better off than he could have ever wanted to be. They would go hungry, but the experience had somehow brought him closer to his brother than he would have ever predicted — they were both tough men, and they would survive.

Ilya heard the shattering of thin ice, and instantly knew its cause. His euphoria was immediately replaced by fear as a sharp crack echoed away from his feet. Instinctively, he threw himself flat as the ice disintegrated under his weight. Panic gripped him as his hands slipped away from the ice and the icy water took his breath away.

His head dipped under.

The bite of the icy water was fleeting. Instead, the pain was replaced by the terror of drowning. Growing up in Oymyakon, neither he or Demyan had ever learned to swim. Controlling his fear, Ilya concentrated on trying to achieve some form of coordinated movements with his arms to pull himself to the surface. He cupped his hands and pulled the water from above downward, as though he was climbing an invisible ladder.

It was a cumbersome movement. One that produced a disjointed and fragmented progress, but eventually his head broached the icy surface.

His eyes swept the surface. An area of several feet had shattered and he was surrounded by icy water. His head dipped under again, and he fought to pull his mouth above the water again. On the third go, he spotted Demyan at the edge of the ice, lying prone, reaching out with his arm.

"Grab my hand!" Demyan shouted, his green eyes fixed with terror.

Ilya didn't have the breath to respond.

His head dipped under again, and again. Each time he kicked and fought to reach the surface. It was a painfully slow process, and with each subsequent dip, he sunk deeper and struggled harder to reach the surface, as his heavy clothes gathered weight from soaking through with water.

Something kept dragging him downward. By the time he realized it was his fur boots that had become heavy weights under the water, he no longer had the strength to do anything about it. He tried, but his hands couldn't even reach the latches, and instead, he concentrated his remaining efforts on reaching the surface.

His brother was shouting at him, but he could no longer hear the words and even if he had, his brain was now so starved of oxygen that he would have had trouble interpreting them. He spotted Demyan's face one last time. The terror seen a few minutes earlier had already been replaced by something different, something entirely more painful—a profound and despondent loss—and dishonorable shame.

Ilya wanted to tell his brother it was okay. There was nothing he could have done. Neither of them could swim. But he couldn't seem to get to the surface. And even if he could make it one more time, he'd never have the breath to produce words.

Fatigue and hypothermia kicked in and fear was replaced with a simple feeling of regret and loss. They say on your deathbed you eventually reach acceptance, but that wasn't the case for him. Instead, he just felt the harrowing torment that he had never escaped Oymyakon.

His burning lungs settled, and he no longer felt the urge to take a breath. Everything slowed. His failing heart eased into a progressively slower rate. His vision turned into a strange purple blur. *That was unexpected,* he thought with surprising curiosity, no one had ever told him about seeing purple before you die. The muscles in his arms and legs jolted, as he vaguely attempted to continue to move them until they simply stopped working.

Ilya heard the final beats of his heart pounding in his water-soaked ears. He heard the very last one, and waited for another… but it never seemed to come.

Every muscle in his body went limp.

Paralyzed, he retreated into the deep subconscious branches of his rapidly deteriorating mind. With the heart stopped and his brain starved of oxygen, he knew it wouldn't be long now.

The pains he'd lived with for most of his life had finally ended. They hadn't been replaced by any sense of euphoria, but the loss of pain was a comfort.

So, this is death.

A calm peace and clarity swept his mind, in a way he'd never experienced in life. Fear and loss disappeared and at last there was acceptance.

This is not too bad…

A split second later, something gripped his leg and yanked. It pulled him downward with the ferocity of an ancient predator. And Ilya retreated into the final branch of his subconscious, where total darkness finally swept him away.

Demyan watched bitterly as his brother disappeared into the icy waters below. At the last moment, the water turned a fluorescent purple, and a strange creature—that looked remarkably similar to a merman—took Ilya, and dragged him deep into the lake.

Unable to grasp what his eyes had seen, the shock stirred some inner desire to survive. There was nothing he could do to save his brother, even if he'd been taken by some mysterious creature from the lake's icy depths. He turned toward the south and spotted the Volk. It was still far away, but getting closer. There was time, but not a lot of it. He might still just make it into the forest.

He glanced at the now dark water below, where he'd lost his brother and cursed Oymyakon and the wretched world that took his mother and brother in the same week. Fear finally broke through the shock and despair as he forced himself to run toward the western edge of the forest.

On the western bank of Boot Lake, he hacked at the fence—cutting through with the third hit—and kept running up the steep slope into the dense forest of spruce.

Behind him, he heard the Volk's massive engine whine as it tried to follow his trail up the slope, followed by the sound of soldiers climbing out and running after him. Demyan was big and at the age of fourteen, was already larger than most adult men in his village. A life of hardship had sharpened his body with the endurance of a professional athlete. Adrenalin surged through his veins and he kept running.

Soon the distant sounds of his pursuers, unused to and ill-prepared for the inhospitable environment, quietened and eventually disappeared.

It didn't slow him down. Instead, he continued running all the way back to his family home. As it became apparent the soldiers were no longer following him, Demyan's mind returned to the loss of his brother and the mysterious purple creature that took him to his death. Fleeting thoughts of despair and wonder distracted him from his burning thighs and slowly numbing toes.

Guilt tore at his soul, and he wondered how he could possibly face his father. He even considered grabbing whatever possessions he could carry and leaving Oymyakon before his dad came home from the mines. That was a coward's path, but he couldn't see any other way out of it.

Demyan never stopped to look over his shoulder. He didn't have to. If they had kept up with him, and followed him, there was nowhere else for him to go. It was early evening by the time he ran down the main road of his village, and stopped just short of his house.

There, someone was waiting for him.

An older man, in a thick fur coat, standing in front of the wooden cottage glanced at him expectantly. *Demyan swallowed hard. Surely, they didn't know where he lived?* His face had been mostly covered the entire time. His eyes swept the rest of the Oymyakon village, deciding whether he still had time to make a run for it—head back into the forest and disappear into the Siberian wilderness where few people could survive more than a few hours in winter.

No. He simply didn't have the strength to run anymore. Demyan decided to face his consequences and be damned.

He stepped forward toward his home.

The man's cold, hard eyes fixed on his. "Would you be Demyan Yezhov?"

It was a relief to give in and stop running. "Yes, sir."

"I'm sorry to tell you this, Mr. Yezhov, but there was an accident at the Yakutsk diamond mine today. Your father was down below at the time. He didn't make it to the surface. I'm really sorry."

It took Demyan a moment to contemplate the news. His father was dead. He was now entirely on his own in the world. A week ago, his family consisted of a proud and violent father, a younger brother who often had a right to hate him, and a mother who he hated for not getting them out of their wretched world. It wasn't a lot, but it was his family, and now he'd lost them all.

He knew he should have felt nothing but grief and loneliness, but as the words sunk in, he felt a different emotion rise vigorously to the surface. There should have been guilt, too — why did he survive when his entire family didn't? — but there wasn't.

Instead, he felt relief. Now he didn't have to face his father and tell him that Ilya had drowned and there was nothing he could do to help him. With time he would feel remorse, but for now, all he could feel was the rush of survival.

Demyan looked at the stranger's face. "Do you want to come in for a tea?"

"Sure," the stranger acknowledged.

Demyan lit the oil heater and poured a glass of Russki chai — AKA, straight vodka.

The stranger accepted the glass and said, "To your father."

Demyan looked at his glass. "To my father."

And both men drank the entire contents of the glass in one gulp.

"I'm so very sorry. It was a terrible accident. But your father did work down the mines."

Demyan nodded. "I know. It was always dangerous."

The stranger held out his hand. "My name's Leo Botkin."

Demyan took it. "My father's mentioned you before. You own the mine, don't you?"

"Yes."

"What are you doing here, Mr. Botkin?"

"I knew your father well." Botkin shrugged, as though he personally handled the visits to all the families of his mine when someone died. "He was a good man. Hard, but fair. He did a lot of good for the company. He will be missed."

"Thank you," Demyan said, and he meant it. "It's more than I expected, and I'm sure my father would have appreciated it."

"There's another reason I wanted to come in person, too."

"Yes?"

"Your father told me of your recent loss of your mother. He was a conscientious man, and has been paying into a company insurance fund for years. It's not a lot but it should help you and your brother out, until you're old enough to find jobs. I wanted to deliver it to you, personally."

"My father left money for my brother and I?" Demyan asked, without admitting that he'd lost his brother today, too.

"Yes." Botkin handed him a receipt. "This has been deposited into the Yakutsk branch of the Bank of Russia, under your name. You're to use it wisely to better the lives of you and your brother. If your family needs anything else, I have left you with a contact number for me, personally."

"That's very kind of you, sir."

Demyan unfolded the receipt. There in front of him was the deposit receipt to an account in his name, for five million rubles—the equivalent of a hundred thousand U.S. dollars.

He looked at Botkin. "Is this for real?"

"Yes. Your father worked hard to ensure that you and your brother would have a good life."

"Thank you."

"Don't thank me. It was simply an insurance policy your father took out on your behalf. Many of my workers do the same."

Demyan smiled at the lie. No one working in the Yakutsk diamond mine could afford to take out such an extravagant policy. He wondered what his father could possibly have been involved in to provide so much money. "All the same, I must thank you for coming all this way to deliver it."

"You're welcome. Is there anything else I can do for you?"

"No."

"All right. I'm sorry for your loss."

Demyan watched as Leo Botkin, the bearer of his great fortune and misfortune, left. He looked at the sorry log hut that a week earlier was considered the home of all four members of his family. Now he was all that was left. *Well, I'm not going to die here.* He packed what few possessions he had into a small rucksack.

When the goods truck came the next morning, he hitched a ride to Yakutsk and from there a flight to Moscow.

His mind was sharp and he was already stronger than most adults. He was now rich. He would survive, and he would make something of his life — someone in his family needed to get out of Oymyakon.

He would leave and never think about the family he'd lost, or his village again.

CHAPTER ONE
————O&3O————

Tepui Mountains, Amazon Jungle, Venezuela — Present Day

The Sikorsky UH-60 Black Hawk banked hard as it rounded one of the fortress-like giant stones that rose from the dark green canopy of the jungle. It crossed the rocky tabletop mountain in almost absolute silence, before dipping its nose and descending the steep sandstone cliffs into the ancient valley below. The nose was soon brought to level, and its angular, radar-disrupting fuselage, heavily modified for stealth, skimmed the tips of the dense forest canopy as it raced by at sixty knots.

Inside, Dr. Billie Swan peered into the inky blackness. Her face displayed all the signs of a person who hadn't slept much in the past 24 hours. Despite that, her intelligent hazel eyes appeared sharp and focused. The dark of the moonless night shrouded the most stunning and potentially deadly landscape as it shot past them. Hundreds of feet of sheer sandstone cliffs, topped with dense jungle foliage, and torrents of water dropping over the edges of the tabletops into pools below — all hid one of the world's oldest and most mysterious cave systems, carved from quartz sandstone.

In the cockpit, wearing military grade night-vision goggles, were Sam Reilly and Tom Bower. Billie smiled at the image. The two men made an unlikely pair. Sam was shorter and stocky, while Tom was tall... and even broader in the shoulders. Both had been good friends since childhood. Both had spent time in the U.S. military as helicopter pilots, before Sam took over the salvage branch of his father's shipping company, bringing Tom with him.

Her lips formed the crest of a half-smile as she watched Tom at the controls. It required constant minor and major adjustments of the three major controls. The collective pitch, cyclic pitch and the antitorque pedals moved in one constantly changing triangle. Despite the complex task, he looked more like someone out for an evening date in a sports car. In this case, the sports car was an experimental, nearly silent, stealth helicopter, worth millions of dollars, on loan from the U.S. Defense Department.

She had dated him for a while. If things had been different, she might have even married him. But things weren't different. Like her grandfather before her, she had dedicated her life to finding the remnants of an ancient race, nicknamed the Master Builders. That life didn't leave a lot of time for relationships. She could live with that. She'd always seen herself as her own master. Besides, Tom was now dating Genevieve, and he seemed happy.

Everyone was still waiting for there to be conflict between her and Genevieve now that she was back, and they were working closely together. It never happened. Never would. Billie never understood jealousy. She'd made the decision to leave Tom to find the Master Builders. By the time she came back, he was with someone else. No harm, no foul. Besides, she liked Genevieve. She had that sort of assertive, hard ass personality that didn't take shit from anyone. Her personality was backed up by the fact that she'd spent many of her younger years as an enforcer in the Russian Mafia. Genevieve kind of reminded her of Geena Davis in that nineties movie, *The Long Kiss Goodnight*.

Tom swore and banked hard.

Billie's head snapped around toward the cockpit windshield. The Black Hawk banked at a ninety-degree angle and narrowly slipped past another giant pillar of stone. Tom audibly thanked divine providence and the Northrop Grumman Corporation for the cockpit upgrade that simplified his instrument panel into a few multi-functional flat-panel displays that alerted him to the close encounter.

Sam just grinned, as though he'd come along for the ride.

It was another day in the office. The Sikorsky UH-60 Black Hawk was ideal for their current mission deep into the Amazon jungle. Equipped with stealth technology, the bird's illegal route across two borders and into Venezuela was untraceable by radar or any other tracking method.

They were flying low and dangerously. Though that phrase was relative when the surface was already an alpine valley some 7000 feet in elevation above sea level. Billie decided it was best not to know how close they were to death, and turned her head to face the other members of the team in the back of the Black Hawk.

Veyron Blanc, Sam's chief engineer, sat opposite her. He made a practiced smile, full of teeth, and a knowing look in reference to their near-death experience. "It's good to be back working with Sam again, isn't it?"

"I'll let you know if we survive." Billie cursed, and then said, "If I could have done this without him, I would have."

Veyron nodded, as though he was enjoying her discomfort.

She'd had a love-hate relationship with Sam for many years now, in their combined search for the Master Builders. There was plenty of respect for him professionally and no interest romantically. Where they clashed often stemmed from their expertise. They were both used to being in charge of any situation. Like the age-old saying goes, you can't have two chefs in one kitchen. She didn't like being anyone's subordinate, even when the pay was good. She was good at what she did, and expected everyone around her to keep up. Sometimes, that need manifested in the form of being a bitch, which had made her highly unpopular at times.

Next to Veyron sat Elise. She was the youngest in their crew. Somewhere around her mid-twenties at a guess, and probably the smartest of the lot of them. She was a computer expert, who provided Sam with access to anything he required—legal or otherwise. Rumor had it, she once worked for the CIA as a hacker. When she lost interest in the job, and the government was less than keen to release someone with her knowledge and skills back into civilian society, Elise hacked into the U.S. Vital Records office and created a new identity for herself.

At the back of the cabin, Genevieve rested in her seat, sleeping. Practicing one of those old battle mottos, *rest when you can*.

The only person missing from Sam's eclectic team of experts was Matthew Sutherland, the master of his salvage vessel, the *Maria Helena*, who stayed behind to ensure they had a ship to return to in the Caribbean Sea, to the north of Venezuela.

Everyone aboard the chopper would have preferred to see what they knew was spectacular scenery below, but the mission required utmost secrecy. Hence the perilous 3 a.m. flight to the top of one of northern Brazil's Tepui Mountains, that left them dodging the vast towers.

Three months ago, Billie had been rescued by Sam and his team from the Amazon jungle. She, along with the entire Pirahã tribe, had spent nearly two years enslaved by the Master Builders. She still didn't quite accept the term enslaved. Instead, she considered it more of an empowerment. A thick, black smoke would come for them along the banks of the Maici River. It would fill them with joy, and wonder, and strength, and then they would be taken somewhere to construct a new temple, in perfect harmony with one another for months at a time.

When a section of the temple was complete, they would all be returned. Although she couldn't recollect what she had done or where it had taken place, she was always filled with a tremendous sense of achievement. As though she'd taken part in something far greater and more important than her mere life. Of course, she had since learned that the black smoke was a strong hallucinogen that shared similar properties to the drug LSD. The drug tapped into an undeveloped and primitive part of her brain to allow a form of communication similar to telepathy. Only, instead of being told what to do, the entire group of workers would simultaneously act as one entity.

Ever since she'd been rescued, Billie had frequent thoughts, images, and sensations occur in her sleep. Too real to be the dreams of a restless mind, they seemed more like flashbacks. She recalled long hours of physical labor, indigenous people, thick smoke, and the smell of the mysterious hallucinogen used to obtain her cooperation to help build a new temple. Awake, she had no recollection of that temple or the location, but she'd known it was buried deep in her subconscious. In secret, and hardly daring to believe the parlor game could provide a clue, she'd used automatic writing to draw a map.

But all she could come up with was a series of mountains that didn't match any known locations anywhere near the Maici River. As the days went on the dreams became more vivid, she knew she had to get back. There was something vitally important she had to do, but couldn't for the life of her remember what it was.

That's when Sam Reilly contacted her and showed her the image of the four stones found inside the megalithic Death Stone discovered in Göbekli Tepe. The instant she saw the strange Greek letters of Theta, Sigma, Phi, and Omega branded below each of the Four Horsemen of the Apocalypse, and she knew where she'd seen the image before. Inside the King's Chamber of the newly constructed temple.

With the cataclysmic event prophesied by the Death Stone fast approaching, she contacted Elise, who scanned the strange images she'd drawn and uploaded them into a huge database of satellite images. A few minutes later, Elise had shown her the Tepui Mountains, and it had all flooded back to her, as though she were reliving a waking dream.

She breathed heavily at the image in front of them. Even in the dark, she recognized the steep cliff line as the one from her dream—but dreams can be mistaken.

"We're here. Wherever the hell here is," Tom said, as he brought the Black Hawk into a hover directly over the coordinates.

They'd all find out soon enough. Night-vision goggles made out tree-tops and tangled vines below. There was no place to land.

Sam said, "I saw a clearing a couple clicks back. See if you can find anything closer. A clearing or even the beach along a stream."

Tom nodded and flew concentric circles over the edge of the mesa. That side wouldn't do. About two miles from the edge, an outcrop presented them with a landing spot clear of trees. They'd have to hike.

Leaving Veyron to hold down the fort with a U.S. military grade M134D Gatling gun and no expectation of using it, the others set out on their two-mile hike to the edge of the mesa. Billie's coordinates were for somewhere 100 feet below.

In addition to their night-vision goggles, each of the five carried military grade respirator masks, personal climbing equipment, and Heckler & Koch MP5 submachine guns. Each also carried a Ka-Bar knife and various non-lethal weapons according to their expertise.

Sam took the lead on the hike, simply following a handheld GPS, with Billie, Tom and Elise following and Genevieve covering their six. The density of the vegetation required they stay close together. There was no trail, or rather, there were many. Small and large animal trails, tiny rivulets and wider streams all crisscrossed in confusing chaos. For so many, they made surprisingly little noise. Every member of the expedition was trained, proficient with their weapons and in some cases in unarmed combat.

Sam came to an abrupt halt, holding up his hand in a cautionary signal. The others stopped in their tracks.

"We're here," he said in a near-whisper. "Billie, now what?"

Billie said, "All right. Follow me."

A large boulder the size of a small van stood twenty feet back from the edge of the sandstone tabletop. She swept the boulder with the beam of her flashlight. Halfway up, the light reflected something metallic.

There were two large PFH ninety degree climbing bolt plates fixed to the stone. They had been professionally inserted, and designed to hold weights far exceeding the strength of their static abseiling ropes, which were rated to take up to 3600 pounds. The ground between the boulder and the edge of the cliff was well worn, as though hundreds of people had abseiled the spot many times previously.

Three hundred feet of static abseiling ropes were threaded through the bolt hold and secured, while the other ends were dropped over the edge. Two sets of ropes, five people. They would need to take it in turns.

Billie clipped her descender onto the rope, and attached the other end to her carabiner. Sam connected onto the second line, and both cross-checked each other's equipment.

Sam asked, "Are you ready to return to the temple?"

Billie pulled her night-vision goggles over her eyes and grinned. "I was born ready."

A moment later, she dropped off the edge of the sandstone cliff-face, and descended into the secret world, far below.

CHAPTER TWO

BILLIE FELT CONFIDENT as she abseiled quickly down the vertical cliff-face. If there were other climbers out there, they might have thought the expedition had taken a distinctly creepy direction. It resembled a military operation, carried out by Special Forces. But instead, it was privately funded by Sam, who had high standards when it came to people with whom he was prepared to risk his life. The three others who were with them tonight were his top choices from everyone else in the world, Special Forces included.

The black rope ran quickly through her descender.

Two thirds of the way down the rope, Billie locked pressure on the anchor and came to a sudden stop. She glanced at the rope. The blue marker indicated she'd dropped a little less than two hundred feet. She had no idea at what point the entrance was, but felt certain she would simply recognize it when she saw it.

Next to her, Sam stopped, silently.

He leaned out, to get a better view of the entrance, although she doubted very much that he would have spotted it. What appeared to be a single piece of sandstone arenite that ran the full length of the face of the Tepui Mountains, now had a cluster of three smaller fragments — two twenty feet high and one a little under ten.

They were thin. A foot wide at most. A fissure no more than a few inches wide, ran behind the stones and was definitely not big enough for even the smallest in their party to slip through. From the front and the sides, it all looked like one single piece of stone. But it was really three separate pieces, superimposed on one another. In the air, or from any sort of distance, she knew that they became visually inseparable from the rest of the face of the wall, molding together like a mirage.

It was impossible to spot the opening from the air. Even now that she was close to it, Billie wasn't entirely certain she'd found the opening. The eerie green glow of the cliff face was different in front of her than the way she remembered it, yet still somehow familiar. The identification rock was lighter, almost neon green in the night-vision goggles, where the rest of the cliff face was darker, as if it was in shadow.

The small rock, no larger than her hand and almost perfectly round was impossible to spot by anyone who wasn't directly upon it. The stone appeared like an innocuous fluke of geometric formations, in an otherwise ordinary piece of geological nature—a round stone among a million vertical ones.

It also appeared as though it were lit by glowing floodlights. Only they weren't floodlights, they were UV-emitting, fluorescent lichen the Master Builders had placed there to specifically identify the place.

Sam shifted his gaze horizontally along the face of the wall, searching for an opening. He stopped and fixed it on her. "Where's the entrance?"

She smiled. "You'll see."

Billie gently took hold of the round stone in her left hand. Her fingertips could feel the tiny metallic grooves behind the façade of sandstone. They were cold and sharp, like the toothed cogwheel on a bicycle. She increased the pressure, until she was gripping the stone tightly, and then began to turn it clockwise.

It rotated more than a dozen times and then stopped.

Gentle vibrations shook the face of the rock-wall and were followed by the sound of heavy machinery making progress. She imagined the series of intricate mechanisms moving within. The finely-toothed wheels of the sprockets inside, turning multiple roller chains, and multiplying the force of her hand more than a thousand-fold, through a succession of complex gear ratios.

The sound finally ceased, and everything was still once more.

Below her, the two, twenty-foot high by five-foot wide stone fragments had separated. Sliding aside, like an automatic door in any retail store. Directly in the center of the two, was a circular opening. It appeared to be carved by hand using chisels, and was large enough for two persons to walk through standing upright.

Billie turned her gaze toward Sam. "Well?"

He smiled, and said in a voice just above a whisper, "The damned stone doors are on rails!"

Billie released her descender, dropping swiftly another eight feet and swung inside the round, carved tunnel's entrance. "Exactly."

Sam followed her down and into the opening. They both unclipped their descenders from the rope. He then radioed the rest of the group to let them know they'd found it and to come down.

His eyes swept the tunnel and the ground in particular. "Are you sure about this, Billie?"

"Yeah. Of course, I am. Why?"

Sam shrugged. "I don't know. If the floor starts dissolving or rocks start dropping at random, I'm out of here. I'm no Indiana Jones."

Billie smiled. "No, you're right. You aren't that handsome."

CHAPTER THREE

———O&3O———

SAM WATCHED AS Elise landed gracefully in the entrance to the tunnel and unclipped. Genevieve's entrance was more dramatic as she immediately crouched and scanned the tunnel with the night-vision scope of her weapon. Tom unfolded his large body just inside the entrance and reflexively looked up. He needn't have bothered to watch his head. The cave was at least ten feet in height, and as Sam played his tactical flashlight around, the ceiling appeared to angle upward farther into the tunnel.

He turned to Billie. "Will these doors stay open?"

She nodded. "Until someone closes them from the outside again."

"All right. Now where do we go?"

"Follow the tunnel. It's not long."

Sam asked, "What am I looking for?"

Billie smiled. "You'll see."

Sam followed the carved tunnel nearly a hundred feet into the mountain. There it opened to a much wider cavern system. His eyes raked the area, and a moment later he ripped off his night-vision goggles.

The active infrared night-vision worked by emitting infrared. But in the cave he'd just entered, that light had simply reflected back at him, magnified greatly.

He switched on his hand held flashlight, and waited for his eyes to adjust. Tiny specks of quartz glittered off the walls of the new cave like diamonds.

Genevieve switched on her own light. "Our night-vision's going to be useless in here. And with these on, our presence here is going to be pretty obvious to whoever's guarding the temple."

"Agreed." Sam looked at Billie. "How confident are you that they specifically wanted you to return for the stone tablet?"

"Reasonably," Billie confirmed.

"How confident?" Sam persisted.

Billie held her breath. "I guess I'm willing to bet all our lives on it."

Sam shined his flashlight at a series of openings up ahead. "All right. We continue. Billie, do you have any idea which of these tunnels we should follow?"

"Not really. But we'll know when we see it."

"See what?" he asked.

She pointed her flashlight down, revealing a floor scattered with sand, and in the sand, thousands of bare footprints. Billie's eyes followed the light. "These. We need to follow them."

Sam wasn't at all certain they should, but in this location, five people with semi-automatics ought to be able to hold their own against a small army of barefoot temple guards. "Sure."

He switched on his headlamp, and turned off the flashlight. With his hands now free, he unshouldered his Heckler and Koch submachine gun, and entered the tunnel. Billie might have been confident that the Master Builders wanted her to return, but he wasn't convinced.

Sam continued along the tunnel and through a narrow opening into a wonderland of speleothems—stalactites and stalagmites—unlike any he had ever seen. It looked like they had melted out of the ceiling of the cave and flowed into fantastic, smooth-sided shapes.

The height of the tunnel slowly decreased until the ceiling was just under four feet, and he was forced to climb through on his hands and knees. Between the thousands of pillars of stalactites and stalagmites, was a grand maze of crystals. The light from Sam's headlamp reflected throughout the labyrinth, highlighting its extreme size.

Sam said, "Lucky we've got this trail to follow. Without it, we'd need days and days to follow each of these small tunnels before we found what we were after."

Billie smiled. "Pity each one of these imprints in the sand represents another pyramid warrior, whose entire purpose it is to protect the temple."

Sam returned her smile. "You said you didn't think they would attack us? That they wanted you to return for the stone tablet?"

"That's what I do think," she said. "But I have been wrong before."

"Great. Let's just hope that was the last time."

It took close to thirty minutes to scramble through the crystal labyrinth. When he emerged between two pillars into a large space, the powerful light from his headlamp was swallowed by the giant, seemingly endless, grotto. He turned on his more powerful hand-held flashlight and shined it toward the ceiling. The faint shimmer of light was the only confirmation they were still underground. Although, for a moment, Sam questioned whether it was merely cloud cover.

He turned to Billie. "Where are we?"

"Follow the footsteps, and you'll see," she replied.

Their voices didn't echo, but instead, simply vanished mysteriously into the distance. Sam paused and listened. If there were still others inside whatever type of subterranean chamber they'd entered, Sam suspected he would have heard their breathing, shuffling of feet, or something at least.

But he heard nothing.

He stepped forward, slowly following the path of footprints in the sand, where Billie had told him hundreds of temple guards had once traveled to take their place.

Behind him, Tom swore loudly. "Sam, you'd better see this."

"What is it, Tom?" Sam asked. "Do we have company?"

Tom unclipped the *Armasight* digital night-vision scope from the top of his weapon and handed it to him. "Not yet, but you're gonna want to have a look through this."

Sam nodded and took the scope.

He slowly placed it up against his right eye, and looked through its telescopic digital lens. Sam held his breath as he studied what he saw, his eye and his mind competing to rationalize what he was viewing.

A wry and incredulous grin formed on his lips. "Billie, where have you taken us?"

"I told you that you wouldn't believe me until you saw it for yourself," Billie said.

Sam increased the digital magnification and brought the lens back up to his eyes. He shook his head, as he stared through it.

"I don't believe it..." he said.

There in front of him were thousands of six foot high, solid quartz sandstone, square blocks stacked upon one another to form an exact pyramid, every bit as large as the Great Pyramid of Giza.

CHAPTER FOUR

BILLIE CLIMBED THE first sandstone block at the base of the pyramid.

It felt more like the world's biggest bouldering room than the grand staircase to the entrance to a temple. To scale each tier, she needed to reach above and perform a partial pull-up, before being able to dig her toes into the rock and shuffle herself forward and over the edge. It wasn't too difficult, but she didn't revel in the idea of completing the process another fifty or more times to reach the entrance to the main descending passage.

She was tall, with an athletic and lithe frame. Despite the heavy backpack she carried, Billie was still the fastest in the group. By the time she reached the triangular entrance to the main descending passageway, she'd gained an advantage of nearly five entire sandstone blocks ahead of Sam, who was the next fastest in their group. Elise moved quickly, too, but she was shorter and consequently had to climb farther to overcome each stone. No one could have ever called Genevieve or Tom's progress slow, but instead of racing ahead, they concentrated on the defense of the team and maintaining a possible exit strategy if needed.

Billie fixed the beam of her flashlight into the entrance of the descending passageway. No light or sound returned. She didn't expect any. It stood to reason that everything of value inside the temple was within the king's chamber. If there were still hundreds of Pirahã temple guards inside, they would be waiting for them at the Grand Gallery.

Confident no one was approaching from within the pyramid, Billie turned to face Sam. In a stage whisper, she called down, "Well, Sam, are you coming?"

"I'm right behind you," he replied.

Spurred on by her taunt, Sam completed the remaining four blocks in under two minutes. He stopped before entering and took a deep breath. They waited until the rest of the team was at the entrance step and ready to go again.

Sam stepped up beside her. "Are you ready for this?"

"You mean after being enslaved here for nearly two years?" Billie replied.

"Yeah."

"I'll be fine."

Billie unshouldered her submachine gun, and descended into the entrance passageway. She was certain the Master Builders had brought her, specifically, back to this place for a reason. But there was no rational reason she should feel so confident about it. Instead, it simply felt like a hidden purpose, or some sort of missing information was stored in the darkest depths of her cerebellum, and that once she returned, it might all be revealed to her.

She swallowed hard, and took another step closer. That didn't mean she would necessarily like what she discovered. Besides, she might have got this entire thing wrong. Instead of coming back because she was a special part of the Master Builder's grand plan, maybe she was simply the fly that got away and was now stupidly returning to the web?

A hundred and fifty feet in and she spotted the ascending passage above her head. She clambered up onto the first step of the ascending tunnel and waited until Sam and the rest of the group reached the same location.

She continued, passing the Queen's Chamber as they went by.

Sam said, "You, Genevieve, and Elise wait here. Tom and I are going to quickly check out the Queen's Chamber."

"Don't bother," Billie said. "The stone tablet isn't in there. It's stored in the King's Chamber."

"So you said." Sam's piercing blue eyes met hers. Then, emphatically, he said, "We're still going to check out the Queen's Chamber first."

"Why?"

"Because I made this mistake when we searched the temple we found in the Kalahari Desert. We got to the King's Chamber, only to get attacked by someone hiding in the Queen's."

Billie shrugged with indifference. "Okay. Don't take too long."

She watched Sam and Tom's lights disappear as they traveled farther down the horizontal tunnel and then returned her gaze upward, where she knew the temple guards would be waiting for them.

The firing switch on Genevieve's Heckler and Koch submachine gun was set to F, for fully automatic. She shined her flashlight behind them and then up ahead.

Elise said, "I'll keep an eye on the tunnel behind us."

"Okay, good idea," Billie said.

Genevieve asked, "Do you still believe this place is guarded by an army of Pirahã warriors?"

"Yes," Billie replied without hesitation.

"Will they try to attack us?"

Billie thought about it for a moment. "I have no idea."

Genevieve spoke with the candor of someone having coffee

with a friend. "I think it's safe to say they will. If the Pirahã simply let you take this ancient stone tablet they would be pretty much useless as guards, wouldn't they?"

"Not if the Master Builders want me to take it."

"So, the question is, do they want you to take it?"

Billie nodded. "And the answer to that is, I have no fucking idea."

Genevieve squeezed her hand in a gesture almost resembling sympathy. "They really did a number on your mind, didn't they?"

"Yeah. But what, specifically makes you say that?"

"I've never seen you doubt any decision before. Even when you left Tom to continue your search for the Master Builders, you did so with unwavering certainty that it was the right thing to do."

Billie said, "It was. I had to leave."

"I know. But it cost you the best man in the world."

She leveled her gaze at Genevieve and smiled. "And you found him."

Genevieve grinned. "Yes. How very lucky for me."

"I would have done the entire thing over if I had it to do again." Billie breathed in and sighed heavily. "Besides, you love him, don't you?"

"Yes."

"Good."

CHAPTER FIVE

BILLIE SPOTTED THE first movement of light flickering from the horizontal passageway.

She waited until Sam and Tom were close enough to recognize and then said, "Find anything?"

"No," Sam conceded.

She smiled. "I told you it was empty."

Sam glanced up, toward the Grand Gallery. "All right. Now the hard part. Do you still think the Pirahã are going to let us steal this thing?"

Billie said, "Question of the day. There's only one way to find out."

She took the lead, stepping slowly and quietly. It was only sixty-odd feet before they reached the guards. The Pirahã warriors stood on either side of the Grand Gallery. They were so still that at first she mistook them for sculptures.

Her eyes glanced across the tunnel, taking everything in. The Grand Gallery was filled with temple guards. She and Sam were fooling themselves if they thought their team of five could defend against nearly four hundred warriors.

She lowered her weapon.

It was pointless anyway.

Billie tilted her head, studying the situation. Sam stepped up beside her. Billie saw their presence didn't seem to have been detected. Everyone in the gallery was facing in the opposite direction. She couldn't determine whether they were mostly men or mostly women, but as she stared she began to differentiate.

More than half grasped spears that looked to be almost six feet in length and carried blades of obsidian that were a foot or more long. Those with spears had what looked like rawhide strings around their waists, but were otherwise naked. They had intricate paint or tattoos covering their arms, legs, and backs. Some had headdresses of rawhide, decorated with feathers, braids, shells and other items she couldn't identify. Those without spears wore the same strings around their waists, but had longer hair and more elaborate headgear. There didn't seem to be any children present.

A cool breeze began to waft toward their party. In the distance, the Black Smoke curled down from the King's Chamber toward them in serpentine movements. Billie stopped, and quickly donned her military-grade gas mask. Sam and the rest of their team followed. For nearly two years the strange, sweet smelling cloud of smoke, had enslaved her within the Amazon jungle. At the time it had provided her with the strength and endurance to work on the construction of this very temple, with the fervor of religious fanaticism.

And for two years, she had felt like she had been chosen to personally help out the Gods — the ancient Master Builders who were so far advanced from the rest of the world's civilizations, that it was impossible to perceive them as anything else.

Since then, she had learned that the Black Smoke was nothing more than a very clever ruse to dominate the Pirahã, in order to provide intense labor in total secrecy for the construction of their latest temple. It relied on the smoke of a strange fungi that shared similar hallucinogenic effects with Lysergic Acid Diethylamide — more commonly known as LSD.

Using the drug and persuasive techniques, communicated through high frequency sound waves, the Master Builders were able to maintain absolute control of hundreds and potentially thousands of people against their will, simultaneously.

It was this ability that most frightened the U.S. Secretary of Defense, who had ordered Sam Reilly to investigate the Master Builder's ability to utilize the weapon. If such a weapon could be mastered, then no one was safe. Military strength became irrelevant. And no one could be completely trusted.

Her eyes turned to the rest of their team. It was hard to imagine how to begin to fight an enemy that consisted of nothing more than a thick, sweet smelling, fog of smoke.

They'd discussed whether the masks would protect them, and the fact was, they didn't know. But it was better to try and fail than not have a plan at all. The only person who didn't don a gas mask was Elise, whose genetic anomalies and hyper-developed brainstem seemed to render her immune to the Black Smoke.

As the smoke touched each temple guard in the tableau in front of them, they turned one hundred and eighty degrees to face them. The warrior's eyes remained fixed straight ahead, with no recognition or deviation toward her or any of her party.

When the last Pirahã turned to face them, the whistling started.

It was high-pitched and eerie. None of the warriors reacted to the presence of Billie's party. It was impossible to imagine they simply hadn't been spotted. But every one of the temple guard's eyes were fixed and glassy, every mouth pursed and whistling the eerie tune.

Billie could now see the men's bodies were painted red, and they carried small shields. The women had small rawhide 'aprons' suspended from their waist strings, along with intricate tattoos on their faces.

The whistling went on until Billie thought she might go

insane, and then suddenly stopped. Like an old movie effect of Moses parting the Red Sea, the tribespeople moved back to each side of the passage, and stayed there, looking straight ahead. Billie's eyes danced back and forth, intently studying what she was seeing.

"What the hell do we do now?" Sam asked. He didn't bother lowering his voice, since the Pirahã clearly didn't seem to care about their presence.

"I think they're going to let us pass," Billie answered.

Sam spoke to Elise. "You have any idea what the Black Smoke wants?"

"No."

"But you understand it?"

Elise smiled. "It's not like what you think. It isn't the sort of telepathy you're thinking of. I have a sense about how the Black Smoke feels, that's all."

Sam persisted. "Okay so what does it feel like?"

"It feels content."

"That's it?" Billie asked.

"That's it," Elise confirmed.

Billie continued through the Grand Gallery. She ignored the temple guards. If they wanted to pretend to be sculptures, who was she to interrupt them? Two minutes later, she reached the King's Chamber.

Sam was right behind her.

In the center of the King's Chamber lay a sarcophagus. Billie felt her arms and legs moving, but it was almost like being in her recurring dream again, knowing what she should do next. She drew a long breath and then let it out on a sigh as she gazed at the sarcophagus.

On it lay a thin stone tablet of some sort of polished black stone. The tablet was illuminated by what Billie could have sworn was a floodlight. *But how…?* And then she saw the dust motes dancing in the beacon. The rays were separated, as if shining through a cloud. Her eyes, accustomed to the darkness of the temple and surrounding cave system, could barely make out the hole far above the sarcophagus.

She pointed, and Sam looked up. He pulled a monocular from a pocket and extended it, searched for the hole above, and found it.

"I can see leaves fluttering in the breeze. It must extend from the mountain's surface, all the way through the tip of the pyramid," he said in a low voice.

Billie paid him no attention. She had stepped up to the sarcophagus and reverently lifted the tablet. Sam looked back at her just as she stowed it in her backpack and calmly walked away. Behind them, the strange whistling resumed.

"Sam, I think it's time we go," Billie said.

"Hell, yes, it's time to go. I don't think the Pirahã are going to be indifferent to us much longer — especially once they work out we just stole their map. You remember what happened to Indiana Jones when he removed that artifact from that temple around these parts?"

She smiled at him. "Sam, that's a movie."

"Even so. It didn't end well for him."

Sam didn't need to tell her twice to get a move on. She wanted out of the temple just as fast as he did. They retraced their steps between the ranks of guards, walking quickly. When they reached the others, all five of them hurried down the passage to the main tunnel, and started up the incline without pausing.

A strong breeze gusted through the pyramid's exit and down the descending tunnel, nearly knocking Billie off her feet. It was followed by a second Black Smoke. This seemed particularly dark, and malicious as it forced its way through her, and the rest of their crew, racing toward the Pirahã guards.

"That's different!" she said.

"What is?" Sam asked.

She swallowed, hard. "I've never seen a second Black Smoke."

To Elise, Sam asked, "Any idea what it is?"

Elise shook her head. "No. Nothing good. I can almost feel its hatred."

Farther inside the temple, the high-pitched trilling sound finally stopped. It was immediately replaced with a new sound. This one was more resonant, like thunder. It took a moment, and they all realized what was causing the new sound.

They'd almost made it to the entrance when the thunder of 400 pairs of feet reached their ears.

Elise said, "Something really bad just happened!"

"You think?" Billie asked, without hiding her sarcasm.

Sam yelled, "Run!"

CHAPTER SIX
———O&3O———

BLOOD POUNDED IN the back of his ears and his chest throbbed with exertion, but Sam continued to climb the final steps of the main tunnel until he reached the giant entrance to the outside of the subterranean pyramid.

He waited until the rest of his team was out and then removed the safety pin from the smoke grenade and rolled it down the descending tunnel. Three hundred and fifty grams of a thick purple smoke, consisting of potassium chlorate, lactose and a purple dye hissed as it was suddenly released from the canister, until it fully obscured the narrow, descending tunnel.

Tom stopped. "Should we hold them here?"

"Yeah, for as long as we can with smoke grenades. I don't want to resort to lethal methods unless we have to." Sam turned to Billie. "Get the stone tablet back to the helicopter."

Billie said, "I'm on it. Genevieve and Elise are already making their way up the ropes. Once she's at the top, Genevieve's going to scout somewhere to cover the entrance to the cave system, where she can pick off any attackers if she has to."

"Sounds like a plan. Now go!"

Sam didn't need to tell her twice. Billie disappeared, and Tom threw another smoke grenade into the tunnel.

It didn't bring them the reprieve they'd hoped for. Instead, their attackers continued through the smoke with the unwavering fanaticism that they'd seen in Billie months earlier. From what Sam guessed, the entire Pirahã tribe were being guided through the smoke-filled tunnel from the same outside source that had told them to attack.

He turned to Tom. "Come on, let's go. They'll reach the surface soon."

"You don't need to tell me." Tom started down the pyramid's steps.

Sam followed him, climbing down the six-foot high stone blocks in a series of fast moving maneuvers in which he swung his legs over the side, while bracing with both hands on the top of the stone—making it appear more like a controlled falling action.

Nearly a hundred feet below, he could just make out the faint glow of a single headlamp, where Billie had finally reached the bottom and was now making her way into the set of narrow tunnels filled with crystals.

They reached the base of the giant stone steps at the front of the pyramid. Behind them, Sam heard their attackers bursting out of the main ascending tunnel. He glanced over his shoulder, running his flashlight across the main entrance. The tribal guards of the sacred temple were spreading out over the giant stairs, taking them in single steps.

Taking the steps as they were, the Pirahã would reach them in minutes.

Sam didn't stop to plan his next move. Instead he ducked down and into the shallow tunnel toward the outside of the cavern and followed the line of footprints in the sand they'd used to enter the temple. The light of his headlamp reflected off the myriad of crystals the size of an adult that lined the walls and surrounding cave-system. Large stalactites and stalagmites broke the cavern into a complex labyrinth.

He rounded a bend, crawling on his hands and knees—and

then stopped. The marks in the sand simply vanished.

Sam shined his flashlight around, expecting to see the footprints and signs of sand being turned over by others shuffling through the sand, but instead he found nothing. There were at least six separate tunnels that branched out of the cavern they were in. He turned around, but there was no sign of anyone back-tracking from where they were.

"What the hell?" he asked.

Tom flashed his headlamp across each tunnel. "The marks couldn't have simply disappeared. Besides, I watched Billie follow Genevieve and Elise into this tunnel only ten minutes ago." He shined his headlamp onto the ground, where a few small handprints remained. "See, these would have been made by Elise."

Sam's gaze swept the ground of the cavern. He looked closer at what he was seeing and felt the prickly finger of fear tease him as understanding finally reached his mind. The ground was completely smooth. Far too much so to be natural. The rest of the cavern floor showed a multitude of pockmarks and deep indents where dripping water had eroded the ground. In front of him were tiny grooves in the sand.

He touched it with his hand. His fingers easily penetrated the loose sand. A wry smile curled his lips, as though he'd finally discovered the answer to a great mystery. Only the discovery itself almost certainly confirmed his worst fears.

Sam said, "Someone's intentionally raked this area. By the looks of things, they've done so after the girls went through here."

"Which means, either they didn't want us to know where the girls went, or they intentionally made sure we couldn't escape." Tom flipped the safety on his Heckler & Koch MP5 submachine gun over to F for fully automatic. "Either way, I think they lost their rights to a fair fight."

"You might be right, although I'm not sure who we're

fighting yet."

The sound of four hundred warriors charging echoed like thunder through the cavern. A sign their pursuers were still closing in on them.

Sam said, "All right, we can't go back the way we came. We'll keep moving and see if we can find a way out. They can't have raked the entire cavern since the girls went through this way."

"Sounds like a plan," Tom said. "You head to the left and I'll go right. We'll meet back here as soon as we find something."

Sam nodded. "Good luck."

By the time Sam reached the edge of the three separate tunnels that headed to the right, he heard Tom call out to him.

"I've got something."

Sam raced along on his hands and knees. "Where?"

Tom pointed, using his flashlight to shine directly on the hand and knee marks in the sand. "What do you think?"

"It looks like only one person went through this way."

"Could it have been Billie?"

"I don't know. It might have been, or they could have come from whoever tried to cover the tracks in the sand to make us lose our way down here. Either way, we're going to have company any minute now."

Tom shrugged, as though he would deal with whatever company they had when it reached them. "So, we follow it?"

"Yeah."

Tom, already ahead of him, led the way through the shallow and relatively narrow cavern. It meandered around a series of stalagmites that were larger than either man, before heading in a straight line for more than forty feet, and then making a sharp turn to the left.

It was the first sign they'd deviated from the route they'd taken on the way in, and Sam instantly knew there was something wrong. Behind him, the sound of the pursuing Pirahã tribe was getting louder. They no longer whistled in a soft, melodic way. Instead they were chanting something. The words were incomprehensible, but there was no doubt about their purpose — this was a war cry.

Sam said, "Not to rush you or anything, but our company's nearly here."

"Just a minute," Tom replied. "I think I can see an opening up ahead."

Sam rounded the next corner and the shallow tunnel opened into a sizeable oval shaped room. It was approximately thirty feet long by twenty wide. He was able to stand up. The entire room — and he thought room not cavern — had been excavated using hand-tools. Rough grooves and indents covered the walls and floors, where rocks and simple tools had been used to hollow out the area. The ubiquitous crystals that had made up most of the rest of the caverns beneath the Tepui Mountains had been removed, and only one single stalagmite remained in the center of the room, as though it had been required to support the ceiling nearly fifteen feet above.

On this giant stalagmite, a man had been bound by his wrist and ankles. The skin over his wrists had been worn off, as though he'd fought to free himself in vain, by pulling his hands through the electrical cable ties. Unable to free himself, the wretched man had spent his last efforts alive staring at something on the wall directly opposite him.

Sam's eyes darted to the wall. There was a large TV monitor. Ninety inches at least. A complete anachronism in an underground temple built entirely by hand using rudimentary tools. The monitor displayed multiple images from secret digital cameras recording video throughout the temple and its maze of stalagmites, stalactites, and giant quartz crystals.

His eyes returned to the remains of the bound wretch. Two bullet holes wept blood from the man's chest. It meant that whoever killed him did so only minutes earlier.

His dead eyes were fixed in a state of abject horror.

Sam felt his stomach churn with fear and a sinister and pervasive sense of impending disaster, as he spotted that the man's eyes were a deep violet color.

There was only one other person he'd ever met who had eyes like that. Her name was Elise, and as far as he knew, she descended directly from the ancient race of Master Builders.

Tom said, "What do you think?"

Sam swallowed. "I don't know, but it raises the question — has there been a quarrel among the remaining descendants of the Master Builders?"

He swept the entire room with his flashlight. There were no tunnels leading out of it. One way in and one way out. And an army of brutal warriors approaching.

"What do you think?" Sam asked.

Tom leveled his Heckler and Koch MP5 submachine gun at the entrance. "I think we're trapped."

CHAPTER SEVEN
———O&3O———

SAM'S FOCUS SHIFTED back to the huge display monitor.

It showed hundreds of Pirahã guards mobilizing quickly through the crystal maze. The giant pieces of quartz were vibrating in a strange harmony with their deep war cry. He stepped closer, and realized his pursuers were now coming through the section where they'd first discovered the raked sand. He put his hand on the screen. The image size changed. It was a touch-screen. He used his thumb and two fingers to expand the image.

He could now see their faces clearly. Their lips were entirely still, but a strange sound resonated out of their open mouths. The tune was completely unrecognizable, but mesmerizing. It gave Sam a momentary pause.

He smiled, mystified. "Truly fascinating, isn't it?"

Tom ignored the comment. "We've got to go, Sam. I thought you were supposed to be finding a way out of here?"

Sam grinned. "So I was."

He opened his hand and then ran each of his fingers together until it minimized the screen into a series of smaller mapped documents. It revealed a dozen separate video images. He glanced over them. To the left corner, an image showed Billie approaching the end of the crystal cavern, where the ropes were still hanging at the entrance. Just past that image, was an external video depicting the sandstone face of the cliff. In the middle of the image, he could just make out the two figures of Elise and Genevieve prusiking up the rope.

His gaze swept downward, where he spotted an image of Tom and himself staring at the computer monitor. Two screens to the right displayed the narrow, empty tunnel, through which they had recently crawled to reach the room they were now in. A second or two later, the first of their pursuers entered the tunnel.

Tom said, "They'll be inside any minute now…"

Sam made a big show of sighing. "Yes… and we'll be gone."

He clicked on the video feed directly above their room and expanded the image by opening his fingers across the screen. The room was a hollowed tunnel, carved using rudimentary tools to chisel away at the soft sandstone.

"Would you look at that?" Sam said. "An escape tunnel!"

He swiped the screen to the left, moving to the next screen, followed by another. On the fourth screen, he spotted the back of a man, climbing onto a rope hanging over the sandstone cliff of the Tepui Mountains. Sam couldn't see his face, but the man had thick black hair with minor graying to the side.

"That's our man!" Sam said.

Tom grabbed him by the shoulder. "That's great, but how do we get there?"

Sam smiled. "I thought you already knew?"

"No."

"Follow me."

Sam walked behind to the back of the giant stalagmite in the middle of the room. He shined his flashlight across the back of the pillar. Small, dark indents had been carved into the back of its limestone structure.

He locked the safety on his Heckler and Koch MP5 and swung its strap over his shoulder. Climbing hand over hand, he scurried up the limestone ladder. At the very top of the stalagmite, three pillars of quartz crystal met together like a giant prism. From the base of the pillar, it was impossible to see that the ceiling went anywhere, but upon reaching it, Sam spotted a secret entrance had been carved out of the sandstone that formed behind them.

Sam slipped through and climbed into the new tunnel. Unlike the rest of the tunnels they'd found beneath the Tepui Mountains, this one went in a perfectly straight line.

Tom squeezed his broad shoulders through the opening. "They're flooding into the room now. It won't take them long to discover the hidden ladder, if they don't know about it already."

Sam switched his MP5 submachine gun to F for fully automatic and turned to face the opening.

Tom met his gaze. "You don't really think we've got enough ammo to stop all of them, do you?"

"Not for a second. Even if we had enough rounds and the time to reload, I wouldn't want to be responsible for the extinction of an entire tribe. I've got a better idea though."

The sound of Pirahã filling into the room below echoed through the secret passage. As expected, their numbers soared. It would be impossible to hope that they simply wouldn't spot the hidden ladder, or that they could be fought off once they climbed up it.

A large fragment of quartz protruded out of the sandstone wall next to the opening to the secret room below. It was roughly one foot wide by six long. If it could be convinced to break free of the wall, the stone would fall into the opening, blocking anyone's progress through it.

Sam removed his backpack and withdrew a single, copper-lined linear-cutting charge of C4. It was used by American Special Forces for cutting through thick sheet steel and solid doors during explosive breaches. He wrapped it around the base of the hanging crystal and attached a twenty-foot line of detcord.

Tom stepped back and nodded. "Clear."

Sam flicked the switch, and the C4 exploded.

CHAPTER EIGHT
———○⚭○———

THE SMALL BLAST exploded in a flash, sending a torrent of rubble and air down the confined space of the tunnel. The blast-wave ripped into Sam, taking his breath away in an instant. Beneath closed eyelids, he watched as the blast lit up the tunnel, and his ears rang with the continuous echo of the explosion.

In an instant it was over.

Smoke wafted out of the rubble, where fractured shards of crystal littered the secret opening. Sam turned his gaze toward Tom to see if he was okay. Confirming Tom was uninjured, he focused his attention on the pile of rubble. His flashlight shined through the fine dust of the tunnel in ghostly silence.

His eyes fixed on the rubble. The top of the pile shuddered. Nothing more than a fine tremor. It could have been the remains of the debris settling into the small opening. Or it could be something much more significant.

Sam held his breath. The movement stopped. Maybe he'd imagined it? It felt like an abominably long time. He breathed out. The plan had worked and the small cave in served its purpose to block any progress from their pursuers.

Then, two hands broke through the rubble.

A moment later, the bloodied hands pulled at the shards of

fractured quartz. Bit by bit the impossible became a certainty. They were going to dig their way out through the pile of rubble.

Sam swore.

Tom said, "Go!"

Sam started running down the escape tunnel. It was tall enough that he could move without fear of hitting his head on the roof, while so narrow his wide shoulders nearly scraped the walls. The tunnel continued for approximately a thousand feet, in a slight upward direction.

The strange humming sound coming from their pursuers gradually increased, until he no longer needed to glance over his shoulder to know they were catching up very quickly.

Sam reached the end, where a giant sandstone boulder rested perpendicular to the tunnel, blocking their exit. It was approximately eighty feet high and thirty or more wide. Between the stone and the escape passageway a narrow crevasse ran in both directions. Sunlight filtered in from both sides. It was a tight fit, but it looked like they could squeeze through it.

The sound of a hundred or more Pirahã guards making their strange and identical war cry was enough to remove any doubt in his mind.

"Which way?" Sam asked.

Tom glanced left and right. "Has to be left."

"Why?"

Tom shined his flashlight to the right. "The sandstone tapers inward here. I'd never fit through."

Sam nodded. "Okay, left it is."

Tom threw his last remaining smoke grenade down the passage behind them. "You go first. You're smaller, and should be faster. I'm right behind you!"

Sam didn't argue.

He slipped into the lateral crevasse. It was an awkward climb.

Although he could see the light of the exit about thirty feet away, the entire gap dipped fifty or more feet below. The result was that he needed to climb and slide his way through it—with the constant risk of falling deep into the narrower section where he might never climb out.

Shifting his weight from his back to his hands, and from his hands to his feet, Sam used opposing pressures—the way rock-climbers do to ascend the rock formations known as chimneys—to shuffle his way across the crevasse. About ten feet from the opening the opposing sandstone walls tapered, and he found the first section where he struggled to squeeze through. He adjusted his position and tried again. Same problem. He turned his head and tried exhaling to reduce the width of his chest. This time he got farther, but was still unable to completely get past the same spot.

He exhaled the last of the air in his lungs, and gravity returned him to where he'd started. Sam shined his flashlight across the opposing walls, searching for any shadows that might indicate a slightly wider section.

Behind him, gunshots fired.

"We've got company, Sam!" Tom shouted. "Forget caution, just get through there!"

Sam said, "I'm on it!"

His glance stopped nearly eight feet above where he was trying to cross the crevasse. There, a small piece of black hair and not yet dried blood marked the way out. Sam shimmied upward and across.

The area was still narrow, but definitely wider than down below.

He glanced at Tom below. "Are you following?"

Tom placed his MP5 strap over his shoulder and started to climb. "Keep going, I can see the route."

Squished between the two immovable rock walls, with his

hands out above his head and his feet pressed against opposite ends, Sam felt his world close in on him. Here, panic could kill as quickly as a bullet. Every part of him wanted to breathe deeply and escape. Instead, salvation only came from exhaling deeply.

He'd gotten past the section where he'd become stuck previously. With his head turned to the left, he could no longer see Tom behind him, but could hear Tom's exerted breathing. In front of him, he could see the light of the opening. He was close. He just needed to get another couple of feet across and then descend until he could reach the opening.

But instead he was stuck.

Fear and claustrophobia, which had haunted him as a child, now reared its ugly head. He concentrated on small movements with his hands and feet to shift his weight, trying not to let the terror override his decisions.

Even so, his fine movements were no longer getting him any closer to the edge of the crevasse. Claustrophobia, it turns out, was only irrational when you could breathe. In this case, so much pressure was being exerted on his chest wall, that inhaling was impossible.

He tried to breathe out further, but there was no more air left in his lungs to exhale.

Beyond the panic, he heard Tom's voice.

"Let go."

Let go of what? I'm stuck!

Tom continued. "Just relax your entire body… and let gravity do its job."

Sam untensed his arms and legs.

Nothing happened.

Then he shifted slightly downward. A moment later, he slipped down into the large area. Several feet down, the narrow section suddenly appeared as wide as a house. He took a deep breath, and reveled in the open expanse.

His gaze shifted upward toward Tom, who was already quickly working his way to the same spot in which he'd become stuck. Sam had learned long ago that caving was as much about technique as it was about size. In this case, despite Tom being physically larger, he was considerably more capable and adept at spelunking—the process of navigating through the narrow sections of a cave system.

Sam focused his flashlight across the crevasse. A beam of light stopped at the entrance to the escape tunnel, through which they'd come. The first of their Pirahã guards came into sight. The man carried a blade of obsidian, slicing at the sandstone wall as though he could enlarge it.

"You've got a very angry looking man with a very big sword on your tail, Tom."

"I see him!"

Sam shifted backward, toward the exit of the crevasse. He braced himself against the two walls with his back and feet in opposing directions. Then, he removed his MP5 and removed the safety.

He aimed the submachine gun at the guard. "Don't come any farther!"

It was a waste of his breath. The man couldn't understand English, and if he had, Sam doubted very much that it would have made any difference. His attacker was following divine orders from a Master Builder, who had no intention of letting them escape.

The guard hadn't spotted Tom above yet. Instead he tried to come straight across the crevasse to attack him. Sam watched in horror as the Pirahã guard moved quickly, with such ease through the narrow section, that he thought the man might just squeeze through and reach him.

He shuffled backward another foot.

His attacker squeezed into the narrowest section of the crevasse directly opposite him, and became stuck. Every muscle in the man's wiry body tensed and struggled to free himself, and when it became abundantly clear that his desire was impossible to achieve, the Pirahã warrior extended his arm and tried to strike with his obsidian sword.

The attack was so swift and unexpected that Sam didn't have time to react to it. The obsidian blade sliced downward, narrowly slipping past his face, so that Sam could feel the rush of wind as it scraped past his eyes.

Sam snapped his head backward.

The sword swung downward without connecting to anything. The momentum pulled the Pirahã forward, and he fell downward. He slid twenty or more feet until his chest became wedged in the vice-like section below.

Sam watched in horror as the man tried to fight his entrapment. He scrambled with his arms and legs like an insect in a spider's web. With each movement, he slid farther downward, until his chest became lodged tight between the two walls of stone. Aghast, Sam noticed the poor wretch was now incapable of moving and unable to breathe. He flailed his arms and legs, moving them faster and faster, until fatigue and hypoxia thankfully took over and suddenly everything went limp.

Sam moved the beam of his flashlight upward, where more Pirahã were now racing toward him. One of them threw a spear. It ricocheted across the sandstone, missing him by a couple of feet, before falling to the ground eighty or more feet below.

Tom slipped down next to him. "What are you waiting for? Let's go!"

"You..." Sam said, exhaling a sigh of relief.

He quickly shuffled to the end of the crevasse and out into the open — onto a half-a-foot wide precipice. His eyes swept his new environment. The ledge was a little over ten feet in length, and positioned approximately halfway up a fourteen-hundred-foot vertical wall of sandstone. The golden wall appeared to be floating in a sea of early morning mist. To the right, where the sun had penetrated the ancient valley earlier, there were speckled views of the jungle. Its dark green canopy appeared like little more than dark green grass. They were on the vertigo-inducing face of the Tepui Mountains.

Sam turned to Tom. "Now where the hell do you suppose we go?"

CHAPTER NINE
―――○ℰ3○―――

SAM TURNED TO meet Tom's hard and steely gaze.

"Maybe we took a wrong turn?" Tom said.

Sam swallowed. "You think we were supposed to go right back there?"

"No. But it is looking more like a possibility." Tom shrugged, as though he was indifferent to having to fight his way back through hundreds of attackers.

Sam faced the precipice, searching for another option. Something that didn't involve killing more than a hundred Pirahã guards who were most likely being used as slave-workers by the Master Builders.

His eyes focused on the sandstone ledge. It narrowed as it reached the end, before disappearing completely. Above and below, the vertical cliff was smooth with no indents carved into it to form hand holds, or metal climbing rungs, like those he'd seen along the Via Ferrata in the Dolomite Mountains of Italy. Heck, there were so few natural cracks in the rock that he doubted many professional rock-climbers could scale the wall.

Then he stopped. Because something silver flickered in the early sunlight. It was so small his eyes had skimmed past it multiple times before.

Sam grinned. "Would you look at that!"

Tom asked, "What?"

"At the end of the ledge, about five feet high — there's the eye of a climbing bolt."

"So there is… too bad we didn't bring about eight hundred feet of rope."

Sam put vertigo aside and carefully walked along the narrow ledge until he reached the end of the sandstone precipice. He touched the climbing bolt. It was hot. A certain sign that someone had only very recently run a lot of rope through it very quickly.

He leaned over the ledge.

A hundred feet below, someone was pulling the excess rope into a separate tunnel. The man glanced up at him. Despite the distance, Sam met his eyes. There was something sinister and evil about the stranger's look.

He could just make out the man's smile.

Sam withdrew his MP5 from his shoulder. With reckless abandon, he aimed the weapon, as though he might still get to kill his attacker before he most certainly became overrun by the Pirahã guards. He aimed the submachine gun and squeezed the trigger.

The small burst of bullets fell harmlessly several feet short of his intended target. The stranger smiled, amused by Sam's audacity, and then disappeared inside the separate tunnel.

Sam swore.

Tom said, "At least now we're only a hundred feet short."

Sam looked down at the small opening in the cliff far below. "It may as well be a mile."

A strange humming sound resonating from the crevasse behind them changed its pitch. Both of them swung around with their weapons aimed at the hidden entrance. Something had changed. Despite the difficult and narrow climb, they had no doubt the army of temple guards would eventually overcome the unique route.

With the distant rumble of the combined war cry in the background, a new, higher pitched wail suddenly shot out of the opening. The obsidian blade was the first thing Sam saw. It jabbed forward toward the ledge, before its owner ran out at full speed — and over the cliff.

The warrior continued to scream his strange war cry as he fell. His voice became distant until they could no longer hear him, and he eventually disappeared into the canopy of the jungle far below.

Tom said, "That poor man simply ran to his own death. He didn't even stop his war cry after he'd gone over the edge!"

Sam's heart pounded in his chest. He swallowed hard. "What a horrible waste of life."

There was no time to discuss a plan, or the morals of killing innocent people from the Pirahã tribe who'd been enslaved by the Master Builders using a combination of hallucinogenic drugs and extremely high-frequency radio waves to persuade the Pirahã to follow their every order. Instead, another attacker came through.

This one had a spear in his hand.

Tom grabbed the weapon as the guard approached the opening. He pulled on the shaft with such sudden ferocity that it slid out of its owner's hand.

"Stop! Stop!" Tom shouted, as though he might be able to somehow get through to the man, and protect him from blindly following the orders of the Master Builders.

The man looked at him, his eyes fixing upon Tom's.

Sam shouted. "That's it! You don't have to do this. You don't want to fight us…"

"Look at me!" Tom continued. "We don't want to fight you…"

The warrior focused on Tom's face and ran forward. Tom

lowered the spear—and the Pirahã guard impaled himself on his own weapon.

The man looked up at them, his eyes filled with confusion, as though whatever magic spell he'd been under had now passed.

Tom said, "I'm sorry."

And the man fell forward into the jungle eight hundred feet below.

Tom fired a few short bursts into the cavern, trying to stop the next set of attackers from following. His eyes glanced at Sam. "Why don't they stop?"

"They never will. It's not that they don't want to. They simply can't. They have no more free-will than a puppet."

Tom checked his last magazine. "I'm nearly out!"

Sam removed the magazine from his MP5 and glanced at the bullets housed inside. "I have four shots left."

"Great. So, we have about ten shots between us. We'd better make them count. How many Pirahã do you think there are?"

"Billie said there were around four hundred in the Maici River of the Amazon when she was there. Inside the temple earlier, she thought the entire tribe must have been moved here recently to guard the temple."

"Okay. Now that's ten shots for about three hundred eighty Pirahã warriors, taking into account the twenty or so who might have gotten stuck or killed trying to reach us. What are our odds?"

"Impossible."

"Exactly."

Another warrior slipped through the narrow gap, and Tom shot him in the head. He turned to Sam. "Have you got any other ideas?"

"None that come to mind, presently." Sam continued to search the sandstone rock face for any cracks or openings through which they could somehow escape. "You hold them off… and I'll see what I can find."

Tom laughed. "All right. You want me just to hold the army here while you do your thing?"

"That would be good."

Fifty seconds later, the best solution Sam could work out was that they might have a better chance at defending themselves at the narrowest section of the ledge. It was then that he heard the distinct sound of the tiny hammer inside Tom's MP5 clicking as it struck an empty cartridge.

Tom said, "I'm out."

Sam removed his own magazine and threw it. "Take this."

Tom inserted the magazine into his weapon. A moment later, Sam heard the sporadic shots get fired, until the last round was finally released.

Sam raced to help Tom.

Tom and a Pirahã warrior became entangled in a death struggle. The warrior gripped Tom by the throat.

The loud report of a sniper rifle filled the ancient valley.

And a red mist defiled the sandstone face of the Tepui Mountains. The strong and wiry frame of the Pirahã warrior spasmed, and then relaxed, before the entire body slumped to the ledge. Tom stepped back, quickly, and teetered briefly at the edge.

Sam turned to the open expanse, where a dark experimental stealth helicopter silently approached.

CHAPTER TEN
———O&3O———

T HE SHADOW OF the Black Hawk shrouded the golden wall of sandstone.

Sam looked up. With its long rotor blades turning overhead, the Black Hawk couldn't get close enough to the vertical wall to throw them a rope. Instead it circled overhead and fired a short burst of several hundred rounds via its Gatling style heavy machinegun into the opening through which the Pirahã were now swarming out. A few moments later, the helicopter banked away from the cliff and increased its altitude, before finally landing on the sandstone tabletop high above.

Two ropes were then dropped right next to them.

Sam smiled. "I told you something would turn up!"

Tom matched his grin as he tested that the rope was secure. "So you did."

Neither of them had to be told to hurry up. The next group of attackers would swarm out through the crevasse any minute, and by that stage they both needed to be out of the range of even the best spear thrower.

Sam looped his pre-tied harness prusik around the static rope and then through his harness with one hand and hauled himself upward to rest on it while he drew his knees upward. He secured his foot prusik to the rope and slipped his feet into the loops at the bottom, then stood upright close to the static rope while moving the harness and foot prusiks up. He repeated the move, inching up the static rope like a caterpillar.

Tom looped onto the second rope and started to climb quickly. Despite his weight, Tom was able to ascend remarkably quickly.

Fifteen feet above the ledge, Sam spotted a single Pirahã warrior climbing out of the crevasse. The warrior ran his eyes along the ledge, down and then up. An instant later, he threw his spear.

"Watch out!" Sam yelled, and quickly shimmied another few feet up the rope.

Next to him, Tom made a slight grunt sound.

"You okay, Tom?" he yelled.

"Just a scratch. But I'd like to put some more distance between us and any of the Pirahã guards before they get another lucky shot in."

"Agreed!"

Adrenaline fueled their efforts, and Sam and Tom soon reached the top.

Genevieve looked at Tom's leg wound. "That looks painful."

Tom smiled. "I've had worse."

Sam glanced at his friend. There was blood oozing out of a small wound to his left thigh. "That looks like more than a scratch."

Tom shrugged. "I'll get a tetanus shot, antibiotics, and some stiches and it'll be fine."

Veyron stepped forward. "Are you sure you're all right? You look pretty pale."

Sam studied Tom for a second. His face was ashen, and small beads of sweat had formed on his forehead. "Okay, let's get him into the back of the Black Hawk."

Sam looked over his shoulder. "Genevieve, are you alright to fly us back to the *Maria Helena*, while Elise stiches up Tom's leg?"

"Yeah, I'm on it," she replied.

Sam waited until Veyron climbed into the navigator's seat and then closed the side door.

In the back of the Sikorsky helicopter, Elise was already in the process of opening the suturing kit. She looked at Tom, "This might hurt a bit…"

Billie studied the stone tablet without looking up, either unaware that Tom had been injured, or indifferent. She smiled broadly, as she studied the ancient map, waiting for its secrets to be revealed.

Genevieve climbed into the cockpit and switched on the main power. The rotors started to turn. She waited until they built up take-off rotation, and then pulled up on the cyclic collective and took off over the tabletop.

CHAPTER ELEVEN

─────○ℰ3○─────

THE HELICOPTER FLEW low and silently north.

Its dark shadow whipped across the tops of the ancient jungle canopies, which made up much of Venezuela. In the cockpit, Genevieve and Veyron were focused, but now settled into their flightpath. In the back, Tom slept well. Elise had cleaned the thigh wound and then sutured it shut. A small drip containing antibiotics and some colloidal fluids slowly ran down a small priming line into his vein. He would be sore for a few days, but he'd recover well. Elise and Sam both attempted to rest sitting up, but their constant subtle movements, and intermittent opening and darting of their eyes, suggested neither was capable of achieving it.

Despite being awake for nearly twenty-four hours now, Billie didn't even attempt to rest. Instead, she spent the flight back to the *Maria Helena* poring over the ancient stone tablet under the beam of a small flashlight, unable to look away from the mysterious inscriptions.

The tablet was made from a single piece of pitch-black jet lignite. The soft rock only scored a three out of ten on the Mohs scale of mineral hardness, making it easy for the ancient Master Builders who worked on it to carve into its soft mineral. It had been polished and cut precisely into the shape of a rectangle.

There was no written description on the surface. A series of fine lines were precisely engraved into the ebony-colored piece of stone, so fine that they were more easily felt than seen against the darkness. They ran both horizontally and vertically, giving it the appearance of a map showing the parallels of latitude and the meridians of longitude.

The Greek symbols for Theta, Sigma, Phi, and Omega were etched in gold, with one at each corner. Below each of those were the four horses, intricately carved out of stone or ivory to represent the Four Horsemen of the Apocalypse.

She studied the first one. It was made of ivory, and its rider carried a sword and wore a crown of thorns. Billie noted the reference to the White Horseman — AKA the Conqueror. The second one was made of pure obsidian. Its rider was carrying a set of scales carved from solid gold, which represented the changing value of barley during the reign of Famine. The third was made of a solid piece of red garnet, which was expertly crafted into the shape of a horse and rider. In the rider's right hand was a broadsword, identifying him as the biblical reference to War. The last horse was made of jade. Its rider carried a scythe. And although some people believed that he rode a pale horse, ashen, or black horse, of all the horsemen his purpose was undisputed — he was the harbinger of Death.

Despite the terrifying meaning behind the biblical references to the Four Horsemen of the Apocalypse, the sight brought reassurance to Billie. Eight weeks ago, when Sam and Tom were trying to track her down and rescue her, Sam uncovered a series of temples, and an ancient covenant based on the Four Horsemen. The covenant dated back to 286 A.D. when Grigori the Illuminator made a pilgrimage to Mount Ararat. What he discovered high up in the twin volcanic peaks, was enough for Armenia's then King Tiradates III to have him thrown into the deep dungeon of Khor Virap, and left to die in solitude where his story could never be told.

Billie thought about that story…

A great harbinger of Death was slowly approaching Earth. Left unhindered, the evil fire from the sky would burn its way through all life on Earth. But the Gods had left the Four Horsemen to protect mankind.

The constant whine of the helicopter's engine softened, and she felt the Black Hawk descend at the northern end of the Tepui Mountains. The nose of the helicopter dipped, and they descended into the valley below, where the dense vegetation of the Amazon jungle ran by at eighty knots, in a mirage of deep green.

Her mind returned to the stone tablet.

Within the inky black canvas were a scattering of identical blue sapphires. Despite the morning's light, which now filtered through the helicopter's windows, she used her flashlight to examine the precious gemstones. They sparkled wickedly under the beam of her flashlight, like a series of stars in the night's sky.

She switched off the flashlight and stared at the stone tablet in the natural light. A curious grin filtered across her open mouth. The entire image looked like a giant constellation of stars. There was a total of twenty-two sapphires.

But what constellation is it?

Her eyes flicked across the rest of the tablet. In addition to the twenty-two precious blue gemstones, there were five empty indentations, where she suspected previous sapphires were once fixed. She brought the stone tablet up to her face so that she could examine one of the empty indents. It looked as though something had once been there. She could even make out the remnant of some sort of cement most likely used to glue the radiant gems in place.

The discovery hit her like a bomb.

There had once been a total of twenty-seven sapphires.

Five were now missing.

Billie looked up. Sam's breathing was deep and irregular. The previously taut expression in his face was now relaxed, as though he'd finally slipped off into a peaceful dream.

She nudged him with her leg. "Sam. Wake up!"

Sam's eyes shot open, and he sat upright. "Did you find something?"

"Maybe." Her voice wasn't certain. More prying, instead. "How many of the ancient Master Builder temples do you know for certain have been destroyed?"

Sam blinked his eyes, still trying to wake from his sleep inertia. "What?"

"The Builder's temples. How many do we know for certain have been destroyed in recent years?"

Sam's blurry eyes darted across to the other crew, all resting in the back of the helicopter. "Three. Atlantis sunk. The one in the Mediterranean Sea was swallowed by the incoming tide. And the one beneath the Gulf of Mexico imploded."

"That's all of them?" she asked.

With her eyes still firmly closed, Elise said, "No. There have been five destroyed, although there may have been others that we don't know about. Including the three that Sam listed, there were also the one in Tunguska in the Siberian Taiga, which was bombed from above. And the one in the Khyber Pass, in Afghanistan, which was destroyed by militants shortly after Sam first investigated it all those years ago."

An engaging smile formed on Sam's lips. His piercing blue eyes were now wide awake with interest. "All right. So, there's five. Why do you ask?"

Billie handed him the tablet. "There are twenty-two stones implanted in small indents within the jet lignite."

"And?" Sam asked.

"There are an additional five indents without stones. When you examine them closely, you will see a small bit of silvery powder, the remnants of a very old form of glue."

"It looks like someone has gone to the effort of removing the gems?" Sam asked.

Billie nodded. "Exactly."

"Or it's just a coincidence, and five stones were randomly lost from the ancient artifact."

"That's always a possibility," she acknowledged. "You want to hear a more likely theory?"

"Shoot."

"This is a map of the world. Each of these gems represents a temple constructed by the Master Builders and interconnected by the strange power of the looking-glass. There were originally a total of twenty-seven indents filled with blue gems. Now there are twenty-two. Someone's been removing a corresponding gem every time a temple has been destroyed."

Sam took a deep breath and beamed with satisfaction. "You know what this means?"

Billie smiled. "We now have a map of the remaining temples of the Master Builders!"

CHAPTER TWELVE

SAM'S HEART POUNDED, and his muscles went tense with anticipation. He counted each of the meridian lines out loud. There were twelve lines in total. On a normal map of the Earth there were a total of a hundred and eighty meridian lines, but a normal map only displayed one line for every fifteen meridian lines.

A wry smile formed on his open mouth. "You're right, it is a map of the world!"

Billie matched his smile. "And it shows where each of the remaining twenty-two temples are."

"But it doesn't tell us which of the four temples we need to take the Four Horsemen stones we found in the Aleutian Portal to, does it?"

"No."

Sam met her inquisitive eye. "Is there anything else you've found?"

"Just this."

"Is there any way we can narrow this down more specifically, or are we going to have to find and search twenty-two temples around the world?"

"You know as much as me. Once we're back on board the *Maria Helena*, I'll run some more tests, and see what I can find."

Billie sighed. "Once we know the map coordinates each of these gems corresponds to, we might be able to recognize a pattern or rule out some of them."

"You're still confident of your theory?" Sam asked.

"Yes, now even more so." She spoke emphatically. "Those four stones found buried within the Death Stone will need to be placed at four separate temples—most likely running along contiguous meridians—in order to protect Earth..."

"How?" Sam asked, incredulous. "The four stones are small enough to fit individually in one's hand. So, what the hell are they going to do to protect us from an approaching asteroid?"

"I have no idea. But previously, we've seen the Master Builder utilize ancient technologies in ways that our scientists can't understand or explain. If they've known about this thing approaching for nearly thirteen thousand years, I'm willing to bet my life they've worked out a way of beating it."

"That's good, because we're all betting our lives that you're right."

The sound of the engine changed its pitch, and the helicopter banked gently to the left. Sam glanced up ahead, out through the windshield. They were flying over water. Most likely they had reached the Caribbean Sea. He glanced at the sea below. It was calm, the rays of light glistening off the ripples beneath the helicopter blades.

Roughly half a mile ahead, a vessel came into view.

It was painted sky blue. And along the ship's steel hull, in large emerald writing, were the words MARIA HELENA and below in smaller writing—Deep Sea Expeditions. From the distance, it looked like nothing more than an oversized tugboat or possibly an old icebreaker converted into a science vessel. On the aft deck a helipad could be seen—the only indication that it was anything more than a tugboat.

The sight of his ship always made him smile.

The nose dipped again, and the Sikorsky dropped its altitude before Genevieve leveled out and brought it into a gentle hover above the *Maria Helena's* aft deck. A moment later, she placed it firmly on the deck and shut down the engine.

The main rotors continued to whir almost silently above their heads. Billie glanced out the side of the helicopter. The sea was still moving swiftly.

Her eyes turned to Sam, and she asked, "We're moving?"

"Yeah," Sam answered, as though it was obvious.

"Where to?"

"We're heading to Belize."

"Belize? What's in Belize?"

"Nothing, but in two days the *USS Gerald R. Ford* will travel through the Caribbean Sea on a routine set of sea trials. We've been instructed to wait at Belize and rendezvous with her to return their experimental Black Hawk — otherwise I'm going to owe Uncle Sam somewhere in the vicinity of forty-five million dollars."

"What are we going to do waiting around here for two days?" she asked, as though the thought of enjoying some much-needed rest and relaxation in paradise was abhorrent and repugnant to her.

"I don't know what you want to do, but I'm going free-diving. There's an annual event. I booked tickets for Tom and I a week ago"

Billie met his eye. "A week ago?"

Sam shrugged. "On the off chance we had to wait for the *USS Gerald R. Ford.*"

She smiled and shook her head at his lie. "Tom's going to be pissed he can't go diving with that leg wound."

Sam glanced over at him. "Yeah, he'll be pissed. No reason I shouldn't have some fun though. Besides, he can come watch."

"I'll have a go deciphering the rest of the tablet and working out where each of the temples are that each of those sapphires correlates to," Billie said. Then, after a long pause, "once I've slept."

Her tone brooked no argument, and Sam didn't even try. His eyes were too heavy, and his body already shutting down for some much-needed rest.

"Yeah, for sure—get some rest. We're no good to anyone in our current state. I'm going to spend the day sleeping, and will probably take a few hours to enjoy the free diving competition tomorrow. After that, let's see what you've found and where we're going to go from here."

"Sounds good."

Sam paused. "Once we know which temples require the stones, and where they belong inside the temple, what then?" he asked.

Billie looked up, a faraway look in her eyes. She shook her head. "Then we wait."

"Wait for what?" Sam wasn't much of a waiter. He preferred action any day. A tendril of fear made the hairs on his arms stand up when he noticed Billie's expression.

She swallowed, hard. "For the signs that the ending of the world has begun."

CHAPTER THIRTEEN

―――――○⛛○―――――

Great Blue Hole, Belize

IT WAS A typical, balmy day off the coast of Belize.

The midday sun glistened in the clear blue and turquoise water, causing it to sparkle with the light of an infinite bed of crystals. Sam edged the *Maria Helena's* inflatable *Zodiac* through the maze of corals that formed the Lighthouse Reef, and then through the gap into the Great Blue Hole. On the opposite side of the small runabout, Tom stretched out his injured leg with a bemused look on his face. They had both dived here extensively when they were in their early twenties. It felt like coming home to a childhood vacation spot.

On an ordinary day, the giant sinkhole would have only had an occasional recreational dive boat and they would have been able to bring the *Maria Helena* right inside.

But today, the entire place was a great flurry of activity.

Boats full of spectators crowded the area where usually only dive boats bearing recreational divers were present. In the very center of the 300-foot, perfectly circular, submerged sinkhole floated a huge temporary diving barge. All the boats had been tied together to make one giant diving platform. At the very end of the flotilla was a single de Havilland Canada DHC-3 Otter Seaplane. Its owner had casually left it tied to the last boat in the flotilla, where it rested peacefully on the perfectly still water at the end of a single fifteen-foot line of rope.

Sam tied the *Zodiac* up alongside one of the larger pleasure cruisers and climbed on board. Tom pulled himself up over the railing, and the two of them made their way across the series of tied-together boats to the main diving platform.

Sam glanced behind him. Tom had a slight grimace he appeared to be working hard to conceal, but otherwise managed to step from boat to boat as nimbly as ever.

"How's the leg?" Sam asked.

"Fine. Never better." Tom grinned. "I told you it was a minor wound, I just needed to rest it for a day."

"That's right. And have some fluids, a dozen stitches, and some antibiotics."

Tom shrugged. "Those, too."

Sam stopped at the main event.

On the surface of the sea, the diving barge was a swarm of activity as well. Competition divers waited their turns to dive.

"How long has it been?" Tom asked.

"Since we last dived here?"

"Yeah."

"Gotta be fifteen years at least."

Sam completed his registration and safety briefing. Afterwards, he waited in silence, making the mental preparations for the dive. Both men had once held record-breaking dives at the site, but that had been a long time ago. Sam had no erroneous belief that he would score highly today. For him, it wasn't about the competition, so much as simply enjoying the event and the rare beauty of the location.

And it was stunningly beautiful.

Sam's eyes greedily raked the wonder before him. The Great Blue Hole was one of many such sinkholes around the world, but maybe the most famous and almost certainly the most beautiful and unusual. In contrast to the green of the surrounding sea, the sinkhole boasted intensely blue water, a result of its depth. Once situated high above the sea, it had begun its life as a cave, complete with karst sandstone stalactites and stalagmites.

The reef was the only remaining vestige of the surrounding land in which the sinkhole had formed, in four events taking place hundreds of thousands of years ago. When the top of the cave had collapsed, the resulting sinkhole descended through what was once about one hundred and thirty feet of surface strata before opening into the cave system, for a total of over four hundred and five feet. Then the sea levels had risen with the melting of the ice caps at both poles, submerging the land and the sinkhole alike. What was once an interesting geological phenomenon was now a spectacular one, beautiful both from above and below, and carrying a mystique that caught the imagination of divers and non-divers alike.

This sinkhole was particularly dangerous for free-diving, though extremely popular. Not recommended for the inexperienced, recreational diving here carried with it the potential to become lost within the stalactites and stalagmites protruding from the back-sloped walls that had formed before the area was submerged. In addition, the speleothems were off-vertical by a consistent five degrees, indicating a land shift and tilting of the underlying plateau in addition to the flooding by a rise in sea level. A diver could become disoriented among them.

Because of those back-sloped walls, diving in the center required absolute buoyancy control to prevent sudden plummeting, as there was nothing to grab and stop one's rapid and likely fatal descent. The depth of the hole meant it was, for all practical purposes to a human being, bottomless.

It would require all of Sam's skill to compete in this annual spectacle.

There was a total of eight freediving disciplines in which

people competed around the world. Today, Sam was participating in what was known as a *Variable Weight* free dive. The concept was to use a heavy sled to sink rapidly, feet-first, before dropping the weight, and using an inflatable balloon to return to the surface. In this case, Sam was wearing a purpose made free-diving vest, which utilized a high-pressured canister of air to rapidly inflate. It had been lent to him by one of the organizers of the event.

Sam's name was called, and he was told to prepare for the next dive.

Tom shook his hand. "Good luck."

"Thanks."

"Stay safe out there."

Sam grinned. "Of course. I'm not going for any record. I just need some time to clear my head and relax."

Tom smiled with genuine pleasure for him. "Good for you. You deserve it. Take all the time you'd like. Preferably under three minutes though…"

"I'll try my best not to stay down too long."

Sam stepped off the diving barge and dipped into the water feet first. The temperature in the Blue Hole at a hundred and thirty feet is a constant seventy-six degrees Fahrenheit all year round, and on the surface, it was closer to eighty. It felt like diving into a bath, only a little cooler than the outside temperature — and yet instantly refreshing.

He surfaced and made a signal to Tom that everything was all okay, before casually swimming across the surface to the weighted dive sled. It was being held by a rope and diving crane that reached out several feet from the diving barge. Two safety divers on the surface gripped either end of it to keep it steady. Sam had always felt the name, diving sled, was wrong, giving a false impression. Unlike a sled, it appeared more like an iron pogo stick crossed with a heavy spade. There was a sixty-pound nose in the shape of a wide shovel, followed by two horizontal pegs on which to stand his feet. At his chest height, was a t-shaped handlebar. All of it was made of iron and came to a total weight of one hundred pounds.

Sam placed his feet on the pegs, and grasped the heavy metal bar. Another diver helped slide a small rubber clasp over his feet to stop him from slipping off and coming away from the sled during his rapid descent.

The judge then said, "Dive when ready."

Sam closed his eyes. He slowly went through the time-honored process of preparing for a free-dive, by reducing his metabolic rate through meditation. He took slow, deep, full breaths, blowing off any excess carbon dioxide in his system, sending his body into a slightly alkaline state and consciously slowing every individual system down. His heart rate dropped from eighty beats per minute down to a staggering forty beats per minute.

He opened his eyes and nodded at the two divers who were keeping the sled from dropping. They let go—the sled lurched downward, and Sam began his race to the bottom of the Great Blue Hole.

CHAPTER FOURTEEN
———O&3O———

THE DIVE SLED picked up speed.

Soon Sam reached a descent rate of two to three feet per second. As cooler water rushed past his face, his mammalian dive reflex kicked in, and the ancient adaptation for conserving oxygen consumption underwater started to manifest.

Blood volume and flow was redistributed toward vital organs, as his peripheral blood vessels constricted. His heart rate slowed further to twenty-eight beats per minute. He swallowed constantly, to equalize the pressure in his middle ear.

Four feet to his left, the vertical dive line raced by.

He closed his eyes.

And found the sort of solitary calm and mental tranquility he'd been unable to achieve in any other place on Earth.

For less than two minutes, his mind was completely empty.

He no longer cared about the unforgiving celestial object rapidly approaching humanity, soon to complete its invisible thirteen-thousand-year-old celestial orbit, that would have it return to Earth.

Nor did he care about the potential conflict between the remaining Master Builders — who he was no longer certain had the best interests of mankind at heart.

Instead, he simply felt at peace.

Sam opened his eyes and glanced at the depth gauge. It read two hundred and five feet. Much less than he'd been able to achieve in his twenties, but more than he had any intention of trying to reach today.

He flicked the release valve and compressed air filled his lift bag.

But instead of sending him upward, he continued to rush toward the bottom. Sam's head snapped around to look at his lift bag. Gas bubbles spurted out through two giant gashes in his inflatable vest. Under normal circumstances, the entire canvas vest would have been folded in on itself until Sam had pulled the release string, and the air super inflated the balloon.

It was impossible to notice the gash without taking the vest apart before the dive to examine, and now impossible to fix. Which meant, he was going to have to somehow make his own way to the surface the old-fashioned route — by pulling on the dive line and kicking his legs.

He let go of the dive sled, but his foot snagged, and he continued to be pulled deeper. He bent down until he could see the problem. The rubber foot clasp had been replaced with a plastic cable tie. It fitted loosely around his right ankle and the vertical rung of the dive sled, so that he hadn't felt it until now.

There was no reason to have such ties on the dive sled, let alone around his ankle. Therefore, it wasn't an accident — and more importantly — it meant someone wanted him dead.

Sam placed his hand and mouth near the small air canister, and took in a deep breath. It would disqualify him from the tournament, but he was more interested in living than breaking records today. There was just enough for a single breath, before the tank ran out.

He kicked his right leg, trying to free his foot. There was plenty of movement, but he remained trapped by the sled — being dragged to the bottom.

The depth gauge now read 275 feet.

He used both his hands and tried to break the plastic. It was impossible. Military Police had been using similar ties to restrain prisoners for years. Without anything sharp to cut it, Sam was wasting his energy by fighting with it.

But what other option did he have?

The alternative was to simply give up and die. He fought with it for another few seconds, and then stopped.

The depth read 350 feet.

He would reach the bottom soon. *Then what?* Even if he could free himself, without the lift bag, there would be little chance of reaching the surface alive. Seawater became clearer the deeper he got, and despite the darkness, he could now see the bottom.

A seabed of sand and limestone raced to meet him.

Stalagmites, twelve feet tall and higher riddled the seafloor, like the pillars of an ancient city, lost for millennia. Below which, large erosions in the limestone formed jagged scars and deep crevasses and cave systems that stretched a further hundred feet below.

Next to him, the end of the vertical dive-line stopped ten feet short of the seafloor. Dangling off the very end of it, and placed there for emergencies, was a single tank of air and attached regulator. It was a divine gift if he could reach it.

The dive sled crashed into the seabed with a hard jolt, sending a thick cloud of limestone several feet high. The narrow, pointy end of the sled dug into the sandy edge. It balanced for a second and then tipped over, like a tree being felled.

It slid deeper, into an opening in the seafloor like a jagged scar — dragging Sam with it another twenty feet — until the sled became wedged horizontally and stopped.

Leaving Sam thirty feet out of reach of the emergency air tank.

CHAPTER FIFTEEN
———O&3O———

SAM WAS RUNNING out of options.

His lungs burned with the desire to breathe. In the darkness, he struggled to determine whether his vision was blurry from an oxygen starved brain, or from the depth where light failed to penetrate. A coldness quickly enveloped him, as though Death himself was wrapping a blanket over him in preparation of the last journey he'd ever take.

But Sam had no intention of dying today.

In the darkness he ran his hands through the coral protruding from the side of the limestone cave. His fingertips felt the sharp edge of a spiral piece of fossilized marine life. His fingers latched around it and gripped as hard as they could. Sam pulled back in one sharp jolt, and the rock broke free.

He felt for the plastic cable tie and ran the coarse piece of stone against it. Whatever he'd found simply slipped off the smooth plastic.

Frustrated, Sam moved his leg closer to the hard stalagmite and searched the surrounding reef for something sharper. He felt his hands cutting against some sort of shell. It felt big in his hand — maybe twice the size of it — and heavy too.

He placed the plastic against the edge of the cave wall and blindly struck it with the shell.

The first missed completely.

The second one slid off the smooth plastic, and scratched his right leg.

But the third one connected!

It sliced through the thin plastic and Sam felt his ankle finally become free. He pushed off the horizontal edge of the diving sled and swam toward the air tank.

A warm glow originated directly above him. Someone was swimming toward him. He couldn't quite see its source, but the light reflected off the metallic cylinder of the emergency dive tank.

It spurred him on and Sam kicked harder with his legs. His oxygen starved and disoriented mind, suddenly focused.

A strong beam of light swept across the Great Blue Hole. It paused on the air tank for a moment, and then continued — finally stopping directly on Sam.

The light shined straight in his eyes.

It made it hard to see the emergency tank. Behind the blinding glare of the light, he could only just make out the shape of another diver. Most likely, one of the rescue SCUBA divers.

Sam felt his vision going again. He kicked harder, but even the movement of his legs seemed to be incredibly difficult.

He was so close. *Another two feet!* Just keep going…

His legs refused to respond.

Sam's world went dark, as his mind shut down. He threw his hands forward. The left one connected with the dive regulator. He pulled it into his mouth and took a deep breath.

The cool air tasted sweeter than anything he'd ever experienced. He took slow, deep breaths in, until his vision started to return. It was intermittent at first, like an old TV that wasn't quite able to receive the transmission.

He opened his eyes and spotted the rescue diver coming in to meet him.

The SCUBA diver stared at him through his full faced divemask with piercing green eyes. They were intense and focused. The man had probably raced from the surface trying to save his life, at great risk to himself.

The man held up his thumb and forefinger together to form the shape of a "Q," an international symbol in diving for, "Okay."

Sam tried to answer, but his arms weren't quite responding yet.

"You okay?" the stranger mouthed.

Sam simply nodded.

Everything was going to be okay.

The rescue diver patted him on the back and smiled. His face said, *You're one lucky son of a gun.* Sam knew he was right, too. Few people could have survived the events of the past few minutes.

Sam took another breath in and stopped.

A sense of panic raged as adrenaline surged through his veins, and his chest burned—because the rescue diver just turned off the flow from his dive-tank.

CHAPTER SIXTEEN

―――――○☙3○―――――

SAM STUDIED HIS attacker's face.

There was something uniquely disturbing about his smile. It wasn't filled with hatred or anger. Instead, the diver's face was set with the cold, hard appearance of something entirely different and much more sinister.

Was it grotesque pleasure?

His attacker gripped Sam in an immovable and giant bear hug, preventing him from opening the emergency dive cylinder again.

Through the full-faced dive mask, the stranger mouthed the words, "It's okay. Just take a deep breath, and it will all be over."

The man was simply enjoying watching him die.

It was enough to rouse Sam into action.

He tensed the muscles in his arms, trying to break free of the restraint his attacker had placed on him. He needed to get his arms above his head to reach the top of the dive tank. It was impossible to break the vice through direct force. Even if his energy hadn't been depleted by oxygen starvation, he wouldn't have been able to free himself.

Instead, he needed a different plan.

Forcing every muscle in his body to relax, his vision darted downward, in the opposite direction he wanted to go. If he couldn't go up to the tank, perhaps there was somewhere he could go down. His eyes paused on his attacker's dive knife, strapped to his lower leg.

Sam moved his right hand slowly toward the weapon. The knife was still out of reach. He had one shot left, and he wasn't about to let it slip past him.

With his left arm, he threw his entire weight into pushing upward. Like a wounded animal in its death throes, Sam fought to reach the top of the dive tank. His attacker applied more pressure from above him — and with Sam's right hand, he shot downward toward the knife.

His hand made contact with the weapon's hilt, but there was minimal movement available to wield it as he withdrew the knife from its sheath.

Sam's attacker, realizing his mistake, tried to tighten his grip again. The man stared at him with those green and intensely malevolent eyes. A sardonic grin formed on his lips. Both men locked in a deadly battle that would determine which one got to live.

It was enough to prevent Sam from moving his right arm at all. But not enough to stop his wrist from driving the knife sideways — where he planted it deep into the diver's calf.

His attacker's pupils widened in pain.

A millisecond later, the binding pressure over Sam's arms disappeared as his attacker punched his right wrist.

A crushing pain seared through the bones of his right forearm.

Sam tried to drive the knife farther into his attacker's calf, but instead, the man used both his hands to pull Sam's hand away. In the process, the knife came free. Sam gripped the knife's hilt as firmly as he could, and the attacker made a desperate play to take it.

Both men were strong, but in his oxygen-depleted state, Sam

knew he wouldn't win a game of might in hand-to-hand combat.

Instead, he opened his hand and let the knife fall.

His attacker immediately dove to grab it, and in that instant, Sam pulled at the diver's face-mask. The quick movement broke the seal, and seawater flooded into his attacker's eyes. It would only take a competent SCUBA diver a moment to clear his mask, but in that moment, Sam kicked hard, breaking free from his attacker and raced toward the surface.

Sam pulled on the dive-line that ran all the way to the surface. He climbed it hand over hand, until he'd built up enough momentum to maintain a constant ascent. Without dive fins, he would have been exerting more energy than he had to try and kick his way to the surface.

Glancing below, he spotted his attacker.

The man had already cleared his dive-mask and was now kicking his fins vigorously in pursuit. In his right hand, the diver gripped the same knife Sam had used to stab him thirty seconds earlier.

It urged Sam on, pulling on the rope as fast as possible as he raced upward. He had a ten to fifteen second head start on his pursuer, who had fins. It was going to be a close race—but he had to win it if he was going to survive.

As the air in his lungs—from the few breaths he'd managed to take before his attacker switched the emergency tank off—expanded, he started to ascend faster than he could pull himself along the rope. Like a small rocket, he shot toward the surface. He opened his mouth, and breathed out in one long and continuous exhale.

He glanced at his depth gauge—just seventy feet to go!

Above him, he could already make out the dark shadows of the flotilla of yachts and dive barges. His view darted downward, where his frustrated pursuer was unbuckling his weight belt and inflating his lift bag. The small, orange balloon filled with air in an instant, and sent the diver shooting to the surface and toward him.

Sam gritted his teeth and kicked as hard as possible. He didn't need to go far. All he had to do was hold in there for another ten seconds, and he'd be on the surface. He kicked again, but his left foot didn't move — because someone had grabbed it.

The diver released the lift bag, and the orange balloon floated past Sam like a shooting star. Sam felt the jolt as the diver tried to pull him down again by his leg.

His attacker had assumed the only way to kill him was to drag him down long enough to drown him, or at least get close enough to him to drive the knife somewhere where it had the potential to kill him. The man probably guessed that Sam, in his hypoxic state, would be unable to concentrate on anything but trying to reach the surface.

It was a mistake.

Instead of fighting to reach the surface, Sam turned his energy to pulling — driving himself downward, to meet his attacker.

With his right leg, he kicked hard — and it connected at the space between his pursuer's dive-mask and face. It wasn't strong enough to do any real damage, but the man relinquished his leg as he tried to fix his mask.

It only took a second, but it was enough for Sam to kick the man's head again. This time, there was enough force to send his opponent off to see stars.

Sam didn't wait to see how much damage he'd inflicted, but instead swam to the surface. His mind struggled to focus, and in his disoriented state, he felt like he was never going to reach it. He felt as though both his legs had been attached to something heavy, which was dragging him under, time and time again. He could see the slight ripples of the water lapping on the surface only a few feet above him — but it may as well have been a mile.

A second later, his head broke the surface.

He took a giant gasp of fresh air…

And the darkness swallowed him whole, as he suddenly blacked out.

CHAPTER SEVENTEEN

―――――○☯○―――――

SAM OPENED HIS eyes.

He was on the dive barge, with his back up against a medical kit, looking out upon the glistening deep blue water of the Great Blue Hole. He must have passed out, and someone had dragged him out of the water. His mouth felt dry. Someone had placed a medical oxygen mask over his mouth and nose. It was working wonders to clear his head, after what had happened to him.

But what had happened?

He was free-diving. That much he felt sure he could remember. Could he have stayed under too long? That didn't seem right. He was only entering the competition to enjoy the peace and mental tranquility free-diving provided—not to get himself killed trying to break records.

So, what went wrong?

A flash of distant memories, almost like dreams filtered through his head, like a movie, fragmented and discombobulated. None of it made sense, but he recalled those eyes.

He sat up, rigid.

Tom said, "Hey buddy, you're awake!"

Sam searched his surroundings. His eyes spotted the orange

lift-balloon floating on the surface. He searched the faces around him. Then stopped and looked directly at Tom. "Where is he?"

"Who?"

"Quick!" Sam removed the oxygen mask. "Where is he?"

With his palms facing upward, Tom asked, "Where's who, Sam?"

"The diver, Tom!" Sam's piercing blue eyes were focused now. "The man who was trying to kill me…"

Sam tried to stand up, but his balance shook with vertigo.

Tom braced him and forced him to sit down again. "Here." Tom handed him the oxygen mask again. "Have some more oxygen."

Sam brushed the mask off. "No time for that, we have to find him!"

"Who?"

"The man that tried to kill me!"

"No one was trying to kill you, Sam." Tom grinned. "Well, no one except yourself! What were you trying to do, staying down there so long, did you learn to breathe underwater? You broke just about every free-diving record this place holds!"

"No… I was attacked!" Sam said emphatically.

"By who?"

"I don't know. He had a pair of intense green eyes. A killer's eyes, cold and hard. He tried to drown me. I got free by stabbing him with his own dive knife."

Tom's dark eyebrows narrowed. "You killed him?"

"No. I only got his leg. Maybe his calf or ankle or something…" Sam tried to recall what had happened after that. Then, with enthusiasm, he said, "He followed me to the surface. We can still find him!"

Tom said, "There was no one with you when you surfaced.

You were on your own when your head broke the surface. An instant later, you blacked out, and two of the rescue divers pulled you out of the water."

"Really? He must have been very close, you didn't see anyone at all?"

"No," Tom confirmed. "Why do you think he wanted to kill you?"

"Damned if I know…" His lips twisted into a wry grin. "It appears my recent dissertation on climate change certainly got someone's attention."

CHAPTER EIGHTEEN
———O&3O———

Tom stood up and scanned the area.

At six foot-five inches, he had plenty of elevation to view the rest of the divers and spectators spread out upon the flotilla, and those on the water. Unable to keep Sam from standing up, Tom helped him balance. His eyes raked the dive platform for any blood or signs of anyone walking with difficulty because of an injured leg.

"I can't see anyone having trouble walking," Tom said. "Maybe he never made it to the surface?"

"All right. Maybe he's still under the water. I don't know how long he'd been down there, maybe he was still decompressing?" Sam thought about it for a moment. "The question is, where will he try to go once he does surface?"

Tom thought about their location.

The Great Blue Hole was surrounded by the Light House Reef and there was only one way for a boat to get in and out. Outside of the submerged sinkhole the reef was too dangerous for boats to anchor.

He turned to Sam. "He'll need to surface somewhere around here and board one of these yachts to escape."

"Agreed, but we'll need to be ready for him." Sam was already searching for a better vantage point.

Tom said, "When did you have time to write a dissertation on anything?"

Sam grinned and started walking toward the edge of the flotilla. "I didn't. Billie did. I just submitted it as my own."

Tom followed, matching Sam's shorter steps.

"Why?"

Sam glanced at the first of eight, expensive pleasure cruisers. Their bows were all tied up together to make one large platform. His eyes searched the edge of the yacht for anyone waiting to tell him to get off their boat, and then stepped onboard. "It was Billie's idea."

"Go on." Tom stepped across the two-foot gap between the dive barge and the first of the pleasure cruisers.

"It all stemmed from our inability to determine who knew about the Göbekli Tepe Death Stone." Sam sighed, as though he'd had better ideas before, and then continued. "As we discovered in the Aleutian Portal, the ancient astronomer's stone depicts an asteroid that orbits Earth. Based on the calculations of a group of astronomers, it's set to return to Earth every thirteen thousand years — or roughly sometime during the next two calendar years."

"Sure. That's why we went to the pyramid within the Tepui Mountains, so Billie could retrieve the stone tablet, and why she's still on board the *Maria Helena* trying to decipher the Code to Extinction — while you're out here having a good time, and trying to get yourself killed."

Sam shrugged. "Hey, I was trying to clear my head!"

"Go on."

"When we found the Death Stone, its previous guardian left a hand-written message informing us under no uncertainties not to allow the Secretary of Defense to discover the stone was still intact, and informing us that she was being watched."

"Yes. I also recall the Secretary of Defense grilling both of us about the stone's whereabouts. So, what does any of this have to do with your dissertation on climate change?"

"Everything," Sam said. "Billie suggested I present a dissertation on the correlation between the shift of the magnetic poles and rapid climate change. There was a convenient global scientific forum, so I got the presentation together and did as she asked." Sam lengthened his stride, and Tom matched it again.

"Why the hell would you do that?" Tom glanced at the water where another diver surfaced, and then back to Sam.

Sam met his eyes, and shook his head. "Not him."

Tom stepped across the next gap between yachts. "I thought the idea wasn't to reveal what we know, and keep the public calm?"

"I didn't talk about the asteroid. The idea was to draw the attention of whoever it is who already knew about it. The easiest way to find them is to dangle me as bait and see who takes it."

"By discussing what might happen if the comet returns as the prophecy predicts, and brings with it some sort of asteroid capable of flipping the magnetic poles?"

"No. By discussing what is happening."

Tom stopped walking, and fixed his steely gaze on Sam's undaunted face. "You can't be serious!"

"I am. The world's changing rapidly. Not like the disaster movies would have us believe the end of days look like, but really no less dangerously…"

"What's happened?"

Sam continued to walk to the end of the row of yachts. "I'll tell you while we walk. I want to be sure he hasn't made it out of the water yet."

Tom nodded. "Okay."

"In the past three months the magnetic pole has shifted nearly two hundred miles farther south. It doesn't sound like much, but in terms of what is considered normal in the Earth's continuously shifting magnetic cycle, that's a giant leap."

"What were the responses?"

"There's been a slowing of the world's thermohaline circulation."

"How much of a slowing?" Tom asked.

"Not a lot, but enough to cause some pretty major secondary problems. Many skeptics of Climate Change have argued that it's merely the result of a statistical anomaly, and that over the course of the past decade, the average temperatures have resided clearly within the mean standard deviation."

Tom stopped at the last yacht within the flotilla. A single-engine de Havilland Canada DHC-3 Otter Seaplane rested in the still water, tethered by a single rope to the last pleasure cruiser. It was painted light blue right down to its pontoons, with a single line of red paint running down its fuselage. The aircraft was close enough that they could see it was empty.

He turned to Sam. "You see anyone?"

"No. Let's head back to the main dive barge and see if anyone has any recordings of the area before the dive. Maybe someone unwittingly captured an image of my attacker."

"All right, sounds good." Tom stared at the perfectly still water of the Great Blue Hole. "You said the thermohaline system has slowed?"

"Yes. As you know the large-scale ocean circulation is driven by global density gradients, created by surface heat and freshwater fluxes. Wind-driven surface currents, such as the Gulf Stream, travel poleward from the equatorial Atlantic Ocean, cooling en route and eventually sinking at high latitudes, forming North Atlantic Deep Water. This dense water then flows into the ocean basins. While the bulk of it upwells in the Southern Ocean, the oldest waters — with a transit time of around 1000 years — upwell in the North Pacific. Extensive mixing therefore takes place between the ocean basins, reducing differences between them and making the Earth's oceans a global system. On their journey, the water masses transport both energy in the form of heat and matter—solids, dissolved substances and gases—around the globe. As such, the state of the circulation has a large impact on the climate of the Earth."

Tom stepped across to another yacht. This one had a small Robinson 22 tied down on its forward deck, surrounded with teak. "You said we've already begun to see the effects of its slowing?"

"Yeah." Sam stopped again. "I had Elise run a search of any irregular weather or seismic activities in the past twelve months."

"They showed a spike, three months ago?" Tom asked.

"One heck of a spike three months ago. Individually, any of the events could have been put down to the oddities and irregularities of the environment and the capriciousness of the weather, but together, they are too much to ignore."

"It's happening now?"

"Not completely. The asteroid is still out there, but it's approaching, and already Earth is feeling the effects of its gravitational pull."

"How long until its effects come into full force?"

"We have no idea. But it won't be gradual when it does. No, it will be exactly what the horror movies make out the end of days to be."

Tom leveled his eyes at a single spectator, still wet from a dip in the water, walking toward him. The man wore board shorts, and Tom's eyes ran toward the man's lower legs. They were wet, but there was no blood.

Sam glanced at him and said, "Not him, either."

Tom sighed. "What I don't understand about any of this is why all the cloak and dagger stuff?"

Sam met his eye, "You mean, why don't we all simply come together globally and try to save the world?"

"Exactly."

"I don't know, but I'm hoping this will help me find out." Sam stopped suddenly and studied the water, where several bubbles making ripples on the surface indicated a diver was somewhere below. "One thing's for certain—the Secretary of Defense has kept some mammoth secrets from us, and I want to find out why. What's she involved in? The only thing I can think of is that someone doesn't want the truth to be told."

"Who has anything to gain from the annihilation of the human race, not to mention the rest of the mammals and most of the sea life, too?"

"Not just mammals. There are a hundred and eight *classes* of animals on Earth, give or take roughly five whose class biologists can't seem to agree on. Based on our oceanographic predictions, if the magnetic poles shift direction suddenly, you can count on at least a hundred of those being destroyed, or reduced to minimal numbers. Brachiopods, cockroaches and water bears will probably get by, because they always do, but who knows? Only extremophiles that live off the hydrothermal vents far under the ocean's surface are going to continue to live happily after this asteroid returns—unless we can stop it."

"So, why's the Secretary of Defense trying to keep its solution, written in the Death Stone, secret?" Tom persisted.

"I don't know, but I intend to find out." Sam held his breath for a moment. "And it appears someone's just as keen to stop me."

Tom met his eye. "You weren't coming here to clear your mind, were you?"

Sam grinned. "No. I needed a public event to draw my enemy out here."

CHAPTER NINETEEN
―――――○⛈○―――――

AT THE MAIN diving barge Sam spoke with one of the organizers, who informed him the entire event was being filmed from the top of *Calypso,* one of the larger pleasure cruisers with a small viewing deck above the main bridge.

Calypso was a one of a kind yacht for the ultra-rich. It had sleek lines and a carbon fiber hull, with a pristine interior of teak, giving it a unique blend of old and new, that was entirely dysfunctional. It was almost perfectly flat, with a small raised bridge, on top of which was an open viewing platform and a digital camera.

Sam knocked on the side of the glass door that led to the main entertainment area inside. "Anyone here?"

A man came out and asked, "Can I help you?"

He was in his early forties, with thick sea-swept hair and thick dark facial hair that fit somewhere between a beard and what is considered unshaven. He wore casual shorts and a loose fitting, long-sleeved white shirt. To Sam, he looked like the epitome of a rich, handsome, successful businessman who'd traded the hardship of modern entrepreneurialism for a life of luxury.

Sam smiled. "Hi, my name's Sam Reilly. This is Tom Bower. I was told you might have got a recording of the dive platform when it was being set up?"

The man's eyes brightened. "Hey, Sam Reilly, it's nice to meet you. I'm Todd Ridley. That was a crazy stunt you pulled off back there. I figured for sure you'd drowned."

"Thanks. I didn't plan to stay down quite that long."

"Come inside. I've got the camera still rolling upstairs." He opened a bar fridge and pulled out a couple of beers. "You guys want a drink?"

"Sure."

Ridley opened both drinks and handed them to him and Tom.

Sam took a mouthful. It was cold and delicious. "Thanks."

Ridley opened one for himself and took a little more than a mouthful. "Follow me upstairs. It's still recording automatically, but you can view what's already been shot, simultaneously." Turning to Sam, he asked, "So what are you looking for?"

"A friend of mine. He's meant to be one of the rescue divers here today, but I'm not sure he showed up. We were supposed to all come together this morning, but he wasn't there, and I don't see his boat around here."

"But you think he's here?" Ridley asked.

"Yeah. It's not like him to miss the event."

Ridley's eyebrows narrowed. "Did you ask the organizers?"

"Yeah, but would you believe it, they don't have a list of the volunteer rescue divers."

"Go figure."

Ridley led them up a spiral staircase and onto the teak-covered top deck. The *Calypso* appeared almost flat from above, with the lines of teak decking on the top deck perfectly aligned with those on the lower decks. To the aft, a two-seater Robinson 22 helicopter rested. On the top deck, a large tripod with a ten-foot periscope held a digital video camera. Next to it, a laptop on a small wooden table displayed the real-time image of the event from high above as it was being recorded. The camera's wide lens showed a two-hundred and seventy-degree arc, capturing most of the flotilla, diving barge, and about a third of the Great Blue Hole's surface.

Sam studied the live video feed, searching the faces of everyone he could see, as well as the few divers on the water's surface. His eyes narrowed as he examined a few faces, but nothing stood out to him.

"No luck?" Ridley asked.

"No."

"All right." Leaving the continuous feed running, Ridley opened a new window that displayed the previous hour of recordings. He clicked play. "Here, have a look at this."

Sam took another drink of his beer, and stared at the video recording. It showed some of the organizers setting up the diving barge. "Can you increase the speed?"

Ridley nodded. Pointing at the video controls, he said to Sam, "Help yourself."

Sam sped up the feed, stopping it intermittently to examine any new divers as they entered the water. Ten minutes later, he reached the end of the recording.

Tom shook his head, "I don't know, Sam. Your man either got here earlier, or he entered the water from behind us?"

Sam turned to face the clear blue water behind them. No one was on the surface, but that didn't mean that his attacker couldn't have entered unseen from that end of the flotilla. It would make more sense to do so, given he'd intended to murder someone.

Ridley looked up. "I've got to go meet someone. Feel free to stay here and keep an eye out for your friend if you want. There's plenty of beer downstairs if you want it."

Sam said, "Thanks, I appreciate it."

Tom scanned the area for any divers getting out of the water. "Now what?"

Sam sighed. "Now we wait."

CHAPTER TWENTY

THE WARM MIDDAY sun glistened overhead, sending rays of light deep into the water.

Tom glanced at the still water and took another drink of his beer. "Tell me about the changes that have already happened."

"What?" Sam asked.

"You said in the last three months the world has already undergone massive global changes due to this sudden shift in the magnetic poles, and the subsequent slowing of the ocean's thermohaline circulations. What were they?"

Sam sighed heavily. "I'll start as far south as Antarctica and work my way back a little closer to home, with what we've found so far. Like I said before, all of it could conceivably have occurred in any given year, but together it paints the picture of an impending doom. Some of these changes are small, but anyone with half a brain can see that it's going to affect the entire world."

Tom nodded. "Okay."

"In Antarctica we have two main areas of concern currently, indicating rising global sea temperatures." Sam removed a digital tablet from his backpack and opened up an image file, handing it to Tom. "Have a look at these."

Tom took the tablet and studied the image. It depicted an

aerial shot over snow-covered Antarctica. In the middle were three stunning blue lakes. Their brilliant shade of sapphire blue indicated the purity of the deep water forming above the ice. Tom recalled that the blue hue of the pure water was a common sight when he was in Antarctica searching for the man behind the Cassidy Project—it was caused by an intrinsic property of water that allowed only selective absorption and the scattering of white light. The effect here was beautiful, to say the least.

He smiled. "They're quite magical."

Sam nodded. "Truly stunning, if they weren't so dangerous."

"How so?"

"They're known as supraglacial lakes and form as warm air heats the surface of an ice sheet to create a pond of meltwater. There are now more than eight thousand of them riddled throughout Antarctica like pockmarks."

"They don't belong there?"

"No. Such lakes are common in Greenland, silently eating away at the ice for more than thirty years, but are an entirely new phenomenon to Antarctica." Sam took another drink of beer. "On the Langhovde Glacier in East Antarctica, these lakes have been draining into the floating ice below, which could have serious consequences for the stability of the entire ice shelf. In other cases, some of the fresh water has been documented to flow directly into the sea at the base of the glacier. This in turn has resulted in a massive influx of icy cold fresh water into salt water, which develops a tornado-like underwater current and further destroys the submerged glacier from below."

"And this is all new?" Tom asked.

"The lakes were first discovered in 2010, but only in the past three months became so significant as to join each other through a series of rivers. The result of which has recently manifested in the calving of a piece of ice-shelf the size of Delaware from Larcen C, off the Antarctic Peninsula."

"Go on."

"In Australia, an entire ecosystem of Giant Kelp off the coast of Tasmania have been destroyed. Do you remember diving there nearly ten years ago, when we first searched for the Mahogany Ship?"

"How could I forget?" Tom's eyes widened as he recalled the unique habitat. "What happened to it?"

"The East Australian Current, which is the Australian leg of the huge gyre that moves water around the Pacific, traditionally pushes warm water south along the coast of the mainland before turning east toward South America, and long before it hits Tasmania."

Tom nodded. He knew the EAC well from his experience sailing the east coast of Australia. "With the recent shift in the magnetic poles something has gone awry?"

Sam nodded. "The warming global climate has discombobulated this once-reliable system. Huge eddies of hot, nutrient-poor water keep spinning down toward the Tasmanian coast. This in turn has caused it to become the fastest-warming body of water on Earth, its temperature rising at a speed of nearly three times that of the rest of the world's oceans."

Sam took another mouthful of beer and then continued. "The warming seas are now hot enough to support the spawning of the long-spined sea urchin, an invasive pest that scours the seafloor. Giant kelp normally booms and busts, ripped away by storms before reclaiming the territory. But now the urchins move in like plague-causing locusts, nibbling away the new strands of kelp before they can grow beyond their reach. The result is miles upon miles of bare rock, covered with black, spiny invaders."

Tom closed his eyes and recalled the reef on which the kelp anchored itself, awash with color. Like some sort of unworldly creature, the Giant Kelp rose more than ninety feet from the seabed to the surface. Hues of red and orange glowed bright among the shifting tapestry of mustard, greens and browns.

He opened them again. "What a loss to the world…"

"It's not just the Giant Kelp that's been lost. An entire ecosystem has been destroyed with the loss of its habitat. Like the Eucalyptus trees that line Tasmania's coastline above the water, the kelp themselves are a habitat. Nearly eighty percent of the marine animals are endemic to the area. With the destruction of their habitat, creatures as unique and strange as the Weedy Sea Dragon, often described as the delicate parrot of the kelp jungle, will also become extinct."

Tom glanced at two divers who climbed out of the water. Both appeared unharmed. A slight nod from Sam indicated that neither was his attacker.

Sam said, "Heading farther north, the Great Barrier Reef, which has struggled with the global rise in sea temperatures over the past decade, suffered tremendously with coral bleaching affecting nearly seventy percent of is unique reef, stripping its coral of its vibrant colors and suffocating the living organisms that have taken nearly eight thousand years to reach their current size."

"I've heard about the coral bleaching. Australia's been struggling with it for years now. I read last year that the predicted cost to their tourism if the reef was completely destroyed would mount into trillions of dollars."

Sam nodded. "It's not just in the southern hemisphere the world's having problems. There are a number of signs here in the north that the delicate balance of life on this Earth is teetering toward our destruction."

"What else?"

"Closer to home. The United States, Canada and much of Europe have suffered more wildfires in the past three months than we have seen in the past decade. There have been multiple minor earthquakes…"

Sam took a deep breath, and then shook his head. "Even last week, Hurricane Hilda formed farther north in the Atlantic than almost any other hurricane in history. It would have destroyed half of Manhattan, if it wasn't for that sudden freak change in direction, that had it move mysteriously north and then east back out into the Atlantic where it dissipated."

Tom glanced at a man fishing off his yacht. Despite being a UNESCO world heritage site and protected, some people ignored the rules. "Have you ever considered whether we're supposed to survive?"

"No. Survival is the one common instinct, shared among all living creatures — we all want to survive."

"I didn't mean whether we wanted to or not — simply whether we should?" Tom's jaw was set firm. "I mean, when you look back on the history of the human race, we haven't exactly been kind to the planet, or the rest of those animals who we share it with, have we? Globally, when things go wrong, we always look at how to save ourselves and our profits, more than what is right."

"That's not always true. Sometimes the human race surprises you in its ability to band together for the greater good — where altruism beats greed."

"Really?" Tom grinned. "Name one."

"The Montreal Protocol."

"The what?"

Sam smiled. It was his *I've won this argument* grin. "The Montreal Protocol was agreed upon in 1987 and entered into full force by 1989. It consisted of two treaties designed to protect the ozone layer by phasing out the production of numerous substances that were responsible for ozone depletion. As a result of the international agreement, the ozone hole over Antarctica is slowly recovering. In comparison, effective burden sharing and solution proposals mitigating regional conflicts of interest have been among the success factors for the ozone depletion challenge, where global regulation based on the Kyoto Protocol has failed to do so." Sam took a deep breath and continued. "The two ozone treaties have been ratified by 197 parties, which includes 196 states and the European Union, making them the first universally ratified treaties in United Nations history. To this date, it's considered the world's greatest unified achievement of the human race for the benefit of the planet."

"I stand corrected. When a gun is put to the human race's head, sometimes it doesn't respond by pulling the trigger itself." Tom grinned and stood up. "Think this yacht has a bathroom onboard?"

"I'm sure you'll find one down below."

"I'll be back in a minute."

Tom walked down the spiral staircase, and used the bathroom. As he walked out to leave, he spotted a muscular and wiry man with pale white skin standing at the back of the yacht. The guy sported a yachting outfit that must have come straight out of the Calvin Klein catalogue. With his right hand, he was dabbing at his nose with a designer handkerchief.

"Are you okay?" Tom asked.

The guy was roughly average height, and had to lift his eyes to Tom's, six inches above. The stranger had the most unusual green colored eyes that Tom had ever seen. Tom thought he could see something in them, too.

What was it, recognition?

Oh shit!

The man reached inside his trouser pocket and removed a small flick knife. He jabbed it at Tom's gut with a quick and well-practiced move. Despite Tom's size he was surprisingly agile. Stepping to the left in an instant, he jammed his attacker's arm holding the knife against the side of the yacht. Putting his entire hundred and fifty pounds of force behind it, he watched the man grimace in pain.

"Sam!" Tom yelled. "I might need a little help down here!"

The man recovered quickly. Unable to move his armed hand away from where Tom had pinned it, he kicked Tom directly behind his right knee. The blow landed on Tom's wounded leg, sending a sharp pain behind his knee and thigh as though he'd been shot.

An instant later, the man changed the direction of his efforts. Instead of trying to push Tom off, he twisted, and pulled.

With the injury to his right leg, Tom was unprepared for the change in force, causing him to fall backward. He recovered in time to take a step backward, where he stepped off the back deck and fell into the water.

Tom surfaced upright a second later. The yacht's freeboard — the space between the waterline and the deck — was too high to reach. Instead he quickly swam across to the diving barge. He glanced backward, and spotted his attacker racing across the flotilla with Sam already running after him.

He lost sight of the chase for a moment when several hands reached to pull him up aboard the barge. At last sight, the guy was leaping over the boat deck, headed for the seaplane at the end of the mooring. Sam was already on his way, climbing down from the top deck to continue the pursuit.

As soon as he'd gained his feet, Tom started after them, gaining on them because of his long legs, but still limping with his injury. He was still yards behind when the guy reached the end.

The guy scooped up the tethering rope to the seaplane and tugged it hard, then clambered in and started the motor. As soon as the propeller started turning, he moved the seaplane away from the barge, just before Sam caught up. Tom watched in disbelief as Sam smoothly dived into the water, swimming powerfully, and caught the back of the pontoon.

Using the pontoon as leverage, Sam heaved himself from the water and climbed on, clinging to the struts and making his way to the cockpit. Tom shook his head, half in admiration, half in dismay. He stopped for a moment to orient himself, and then headed for Ridley's pleasure cruiser. The tiny Robinson 22 helicopter looked like his only choice.

Ridley looked out at Sam climbing onboard the back of the seaplane's pontoon as its pilot circled around, ready for takeoff. "What the hell does he think he's doing? This time he's definitely going to get himself killed."

The de Havilland Canada DHC-3 Otter was a single engine, propeller driven seaplane. With its high wing, and high power to weight ratio, it was designed for short take-offs and landings. Its single propeller whined loudly, and the aircraft started to skip along the still water of the Great Blue Hole until it built up enough speed to break the confines of gravity. It was setting up on a direct approach to the flotilla.

Ridley looked at him, his mouth wide open. "What the hell is the pilot trying to do?"

Tom yelled, "Duck!"

The aircraft took off right over their heads. Tom and Ridley instinctively dropped to the floor as the pilot banked sharply to avoid the collision.

Tom stood up and moved toward the Robinson 22. "Is your helicopter fueled?"

"Of course, it's bloody well fueled and ready to fly. Why?"

"I need to borrow it."

Ridley shrugged, as though the three hundred-thousand-dollar helicopter was a trivial possession. "Sure. What are *you* going to do?"

Tom grinned, and called over his shoulder. "What I always have to do. Make sure my mate doesn't get himself killed in the process of being a hero."

CHAPTER TWENTY-ONE
————○₰3○————

THE DE HAVILLAND Canada DHC-3 Otter was designed to carry ten passengers and one pilot to remote areas where other aircraft simply couldn't reach. This one had been upgraded with a STOL kit that allowed a short take-off and landing, by modifying the wing with a contoured leading edge and drooped wingtips for increased performance. Without it, Sam doubted the floatplane would have gotten off the water within the Great Blue Hole.

The narrow and robust aluminum fuselage was connected to two slender floats by a total of six struts—joined by three on each side—and a single boarding ladder that led to the rear hatch. There was also a forward hatch next to the pilot, but no ladder, which made it impossible to reach while the aircraft was moving.

Sam gripped the side of the ladder until the whites of his knuckles shined bright. He breathed heavily, and his heart pounded in his chest. And like a child who'd climbed the highest tree only to realize the inherent dangers, Sam glanced down at the water racing by and swallowed hard.

What have I just done?

He planted his feet hard on the slender float below.

The floatplane banked heavily to the left. The pilot's movement was more of a swift jerking motion than a controlled maneuver. Sam's weight instantly shifted with it, and the soles of his wet bare feet slipped off the pontoon.

Sam's legs fell into the open void and his hands slipped, falling to the second rung of the ladder. The wind rushed over him, trying to drag him away with it. The pilot straightened the floatplane and its 450-kW Pratt & Whitney R-1340 geared radial engine grunted as they started to climb.

Sam gritted his teeth and in one quick motion pulled himself up onto the pontoon again. He crossed his legs around the boarding ladder and entangled an arm through a rung so that his elbow formed a permanent lock, while his other hand gripped the edge of the ladder. He breathed heavily again catching his breath.

He shot a glance at the water. It was more than fifty feet below now — much too far to jump, even if he had wanted to. He returned his attention directly above, and his eyes trailed the row of windows along the fuselage. Except for his would-be-assassin, who was piloting the floatplane, the aircraft was empty.

That meant the pilot would have trouble defending himself, but also presented the problem of how to incapacitate the man without crashing the de Havilland in the process. Either way, he needed to come up with a solution before the pilot reached the mainland, where, chances were, his attacker would have reinforcements.

Sam climbed the four rungs up the ladder. His right hand reached the cabin door and tried to turn the handle. It didn't budge. His luck had run out. The door was locked, and he was fresh out of keys. Or anything else to force the door.

Inside, the pilot glanced over his shoulder and smiled at him with all the confidence of a man who knew he'd already won.

Sam returned the smile. He didn't lose very often, and when he did, his opponent's victories never came easy. He had nothing more than the shirt on his back, but there were still a few cards left to play. On the other hand, so did the bad guy. The pilot's eyes returned to face forward and a moment later, he banked hard to the right.

This time, Sam was prepared for it.

His hands gripped the rungs of the ladder, and his legs kept their footing at the base of the ladder. The plane leveled out again, and the pilot started to seriously put the little seaplane through its paces — banking sharply, diving, and then climbing to shake Sam off. As the plane dipped again, Sam considered his best option may still be to jump next time the aircraft dipped low enough that he might survive the fall.

He glanced back at the Lighthouse Reef to see how far they'd traveled. It was already more than a couple miles away. An impossible distance to swim in the open ocean, where the currents would constantly pull him off course.

The seaplane banked hard enough that it nearly rolled. The airframe gave a distinct creak with the greatly increased wing loadings and g-forces. Sam gritted his teeth and locked his hands together through the ladder's rung. It was obvious the pilot was willing to risk crashing the aircraft to win. Sam shook his head. His forearms burned.

Could his grip outlast the strength of the airframe?

The pilot could keep playing all day until the seaplane ran out of fuel, or its structure finally gave out. Either way, Sam couldn't hold on that long. He needed to do something, and whatever action he was going to take, he needed to take it soon while he still had some strength in his reserves.

He glanced across the horizon, trying to get an idea where the pilot was heading. The afternoon sun was somewhere to the right of the aircraft's nose, which meant they were heading west, toward the Belize mainland. Up ahead, Sam could make out the sandy outline of a beach and surrounding shallow green waters of Turneffe Atoll.

His eyes darted backward toward the Great Blue Hole,

confirming his predictions about their location. The sky looked clear and the water inviting. Sam squinted. There was something else on the horizon. Between him and the rapidly dwindling sight of the reef was the most welcome sight he'd had in at least a week.

Was it a small helicopter?

Sam remembered the tiny Robinson 22 on the back of Ridley's pleasure cruiser. He didn't know how, but he was willing to bet his life that Tom had either appropriated the helicopter or convinced its owner to follow them.

Maybe he wouldn't have to swim after all.

Now all he had to do was force the seaplane down, so the fall wouldn't kill him. Sam's daredevil nature had put him in many crazy predicaments, but the sight of his old friend once again coming to the rescue somehow made him braver than he probably should have been. They were approaching the mainland rapidly now, and Sam could see Belize City on its little pimple of land sticking out from the mainland.

Sam mentally checked his resources. There wasn't much. He'd simply thrown on a casual shirt over his board shorts after peeling out of the wetsuit. He climbed the top step of the ladder and gripped the large strut fixed to the wing. It gave him a clear view of the pilot. The man looked at him, and then dipped the wing to the left, trying to throw him off.

The pilot was close to succeeding at it, too. With his elbow wrapped around the strut, Sam ruefully considered his $4000 titanium dive watch. It wasn't the price tag that upset him. The watch was a gift from his dad, and he hated the thought of losing it. Deciding his life was worth more than the watch or the sentiment, he unclipped the lock clasp and waited.

When the pilot banked again, Sam was ready for it.

The aileron—that small hinged flap at the trailing edge of the left wing—jolted upward. The immediate reduction to the overall camber of the wing reduced lift and caused the left wing to dip. The seaplane rolled to the left.

Sam gripped the strut fixed to the wing, and then using his left hand, he shoved the titanium wristwatch into the small gap between the aileron and the leading edge of the wing, so the aileron was now permanently locked in an upward position.

Under normal circumstances, ailerons worked to turn the plane by creating more lift on one wing while decreasing the lift generated by the other. The upward aileron reduced the overall camber of the wing exposed to the relative airflow, which reduced its ability to create lift. As the wing dips, the aircraft rolls and then turns to that side.

Sam watched as the pilot tried to bring the steering column back to straight and level. It didn't budge. Instead, the seaplane continued to dip farther to the left. The loss in the overall lift of the wing caused the nose to drop, and the entire aircraft to stall — entering what is known as a death spiral, losing altitude as it spun in a tight circle.

The contents of Sam's gut raced upward as the seaplane plummeted to the ground. He held on and cursed himself for having so much success with his plan, as he raced toward the sea with deadly speed. He wanted to force the aircraft to crash, but hadn't planned to kill himself in the process.

He glanced toward the pilot, who was madly working the other controls to compensate. The engine whined, as the pilot tried to extract every pound of lift, and the tail rudder was hard all the way over to the right, in an attempt to counteract the roll.

The pilot's damned good, Sam noted — but not good enough. They were going to crash, and they were going to crash hard.

He had no intention of dying today. It wasn't just his life at stake. The code to extinction needed to be broken and right now he was the most likely person on the planet to do so. If he died, billions of others might soon follow.

Sam swallowed and pulled the watch free from the hinge.

Instantly, both ailerons started to move wildly. They settled into a neutral position and the calm sea below raced to greet them. Sam's eyes turned from the sea to the pilot. The man had dipped the nose to gain airspeed. It was probably the only option, but risky too. If he didn't have enough time, all the pilot would have achieved by doing so, was to ensure that he struck the water faster and harder.

With his heart in his mouth, he yelled, "For God's sake, pull up, man!"

The pilot glanced at him. His blue-gray eyes were malevolent, and he grinned like a man possessed — a man who'd risked everything and lost. For such a person, all options were available.

Sam felt his gut churn with fear, as comprehension greeted him like an unwanted stranger — *he's going to kill himself just to be certain I don't survive.*

CHAPTER TWENTY-TWO
──────○℘3○──────

SAM KNEW HE was out of options.
If he or the seaplane struck the water at this speed he would be dead. There was no point trying to jump. His downward momentum was already deadly.

There's an odd feeling of peace that comes across a person who realizes that death is imminent and that there is nothing they can do to change it. If there had been more time, he might have reflected that his life had been extraordinary. That he'd lived more days in his short life than most could have in ten lifetimes. But instead, his final thoughts turned to the future of mankind.

Best hope to hell you can break the code to extinction, Billie!

In the cockpit, the pilot firmly pulled the control wheel toward his chest. At first, the de Havilland's nose refused to move. But a split second later, it was coaxed to rise.

The dark blue of the deeper water appeared to race faster to meet them, as though it was eager to reach them, before the seaplane could be manipulated into leveling out.

The sea lost and the little de Havilland won.

It leveled out precisely as it reached the water. The slender pontoons skimmed across the top of the water, as the pilot pushed the throttle all the way in, and the floatplane started to climb again.

Sam grinned as he struggled to maintain his grip on the wing's strut. He gazed at the pilot, who'd now recovered full control over the aircraft.

The pilot glanced backward and met his eye, grinning wildly and laughing at the same time. "Sam Reilly — you sure are one crazy son of a bitch!"

Sam stared at him, trying to read some sort of purpose in his attacker's face. "I did ask earlier to get off the ride…"

The pilot laughed. When the laughing eventually stopped, he smiled. It was a surprisingly engaging smile. "I'm glad I got the chance to meet you. This has been one hell of a fun day, hasn't it?"

"I'm glad you enjoyed yourself." Sam returned the smile. "Now what happens?"

"I'm afraid you're really going to have to die. It's nothing personal. Bigger things at stake than you or me. But you already knew that, didn't you?" The pilot grinned like the devil. "If it's any consolation, you weren't going to live much longer anyway. No one is. Now at least your death will serve a purpose. The colony thanks you."

Sam wanted to ask, *what colony?*

But he didn't get the chance.

The pilot shoved the control wheel hard to the right and the aircraft started to roll. Sam had braced, expecting to be thrown downward, but instead, his attacker had rolled to the right — sending Sam's side of the wing upward.

This time, the pilot didn't attempt to level out again.

Instead, the de Havilland Canada DHC-3 Otter, continued to roll. Against its structural recommendations, and as a tribute to her strong airframe, she continued to roll a hundred and eighty degrees.

The pilot brought her to straight and level in an upside-down position.

Sam's heart raced as the bulk of his body came to rest on top of the wing. Staring downward at the fuselage, he spotted a small cylindrical opening.

It was the air intake manifold.

Sam pulled off his shirt and stuffed it into the opening. The engine quickly drew it further inside, until it became wedged hard and all airflow ceased.

The engine coughed.

Sam clenched the side of the wing strut with all his might. The pilot, as expected, assumed that the roll had caused the engine to flood the carburetor, and consequently completed the maneuver until they were once again flying straight and level in an upright position.

The propeller continued to spin, but already it was losing strength.

With the carburetor starved of air, the engine sputtered and choked.

And then cut out completely.

Inside the cockpit, the pilot dipped the nose to maintain airspeed. Unaware of the cause of the engine's problem and suspecting it to be flooded, he went about setting the fuel mixture to idle cut off and the throttle to wide open while cranking the engine. The idea was to attempt to allow excess fuel to exit the engine through the exhaust. Then, once enough fuel cleared the cylinders and a proper ratio of fuel to air was achieved, the engine would begin firing.

It probably would have worked, too — if the engine had been flooded.

If the air intake manifold hadn't been blocked by me...

Sam stared at his attacker and smiled.

The pilot was working hard to resolve the problem. They

were losing altitude. The aircraft had a decent glide ratio and already the pilot set a new course directly toward the closest piece of land — the city of Belize.

Sam grinned and then shouted, "You broke your toy airplane... I guess we're both going to meet our maker together."

"Speak for yourself," the pilot replied. "See that land up ahead?"

Sam glanced at the sandy peninsula jutting out into a sea of shallow green and turquoise water. "Yeah, it's the city of Belize."

"I think I can reach it."

"You think?" Sam teased.

"Yeah, I fucking think. Then I'm going to get out and kill you."

Sam started to laugh uncontrollably.

The pilot snapped his head around. "What the fuck are you laughing about?"

Sam stopped laughing. His jaw was set firm and his piercing blue eyes were fixed on his attacker. "I don't die that easy. Oh, and by the way, if you glance over your shoulder you'll notice my friends are right behind us."

The pilot glanced over his shoulder and swore. A moment later, he lowered the nose and set up for a landing. At the edge of the city a rocky cliff, thirty feet high, jutted out into the sea. On the other side of the cliff a single road led to the popular southern end of the city, filled with tourists and locals wanting to have a good time.

Sam studied their glidepath. It was going to be close. Too close for him to be certain they would clear the cliff at all. He glanced at the water. It was still fifty feet below, but as they got closer he might just make it if he jumped.

He dismissed the idea. The priority was catching his attacker.

He needed answers, and right now, the man piloting the aircraft was just about the only person who could provide them.

Sam held on, and the seaplane gradually approached the land.

The aircraft crossed the rocky cliff, clearing it by a full three feet. Sam waited. A split second later, its twin pontoons struck land.

Sam jumped.

He hit the grass and rolled.

When he finally stopped, Sam stood up.

Disoriented, he scanned the area for signs of his attacker. A long line of white scratch marks from the pontoons ran along the blacktop, leading to where the wreckage of the de Havilland Otter rested on the edge of the road some eighty feet farther away.

From the edge of the crooked fuselage, the pilot was already scrambling out. Sam met his attacker's eye. The man cursed and then started to run.

Ahead of him, Tom was already bringing the little helicopter around at a punishing pace, settling into a hover, ready to land.

Another two hundred feet away, he spotted his attacker entering a bar as if nothing had happened, and his seaplane wasn't parked in the middle of a resort city street. Sam shook his head to clear it and scrambled to follow the pilot, not waiting for Tom.

Inside, the bar was rollicking. Despite the hour, party-goers were drinking and dancing as if they were celebrating the ending of the world. Sam pushed his way through the crowd, looking for his target. He was halfway through when he spotted the man opening the back door. Some woman grabbed him and pulled his head down to hers for a drunken kiss. He smiled and set her gently aside. Someone else thrust a beer in his face.

He kept going, racing to reach the door.

Sam opened it, and spotted his attacker getting into a cab, which peeled away with a screech of tires. Sam looked around wildly for another cab, but there were none to be seen. The adrenaline surge was over.

Dejected, he slid down the doorframe to land on his butt.

He felt something digging into his left hand. *What could this be?* He opened his hand. He glanced at the contents and smiled. He was still holding his wristwatch. *Well, what do you know? It still works.*

Seconds later, Tom opened the door.

"Where did he go?"

"He got away." Sam swallowed hard. "Which means we're back to square one."

CHAPTER TWENTY-THREE

―――――○⊰३○―――――

Batagaika Crater, Russia — Gateway to the Underworld

THE OLD MAN had once worked deep in the Mir open-cut diamond mine in Yakutsk. In 2004, its seemingly endless supply of gem-quality diamonds ran dry, and the production was forced to close. In 2009, the mine was reopened, but this time with deep underground shafts.

He told the very few people who asked, that a cave-in at one such mine shaft had caused his left leg to become grotesquely crushed. A local medicine man was able to set his leg so that he could one day walk on it again, but the foot was left a permanently disfigured mess of mangled bone and skin tissue. With a gregarious smile and a once handsome face, he would then hint at the more somber reflections of his past. Telling them that suffering is a good way to pay penance for the mistakes of his youth, and then he would refuse their kindness and continue on his way.

Because he alone knew the truth.

It was all lies.

His leg had indeed been crushed in a mine collapse. But it wasn't at the underground Mir mine in Yakutsk. The accident had taken place at the end of a very different mine altogether. And there was nothing accidental about the cave-in.

It was the last week of their extensive mining project, which had taken years to complete. They were all meant to go home to see their families. But they couldn't, could they? Not anymore. They knew too much. It would be impossible to stop them from revealing secrets the world wasn't ready to hear.

When he heard the distinctive sound of dynamite charges being triggered and the shifting of earth beneath his feet, he didn't try to flee like the rest of the men. Instead, he ran deeper into the tunnel. The entire shaft led nowhere, and it soon became apparent the entire place was set to collapse.

But deeper still, a ventilation shaft had been bored.

It led eighty feet to the surface. He was close. If he had left a couple seconds earlier, he would have reached it without harm. As it was, he'd left it too late. The cave-in continued, like a chain-reaction, until it was over the top of him.

A single boulder caught his leg as he was climbing into the entrance of the ventilation shaft. It took him nearly an hour to break the stone apart using a chisel and hammer normally used to set dynamite. When he was free, his foot and lower leg were badly damaged.

He looked up, where the slim light of the night's sky shined down from the opening of the ventilation shaft. It would have been a struggle to climb had he been uninjured. In his current state, he knew it was closer to impossible.

But then he had thought about the secret, and he knew he had to escape. He had to live long enough to tell someone, so that his family could be spared. He alone survived through tenacity and sheer will. He had a purpose. He needed to tell a secret.

It took him three weeks to reach his old home, and when he got there, he discovered that everyone he'd ever loved had been taken from him.

His secret no longer seemed important to him. He wanted nothing more than to die, but even that seemed too easy a way out for him. So, he continued as he had always done, striving to survive through any means he could.

Without a family to support him, that means had recently taken him to the Gateway to the Underworld—a massive crater in the frozen heart of Siberia.

The old man took another step closer. His disfigured foot hurt like hell. It always had, but recently the combination of age and cold seemed to worsen it tremendously. He slowed his pace as he got closer to the dreaded place. He'd been three years old when the massive crater first made its appearance, and in the nearly fifty years since, he and everyone he knew had believed it was evil, the gateway to the underworld.

Each year, it had claimed more and more of the surrounding land, devouring all vegetation in its path. Those who lived in the closest village of Ese-Khayya, in East Siberia, knew it to be a living, breathing monster from hell. It was growing rapidly, and the foreign scientists who came to study it during the summer months said nothing would stop it. Its very nature meant that it would grow faster and faster each year—until the end of the world.

He forced himself to smile.

It had been decades since he'd viewed the place and much had changed in that time. He grew up in the nearby village of Ese-Khayya. Born to a poor family of the local Yakutian tribe that barely eked out a living in the frozen north, he'd dreamed of one day leaving this place.

As a teen, he'd thought it might be a dinosaur egg, or even an intact skeleton. His imagination was captured by the great lizards for several years. Now an old man of 52, he knew that the secrets of the monstrous crater were more likely to be mammals from 4000–5000 years ago. Perhaps a musk ox or mammoth. One year, the thawing permafrost had disgorged a horse from what the scientists called the Pleistocene. He'd even heard that the walls of the crater showed bands of forests like those that covered the land now, indicating it had once been warmer here.

Already it was warmer in summer than it had been during his youth. Somehow, in a way he didn't quite understand, the melting and caving in of the crater meant that it would continue to be warmer each year. He couldn't wait for that. His bones craved a place where he didn't freeze for nine months of the year. It was time to put aside the superstitions that had kept him from entering the crater all these decades. This would be the summer he either found a treasure that would allow him to leave this place, or die trying.

The half of him that clung to the stories he'd been told all his life fully expected to die trying. Either the earth would open and swallow him as it had done when others went to explore the crater, or the denizens of the underworld would capture him and carry him away. But even that was better than to endure another winter here.

He plodded along beside his oxcart. The crater was only three miles from the village, but no roads went there. His route skirted hills and crossed streams from the closest road, forcing him to spend a night under a canvas in the cart. Today he would gain the edge of the crater, and God help him with whatever came next. He was getting too old to spend a freezing night with no more than canvas to shelter him.

An hour or two after dawn, he stopped his ox and cautiously approached the edge of the crater. The unstable soil, mixed with frozen moisture, was vulnerable to crumbling. The edges tended to collapse, which was what kept the monstrous gash growing ever deeper and wider. No one knew how deep it would go, but the scientists had said it would likely eat through the entire hillside before it stopped or even slowed. Each year, the more surface that was exposed, the more the crater outgassed the carbon dioxide trapped in the frozen water. That in turn, they said, warmed the area, thawing it more, causing it to collapse more, and warming it more. It seemed to the old man that such a cycle would never end, until the hole reached the very center of Earth, Truly he believed the fiery center to be hell itself.

He drew a deep breath and paused to look around for perhaps the last time in his life before he would descend into the crater. The landscape was filled with thick vegetation. Dense forests of Dahurian Larch stretched to the horizon in the north. Siberian Pine and deciduous forests composed of birch and poplar species lined the Batagayka tributary of the river Yana to the south. It was beautiful in its own stark way, and he understood that it was only because of the warming of the earth in general that he had these forests to view. Only a small percentage of the trees were older than he was. Some of the scientists had said it was because of deforestation when he was a baby that the crater appeared in the first place.

He didn't know. All he knew was that now, only two weeks past summer solstice, was his last chance before winter set in again and it was too cold to make the overnight trip. And that the crater into which he was about to descend was dangerous, treacherous, and his only chance of making a better life for himself. With that final look around, he sighed and picked his way carefully down the steep cliff face, occasionally slipping and reaching in vain for something to slow his slide into hell.

The interior of the crater looked a little like melting blobs of ice cream. Vegetation couldn't take hold before the fragile soil collapsed under it. Steep hills inside dotted the lower reaches of the two hundred and seventy-eight feet of depth. Once inside, he despaired of finding anything because the landscape was so broken. Nevertheless, he walked slowly around the nearest wall, examining the surface of the cliff face closely for any hint of a fossil or frozen carcass.

He became so focused on not missing anything that he didn't watch where he set his feet. He'd just seen something he wanted to examine more closely when the ground below him shifted and collapsed, throwing him to the side. He staggered, trying to catch his balance, and in the process, twisted his ankle painfully. A thrill of fear went through him. No one would come looking for him if he couldn't climb out of this place.

Just once I wish something would go right.

He sat down right where he was, on the cold, damp ground, and allowed himself to feel sorry for himself for just a few moments. Only a few moments, though, because he knew he'd have to rescue himself.

To make matters worse, a strange, stinging precipitation began to fall. He huddled miserably by the giant roots of an upturned conifer tree, until he noticed that the downfall pelting him wasn't moisture at all. Dozens of tiny, clear stones lay near him. He picked one up and held it gingerly between his fingers, bringing it close to his eyes. The stone was minuscule, but very pretty. It sparkled in the weak sunlight.

No sooner than the old man observed that, he looked up. The sky was a clear blue expanse, with the small stones still falling…out of nowhere. When several hit his face, he hastily looked down again. He caught his breath and carefully examined the stones.

Could these be… diamonds?

The idea made him gasp. Was it really this simple? He wished for his fortune to turn, and suddenly he was showered with diamonds?

The old man staggered to his feet and started to dance a joyful jig, thinking better of it when his weight fell on his injured ankle. Without pausing to analyze the why and how of the windfall, he fell to his knees again and began scooping up dozens of the tiny stones. No one in the village would believe this!

On second thought, he shouldn't tell anyone. No, these stones could be dangerous to his health if anyone else knew about them. He felt a prickle on the back of his neck, imagining he was observed. He huddled over his small pile of diamonds and looked up. There… in the bushes at the edge of a crater, he imagined he saw movement. A moment later, a rustle of noise above the *ping, ping, ping* of the stones gave him even more evidence that someone was watching.

His attention was snagged by a larger *ping* close by. He whipped his head toward the sound and was stunned by the sight of a much larger stone lying on the ground about a meter away. He scrambled toward it and snatched it up. He opened his hand, with the stone resting in the center of his palm. He'd never seen one, but he knew beyond a doubt, this was a diamond. A flawless diamond, bigger he thought, than a normal diamond. All his dreams were about to come true.

He placed the diamond reverently in his watchpocket, a place that had never seen a watch deposited. Then he scooted back to the little pile of smaller stones he'd collected and stuffed two handfuls into his jacket pockets. Fearful that the watcher was human rather than animal, he didn't want to stay where he was vulnerable to attack. Instead, he searched for a way to climb out of the crater.

It was difficult going with the cliff sides crumbling half the time, but he finally gained the top several meters away from where he'd left his ox. The patient animal still stood there, munching on what vegetation it could reach. He turned the ox and pointed back toward the village. This time he would walk through the night if he had to. His find was too precious to wait longer than necessary.

He'd walked for several hours when he encountered the path he'd taken away from the road. It led through a particularly dense area of larch forest. He was watching his footing, loathe to turn his ankle again, when a noise made him look up and his heart skipped a beat.

Twenty feet ahead, a man stood quietly in the path. He looked young and heavily overweight. The stranger stepped forward to greet him. The old man instantly thought uneasily of the treasure in his pockets.

The stranger greeted him through dark, hooded eyes. Examining him with the wry curiosity of a scientist assessing a primitive creature. The man had striking features — very pale skin, even for this region, and intensely dark eyes. There was intelligence in those eyes, and pain behind them, too. Something else was there as well. The old man couldn't put his finger on it.

Was it triumph?

The stranger gritted his teeth and stared at him with eyes so dark they appeared almost black, with tiny specks of gold, like the devil.

The old man felt his chest constrict at the sight. He closed his eyes as though it might protect him from his past. There was only one person he'd ever met with such eyes, and that person had died a long time ago.

The man fixed his penetrating gaze at him and said, "Pressure! Everything of value in this world requires pressure to achieve its potential!"

When the old man opened them again, the stranger was gone.

A few minutes later, he heard the deep, guttural sound of a large diesel engine starting up. He stepped through the thick vegetation, and caught the glimpse of an oversized, Russian quarry truck. On the back of it, was a large dish—the sort found on a microwave tower.

He sat down and watched the truck disappear to the north.

There was something about the stranger. He looked familiar, yet distant too… he stared at the overweight man and shook his head. It was impossible. There were similarities, but more differences, too.

He shook his head. It was impossible. Besides, he didn't believe in ghosts.

Yet he was still unable to shake the feeling they'd met before…

CHAPTER TWENTY-FOUR

―――――○⋲⋗○―――――

Philip S. W. Goldson International Airport, Belize

THE GULFSTREAM G550 taxied along the blacktop, gently easing to a stop at the end of the runway. Ilya glanced out the window and watched as a commercial jet passed overhead. A moment later, he heard the roar of the Gulfstream's twin Rolls-Royce engines and the luxury jet bounded down the runway, before defying the effects of gravity at a steep incline.

He rested back into the Italian leather and closed his eyes.

A computer search for Sam Reilly had identified that he was going to be diving at the Belize Great Hole free diving competition. It should have been a breeze, but there were complications. The man simply wasn't that easy to kill. Everyone could be killed, but he'd gone about it the wrong way. He wanted to make it look like an accident. Sam wasn't the sort of guy who had accidents. Ilya knew that now. Next time he would simply walk straight up to the guy and shoot him.

His mind returned to the way Sam had tried to disable the seaplane, so it would crash. It had been an invigorating experience. It wasn't the first time the man had nearly killed him, either. A week ago, Sam had trapped him inside the Aleutian Portal.

The thought of death made him recall how close he'd come to drowning as a kid. He and his brother fell through a sheet of ice on a lake in Siberia. His brother had died, but he was rescued and resuscitated by someone working below the ice. That's how he came to meet Leo Botkin. One of the most powerful and dangerous men on earth.

The experience had changed his life. Not only did he lose his brother, but it had made him stronger and tougher, mentally and physically. There was a certain comfort in knowing that death was not so bad. It was only in life that you experienced pain—it had made him far more callous and capable as an assassin.

The Gulfstream banked gently, and his cellphone rang.

He answered it immediately. "Yes?"

It was Leo Botkin. "Do you want to tell me why I had to send you my private jet?"

Ilya sighed. "There were complications."

"Is it done?"

"No."

"Why not?"

Ilya looked out the window, at the turquoise water intermingled with a series of shallow reefs below. "There were complications."

"That doesn't normally stop you from doing what I ask." Botkin's voice was cold and hard.

"You don't normally ask me to kill Sam Reilly."

"When will you finish the job?"

"I'll start tomorrow. I can't find anything about where he is right now, but I will." The Gulfstream straightened up, and Ilya rested his feet on the soft leather chaise. "Any idea what he was doing at the Great Blue Hole?"

"You said he was entering some sort of free-diving competition."

"Sure, but why?"

"He likes diving. Why not?" Botkin asked.

Ilya sighed at the obvious discrepancy. "Sam Reilly's got the Death Stone. He's a smart guy. By now he must know what the future holds. Time's running out. He's got one chance to survive."

"So?"

"What the hell was he doing here looking like he's on vacation?"

"Beats me?"

"Really?"

"Yeah. Your guess is as good as mine. When you work it out, let me know."

Ilya knew he was lying, but had learned long ago that Leo Botkin let you know precisely what he wanted you to know and nothing more.

"Okay."

Botkin's voice took a dangerous tone. "Do you have any idea what's at stake here if he works out what to do with the stones?"

"I know," Ilya confirmed. "Don't worry, he won't be around long enough to work it out."

"You'd better hope not."

CHAPTER TWENTY-FIVE

―――――○☾३○―――――

Onboard the Maria Helena — Coast of Belize

THE DARKROOM WAS positioned on the lowest deck of the *Maria Helena*, toward the bow and below the waterline. The steel hull and purpose-built door barred any light from entering. In the days before Global Shipping had purchased the vessel and reconditioned her from an Ice-breaker to a Salvage and Rescue ship, the room had been used by its previous occupants to develop film — in the times before digital cameras, when photos needed to be developed and every shot counted. Now, the room was set up with a range of lights across the UV spectrum that could be used to examine artifacts or antiques.

Under the soft red light, Billie stared at the ancient stone tablet.

Stolen from the temple hidden within the sandstone quartz caves beneath the Tepui Mountains, it had already revealed a number of secrets. She'd already discovered that it was an ancient map leading to all twenty-two of the remaining temples, but so far, there was nothing she could do to interpret it.

The colors visible by unaided human eyes are controlled by the wavelength of light vitality. Unlike some insects, people can just view the spectrum from red to violet. Other invisible *colors* exist above and below this spectrum. The color above red is called infrared, the same as they used in their night-vision goggles to access the Tepui Mountains at night. The color below violet is called ultraviolet. Ultraviolet light will make fluorescent or luminous pigments fluoresce, emanating visible light.

It was inside the ultraviolet color range that she hoped to find some hidden clue left by the ancient Master Builders.

There were four main types of ultraviolet light, each one separated into categories based on their wavelength. Unaided, human eyes can view violet light between four hundred and fifty and four hundred nanometers. To see light in the wavelength spectrum of four hundred to three hundred and twenty, also known as ultraviolet A, long wave, light, one needed the assistance of a black light. Moving further down into a range of three hundred and twenty to two hundred and eighty, ultraviolet B is highly harmful to one's skin, yet small exposures are vital for the production of vitamin D3 that allows the human body to absorb calcium in the bowel. At the lowest end of the spectrum, medium wave length light and two hundred and eighty to one hundred nanometers, the short wavelength light was considered germicidal, and used in medical practices or food-processing to eliminate any bacteria.

Billie switched on the handheld black light wand.

Electricity passed through the small tube loaded with inert gas and a small amount of mercury. Now energized, the mercury molecules radiated energy as light photons. Some of these were visible, but most of the photons produced were inside the ultraviolet B wavelength range. Since UV light waves are invisible to the human eye, the black light wand needed to change this energy into visible light, by covering the outside of the tube with phosphor.

Black lights have been used for many years for a variety of purposes, ranging from antique inspection through forgeries, crime scenes, and mineral identification. Various chemical properties end up noticeably evident when exposed to black light. Current paint will incandesce or sparkle when exposed to black light while older paints won't. This can be used to determine if a painted material is an antique, or a newer reproduction, or a modification of the original. Many banknotes from around the world incorporate fluorescent colors, which sparkle under exposure to black light. To enable fluorescence, dye is infused with luminous solids that emit a specific colored gleam when exposed to UV light. In geology, a few minerals show photoluminescence, meaning they glow when introduced to a black light. Minerals such as opal, fluorite, willemite, calcite, dolomite, apatite and quartz all glow under black light.

 Billie took the wand, shined it over the stone tablet, and gasped.

CHAPTER TWENTY-SIX

―――――○☙○―――――

SMALL MARKINGS AND lines of purple luminescence lit up across the ancient stone.

Someone had used ink made of fluorite to make notes and markings throughout the stone. Billie glanced at the sapphires. Most of the blue precious gems had been visibly crossed out with the strange purple ink. Her eyes stopped at the four unmarked sapphires. Next to each one, was a symbol for one of the four horsemen of the apocalypse, followed by their respective Greek letters—identical to the ones she'd seen on the MRI scans of the stones hidden inside the Göbekli Tepe Death Stone.

It made her think about the Sacred Stones—the name Sam had started using for the four stones still locked inside the Göbekli Tepe Death Stone. It begged the question, what was so special about these stones? And were they supposed to be taken to each of these four temples? Billie thought about it for a moment. She still didn't have a clue where any of those temples belonged. When she'd first studied the stone tablet, she was certain it was an obvious map of the world. But since then, she'd discovered that none of the sapphires led to any temples. There was no benefit knowing that the sacred stones needed to be taken to specific ancient temples, if she had no way of finding the temples.

She put the thought out of her mind and continued studying the stone tablet. A line had been formed between ten sapphires, which looked like stars imbedded in the jet-black lignite. Without the lines, the gems appeared to be placed at random, but now stood out as a constellation of a bird. Although which constellation, she had no idea. Inside that set of ten stars were the four unmarked sapphires.

Billie smiled. She was making progress.

It was slow, but it was movement. The new revelation said to her, *find the constellation and you'll find the four temples where the sacred stones need to be laid to rest.* She continued searching. In her right hand she held the black light wand, and in her left hand, a magnifying glass.

There were fifteen new meridian lines that ran vertically and horizontally throughout the stone. Each line was only slightly off the previous line that had been etched into the stone. She sighed. What the hell did that mean? Had someone decided to move the shape of the earth?

She took several photographs of the stone, and made full-size prints on A4 paper. She then walked upstairs to Elise's office.

Inside, Elise was working at tracking down the man who had attacked Sam.

Without preamble, Billie said, "You have a photographic memory. Tell me you were paying attention in school when you were introduced to geography!"

"Technically, it's considered eidetic, but yeah, my memory's good, and I studied geography at school. What do you want to know?"

"How many meridian and parallel lines are there in total?"

Elise answered without hesitation. "Three hundred and sixty, but most standard maps have fifteen."

"Are you sure?"

"We just agreed I have an eidetic memory, didn't we?" Elise

looked up at her, with those intense purple eyes. "Yes, I'm sure. Why? What are you trying to work out?"

Billie placed a full-size print of the stone tablet on the table next to Elise. Its background was colored black as the night's sky. The image of twenty-two blue stones speckled the paper, and there were five empty spots roughly the same size. Fifteen fine lines, marked in red to emphasize their visibility, ran lengthways and vertically. The Greek symbols for Theta, Sigma, Phi, and Omega were etched in gold, with one at each corner. Below each of those were four horses, intricately carved out of stone or ivory to represent the Four Horsemen of the Apocalypse.

"When Sam and I looked at this, we were certain it matched a standard world map. All we had to do was work out the locations these stones correlate with, and we find the temples."

Elise ran her eyes across the paper. "Okay, so what's the problem?"

"No matter which way I looked at it, none of these stones seemed to match any corresponding locations with temples."

"Are you certain?"

Billie nodded. "Most of them are in the ocean somewhere."

"They might be submerged temples, like the one Sam and Tom found in the Gulf of Mexico?"

"No. I could have believed that for one or two of them, but not all of them." She looked at Elise. "I need to understand more about how latitude and longitude work. I've placed this next to a world-globe map and tried to estimate where each of these blue stars correlate to."

"And?"

"None of them seemed to correlate to anything. But then I ran the stone tablet under a black light. It revealed that someone had made notes using purple ink of fluorite. All of the sapphires were crossed out, except these four." Billie pointed to the four sapphires at the center of the constellation of a bird. "These are the only unmarked sapphires left. My guess is this constellation might lead us to the four temples."

Elise smiled. "Astronomy's not really my strong point."

"It's all right. We're seeing the astronomer who's examining the Göbekli Tepe Death Stone tomorrow afternoon. I'll talk to him about how we can locate the constellation, and more importantly, where it could be viewed from."

"So, what do you want to know?"

Billie placed a second A4 piece of paper on the table in front of Elise. This one had been shot under natural light. "What do you see?"

Elise studied the two images. "With the exception of the missing purple phosphorescent marks, they're identical."

"Is that all that's different?"

Elise ran her eyes across the two images again. Her lips formed a curious smile, revealing a set of evenly spaced, white teeth. "The meridian lines have shifted."

"Exactly!" Billie held her breath. "I was hoping you could tell me why?"

"There's a number of reasons the person who marked this might have changed the placement of the meridian lines."

Billie raised her left eyebrow, slightly. "Really?"

"Yes. But the most likely reason is simply that the meridians have moved over time."

"The shape of earth moves?" Billie was incredulous.

"Sure it does. Not much, but over thousands of years, there's definitely likely to be some sort of change."

"Based on the new position of the meridian lines, can you recalculate the location of each of these four sapphires?"

"That, I can do." Elise took the piece of paper and placed it in the scanner. "What I can do is superimpose this on an identical scaled world map on my computer, using my Global Information System software. Then I can tell you precisely where each of those dots correlate to."

"That would be perfect, thanks."

Elise waited as the image uploaded, pointing to a saved document that displayed a visual map of the earth over a rectangular image. Although it looked like any other map you'd find in a geometry classroom, it was an advanced Global Information System, based on software developed for the US military, with the ability to change the scale constantly and zoom into any given location, like Google Earth.

Elise pointed to the outline of the image on her laptop, and said, "Graticules are lines showing parallels of latitude and meridians of longitude for the earth, like a grid map. Latitude is a geographic coordinate that specifies the north–south position of a point on the Earth's surface. Latitude is an angle which ranges from 0° at the Equator to 90° at the poles. Lines of constant latitude, or parallels, run east–west as circles parallel to the equator."

The scanned document opened on her laptop. She copied the image and then attached it to her map program by superimposing the image of the stone tablet over the world map. The red grid lines, representing fifteen lines of longitude and latitude of the stone, lined up identically between the two maps.

"What do you think?" Billie asked.

"Well, if it's not a map of the earth, I don't know what it is." Elise pointed at the prime meridian. "Did you know that the term *meridian* comes from the Latin word meridies, meaning, midday?"

Billie sighed. She didn't know and didn't care.

Elise continued. "The sun crosses a given meridian midway between the times of sunrise and sunset at that meridian. The same Latin stem gives rise to the terms a.m. meaning ante meridiem and p.m. meaning post meridiem, used to disambiguate hours of the day when utilizing the 12-hour clock."

"That's really fascinating, Elise... but I'm kind of pressured for time."

"What do you want to know?"

Billie pointed to the four sapphires that hadn't been crossed out. "What's at these locations?"

Elise ran her eyes across the map. "Nothing."

"Nothing what?"

"I'd need to study a similar map with maritime landmarks and bathymetric imagery of the ocean floor to tell you specifically, but already I can tell you they're not the locations of any temples we're looking for."

"Why?"

"Because if they were, they would all be under water."

"All of them?" Billie asked.

Elise stared at the four unmarked stars. "Possibly not this one. It might just hug the coastline."

"Why?" Billie looked at the third empty marker. "Where on earth does this one correlate to?"

"The western edge of Big Island, Hawaii."

CHAPTER TWENTY-SEVEN

SAM STEPPED INTO the main computer labs on board the *Maria Helena*. Billie and Elise were staring at the projection wall, where a series of maritime and bathymetric maps depicting the water around Big Island, Hawaii were displayed.

Elise acknowledge his presence with a curt nod, but her eyes remained fixed on the projection.

Billie looked up, and met his eye. "I hear you had an eventful day at the Great Blue Hole?"

"Yeah, you could say something like that. But I lost my attacker, which means we're back to square one regarding who knows the truth about the Göbekli Tepe Death Stone." Sam looked at the map of the stone tablet superimposed on the maritime maps. "Tell me you found something on your end."

"I've found plenty of things. This seemingly simple stone is riddled with puzzles and mysteries. But very few answers. Every door I open leads to another three directions."

"Did you find the locations of the missing temples?"

"No."

Sam raised his eyebrow. "What have you found?"

"Where do you want me to start?"

Sam shrugged. "The beginning I suppose."

"The tablet itself is smaller than an A4 piece of paper, with the following dimensions: 11.69 by 7.225 inches, making it a Golden Rectangle."

Sam's eyes narrowed. "A what?"

"A Golden Rectangle is a rectangle whose side lengths are in the Golden Ratio of Phi — which is sometimes referred to as the Divine Proportion, is 1.618 — followed by a whole bunch of numbers that only Elise would bother to remember."

Sam glanced across at Elise.

She nodded and said, "You want them?"

"No thanks." Then, to Billie he said, "In English, without the calculations, how is a Golden Rectangle any different from every other four-sided shape with straight sides where all interior angles are at ninety degrees?"

Billie smiled as though she was enjoying this. It wasn't very often she was in a position to teach Sam Reilly something, and she was going to make him pay for it.

She drew a simple square. "Here's a standard square."

Sam nodded, but remained silent. He asked the question, now he was going to have to listen to the answer.

Billie drew a line from the midpoint of one side of the square to an opposite corner, and then used that line as the radius to draw an arc that defined the total height of the rectangle. She increased the length of the original square to meet the tip of the arc, thus making a rectangle. Billie smiled triumphantly. "That's a Golden Rectangle."

"Really?" Sam wasn't impressed.

"A distinctive feature of this shape is that when a square section is removed, the remainder is another golden rectangle. That is, with the same aspect ratio as the first. Square removal can be repeated infinitely, in which case corresponding corners of the squares form an infinite sequence of points on the golden spiral, the unique logarithmic spiral with this property."

He watched the imaginary sequence unfold. It was interesting, but he wasn't convinced the Master Builders considered it when they'd built the map. He eyes fixed on the real stone tablet. "Billie, it's a rectangle… don't you think you might just be over thinking this one?"

Billie shrugged. "Not just any rectangle. A Golden Rectangle, using Devine Proportions, that are aesthetically pleasing in nature and in science at a mathematical level."

"My credit card looks just like that."

"And why do you think the banks designed them in that shape?" Billie asked.

Sam shrugged. "It's not because that's the shape of my wallet?"

"No."

"You know who made the Golden Number popular?"

"No… who?" Sam thought about it for a minute. "Wait… I do remember something about this… go on, who?"

"Leonardo da Vinci. He applied the Golden Number to art. Some say that's why it was considered so perfect."

"Oh yeah, da Vinci, that's right…"

"Who were you thinking of?"

"Dan Brown… in that popular book of his."

"Really?" Billie said. "I once thought you had an IQ off the charts?"

"It's on the charts—just. People just think I'm smart because I fill my world with people like you and Elise, who answer all my questions." He sighed. "All right. Let's assume you're right about the stone tablet being an intentional Golden Ratio."

"I am right," Billie said, emphatically.

"Sure. Now what? How does it help us find where we're heading?"

"It doesn't. But what it does tell us is that the Master Builders were very specific about the dimensions of this tablet."

"What else have you found?" Sam glanced at the sheets of astronomy notes, with dozens of constellations, scattered along the table. "What's the story with these?"

"Those are kind of a dead-end at the moment. We're looking for the four temples that might just hold the key to saving the human race."

Sam grinned. "In the stars?"

"No. I found a series of markings on the stone tablet, written in fluorite."

"Really?" Sam was intrigued. "Visible only under a black light?"

"Exactly."

"What did they show?"

"That the shape of the earth has changed slightly since the tablet was first put together, for one thing. We found the meridian lines had shifted, slightly."

"And now?"

"They still don't show where to locate the ancient temples." She pulled out the A4 piece of paper with the UV highlighted image of the stone tablet. "I had Elise do her thing where she blended the old and the new map with a current precision map of the world and it spat out virtually the same answers — the stone by itself doesn't indicate where the temples are."

"Okay, what did the phosphorescent writing tell you?"

"Every temple — assuming the sapphires represent ancient temples at all — has been crossed out, with the exception of these four." Billie looked up at him with a raised brow. "See the pattern?"

"Four Horsemen of the Apocalypse, four Sacred Stones buried inside the Göbekli Tepe Death Stone, four remaining temples… I get it… the ancient Master Builders had a thing for the number four."

"I guess, something like that."

"What's the story with the constellations?" Sam asked.

Billie handed him the A4 piece of paper with the image of the stone tablet underneath the black light. The image was focused on the sapphires all joined together. "I don't know yet. But someone obviously thinks this constellation of a giant arrowhead means something. We haven't found it yet, but we were hoping to be able to work backward once we found the constellation."

Sam looked at the image. "That's not an arrowhead."

"Then what is it?" Billie asked.

Sam grinned. "It's an eagle, and the constellation's name is Aquila."

CHAPTER TWENTY-EIGHT

―――――○ℰ3○―――――

SAM FELT HIS heart race. They were finally getting somewhere.

"Aquila is a constellation on the celestial equator. Its name is Latin for *Eagle* and represents the bird that carried Zeus and Jupiter's thunderbolts in ancient Greek mythology." Sam pointed to the biggest star, defining the head of the eagle. "Its brightest star, Altair, is one vertex of the Summer Triangle asterism. The constellation is best seen in the northern summer, as it is located along the Milky Way and can be used for navigation."

"What's its story in Greek mythology?"

"Aquila was the pet eagle of Zeus." Sam made a theatrical sigh and then said, "Like all pets, it was kind and loving to its master, but could be exceedingly vengeful to those who upset its master, as Prometheus discovered."

"Who?"

"Prometheus, one of the last of the Titan gods, who became an advisor to Zeus. He was protective of the human race, and seeing how they suffered because they had no fire, he stole a ray from the Sun, which he smuggled down to earth in a hollow stem. Zeus did not believe that man was worthy of such a gift and was furious that Prometheus had acted without his permission. The well-meaning Titan was chained to the side of a mountain, stripped of his garments, and was continually attacked by Aquila."

"But Prometheus was a god!" Billie pointed out.

"Exactly, and since he was immortal, his dreadful wounds healed themselves every evening, only to be opened up again the next day by Aquila. After many years Prometheus was saved by Hercules, who agreed with his kind deed to mankind. Using his bow and arrow, he killed Aquila, who was then placed by Zeus to soar in the heavens."

"Nice story." Billie smiled. "Any idea what any of it has to do with the Sacred Stones or finding the four remaining temples?"

"No. Prometheus was trying to save the human race from suffering. The ancient Master Builders were trying to save the human race from extinction. I don't know. We'll ask the astronomer when we see him tomorrow."

Billie said, "All right. We'll go from there."

"Was there something else?" Sam asked.

Distracted, Billie looked at the Aquila constellation. "What?"

"Before. When I walked in, you said you had something extraordinary to show me and that you'd tell me all about it afterward."

Billie smiled. "This stone weighs precisely eight pounds."

"Exactly?"

"Well, technically, it would have if the five missing sapphires were still in there."

Sam sighed. "And that's interesting, because?"

"Everything the ancient Master Builders did was precise. There are no accidents."

A wry smile of incredulity crossed Sam's face. "You think they pre-planned the exact weight of the stone tablet?"

Billie nodded. "I don't think it—I'm certain they did. Don't you want to know what eight pounds relates to?"

"All right. What does eight pounds correlate with?"

"It's the precise distance between each of these sapphires when depicted on a world map!"

Sam glanced at the map in front of him. "All of them are identical?"

"Yes."

Sam smiled, still unsure if she was playing some sort of joke on him and unaccustomed to Billie overlooking clear errors of mathematics. "You think there's only eight miles between each of these temples, spread out evenly around the world?"

"Not eight miles, eight hundred."

Sam met her hardened gaze. "Okay. If the distance was eight hundred miles and not eight, why make the stone eight pounds?"

"Because it's too hard to carry an eight-hundred-pound stone."

"I can buy that argument, but I still don't understand where you came up with the number eight hundred? Especially given, as you said, the Master Builders knew a thing or two about precision."

Billie handed him a magnifying glass and pointed to the upper right-hand corner. "Have a look for yourself."

He knew better than to judge Billie's ability on face value. He stared at the horse made from pure obsidian. Its rider was carrying a set of scales carved from solid gold, which represented the changing value of barley during the reign of Famine. Written on the side of the scale in numbers barely visible with the magnifying glass, was the number one hundred. It indicated that during the reign of Famine, the value of barley would be inflated by a factor of one hundred.

Sam grinned. "Eight pounds inflated by a factor of a hundred equals eight hundred."

"The same number of miles between each of the temples,"

Billie said, matching his smile. "That means once we work out where some of the temples are, we can use this number to calculate the rough location of the subsequent temples around the world."

"That's great!" Sam ran his eyes across the equations Billie had scribbled on the side of the map. "But we don't even know for certain what method of measuring weight the Master Builders used, so the eight pounds couldn't possibly be correct."

Billie raised her eyebrow. "You think the Master Builders accidentally made this stone tablet precisely eight pounds?"

"It's unlikely, but less likely than the theory they used the same measurement of weight as we do today."

"That's not true."

"Really?" He turned to Elise, "Is she right?"

Elise nodded. "The grain was the earliest unit of mass and is the smallest unit in the apothecary, avoirdupois, Tower, and troy systems. The early unit was a grain of wheat or barleycorn used to weigh the precious metals silver and gold. Larger units preserved in stone standards were developed that were used as both units of mass and of monetary currency. The pound was derived from the mina used by ancient civilizations dating back to four thousand years B.C."

Billie said, "So it's possible the Master Builders were working on the same units of measurement as we are today."

"Only in the U.S. The rest of the world is on the metric system, and would have used kilograms, not pounds."

She shrugged. "It doesn't matter. I know I'm right."

"How?" Sam shook his head. "We don't even know what the Master Builders used to measure distance. I'm guessing it wasn't the mile."

"Because 800 miles equals 281600 cubits."

"Go on..."

"As you know, the Egyptian cubit was the earliest known unit of measurement used by ancient people to measure length, dating back to the third century B.C. The cubit was the length of the forearm from the elbow to the tip of the middle finger. The Royal Cubit, which was a standard cubit enhanced by an extra palm — thus 7 palms or 28 digits long — was used in constructing buildings and monuments and in surveying in ancient Egypt. The inch, foot, and yard evolved from these units through a complicated transformation not yet fully understood. Some believe they evolved from cubic measures; others believe they were simple proportions or multiples of the cubit. In whichever case, the Greeks and Romans inherited the foot from the Egyptians."

"Go on!"

"There are 3520 cubits to the mile, which means we're dealing with a distance of 800 miles between each temple."

"That can't be right," Sam protested.

"It's right," Billie said, emphatically.

"No, it isn't. Let's take the temple at the distance between the Pyramid of Giza and the one that sunk in the Mediterranean Sea as a reference point. You would agree that if all the distance between each of the temples is equal, then all we need to do is work out the distance between any two temples closest to each other to determine the distance?"

"Sure."

"The distance between the Great Pyramid of Giza and the submerged temple in the Mediterranean Sea is 1152 miles. I know, because I looked it up when we first examined the stone tablet and noted that there was an even spacing between each of the sapphires."

"That's right," Billie agreed, undeterred.

"But if 3520 cubits make a mile, then 281600 cubits is nowhere near 1152 miles."

"No. It's 800 miles"

Sam ran his palms through his thick hair. "But you said you were certain you were right?"

"I am."

"How?"

"Because ancient Master Builders didn't work on a base ten system."

"Of course, they worked on a duodecimal base of twelve."

"Yes. And would you like to guess what 800 in base twelve converts to?"

Sam grinned. "Let me guess, 1152."

CHAPTER TWENTY-NINE

SAM CONSIDERED THE revelation that Billie had discovered.

"If this is right, you know what this means?"

Billie said, "We map out the known temples to work out the rest of the map?"

Sam nodded. "It also means that the stone wasn't the original map."

"It's not," Billie agreed. "I've already checked."

"How old is it?"

"I carbon dated the ivory horse representing the Conqueror. It's roughly four hundred years old."

"About the time the previous stone was damaged and one of the remaining Master Builders made a replica, working the weight out in base ten, but continuing to calculate the distance using base twelve." He was genuinely impressed. "Remarkable that you worked it out."

"I got lucky, and Elise helped. You're the one with a lifetime of maritime experience and searching for hidden treasure under your belt, so now what do we do?" Billie asked.

"Map out every known temple and see if Elise can run a computer program to fill in the gaps, by inserting the distance of 1152 miles between each one. Also, see if you can find out anything else on the constellation of Aquila. In the meantime, my attendance has been formally requested by the Secretary of Defense."

"What does she want?" Billie asked.

"She didn't say. She's probably just found out we borrowed the Sikorsky Black Hawk experimental stealth helicopter without her permission, and now she wants to know why."

"What are you going to tell her?"

"The truth."

"But the note you and Tom found attached to the Göbekli Tepe Death Stone specifically warned you that she was being watched, and that it was imperative we don't tell her the ancient astronomer stone still exists?"

Sam smiled, sardonically. "Not the whole truth, simply that we needed the helicopter to locate something regarding your abduction. The Secretary of Defense still wants us to find out as much as we can about the Master Builders. It's a matter of national security that we stay ahead of them."

"You think she'll buy it?"

"Not for a minute."

CHAPTER THIRTY

───────○⊰⊙⊱○───────

47th Street, Manhattan—Diamond District.

SAM APPROACHED THE address the Secretary had given him on foot, after traveling from the airport to the Diamond District by taxi. She'd told him the building where they'd meet was just one block north of the famous 47th Street stretch of diamond commerce. He'd walked along 47th Street from 5th Avenue to 6th, and then gratefully turned north after dodging dozens of hawkers claiming to have the best deals on diamonds if he'd only follow them.

Sam wasn't in the market for a diamond, nor much in the mood for hawkers. The Secretary's summons had, as usual, come at a time when he had important business elsewhere. Furthermore, she knew he did, and she knew just how important and urgent it was. He could only assume this was just as important and urgent. Why the meeting had to take place at a gemstone appraisal lab was beyond his understanding.

When he arrived and stated his name, the receptionist rose and had him follow her to a room where he found the Secretary waiting. The room was clearly a laboratory, with microscopes, spectroscopes, a jeweler's loupe, and various other tools and electronic equipment that he couldn't identify. With the Secretary was a small, elderly man who resembled Albert Einstein, with a shock of wild, wiry, white hair, a bulbous nose, and a pair of thick, black-framed glasses that looked two sizes too large for him.

"Mr. Reilly, thanks for finally joining us," the Secretary greeted him.

He turned his palms upward. "I came as soon as I could…"

She didn't let him finish. "This is Simon Greenfeld, an eminent gemologist. He has confirmed what I'm about to tell you." She turned to the older man. "Mr. Greenfeld, please give us the room."

Greenfeld had not spoken, nor acknowledged Sam in any way. He gave an odd little bow to the Secretary and left the room without any apparent reaction to how strange it was that someone could dismiss him from his own laboratory. The Secretary waited until the door had closed, and then brought her hand forward, palm up. In it lay an uncut diamond half the size of a chicken's egg.

"Wow, nice stone," Sam said. "What is it?"

"That's potentially one of the world's most valuable diamonds," the Secretary answered.

Sam looked at her face. She hadn't cracked a smile since he walked in. "That's great news. So, who's the lucky guy?"

The Secretary ignored his comment. "Two weeks ago, it turned up on the New York diamond exchange, with an estimated value of one hundred million dollars."

"Wow," he repeated, this time genuinely. "And they let you walk out of the shop with it?"

"Well, it would have been, if it was real." The Secretary laid the stone on the lab counter and folded her arms.

"It's a fake?"

"Yes and no."

"Really?" Sam smiled. "I figured it either is or it isn't, right?"

"Technically, it's real. It has the same properties as a diamond that was formed by heat and pressure deep in the Earth. However, that isn't the way this one was formed. You might have heard of synthetic, or lab-grown, diamonds?"

"Sure. They use them for industrial purposes."

"Right," she confirmed. "They've also been growing them for the jewelry industry for more than twenty years, and it takes real expertise to distinguish them from mined diamonds."

"I thought fake diamonds could be easily distinguished."

"You're talking about diamond simulants, like cubic zirconia or moissanite. They are different chemical compounds from diamond. This stone, other than the way it was formed, is indistinguishable chemically from a natural diamond."

"Okay, I'll take your word for that. So, what's your interest in all this?"

"Well, first, even though it's technically real, as a synthetic diamond, its true value is only about sixty percent of a natural diamond."

"Why?"

"Mainly because of the natural diamond industry. They have created a mystique and romance around natural diamonds that has inflated their value even more than centuries of people coveting them for their beauty. And that's despite the troubling human rights issues that have come to light about diamonds."

"Blood diamonds, you mean," Sam observed.

"Yes. And the fact that they're still being used to fund terrorism in some parts of the world, despite the industry's efforts to clean up their sources."

"So, back to *this* diamond," Sam prompted. "Someone attempted to pass it off as a real, or natural diamond. That's fraud. Why is that of interest to the Defense Department?"

"Not just this one. There have been more than two hundred sold throughout the world—all perfect diamonds. Together they're worth billions of dollars, and all of them fake."

"Madam Secretary, what's your interest?" he persisted.

She continued as though she hadn't heard or wasn't interested in his question. "Unlike synthetic diamonds that are grown in a laboratory, these are nearly impossible to distinguish from the genuine version."

"Okay."

"The process works by placing a tiny fragment of diamond, called a carbon seed, into a microwave along with varying amounts of a carbon-heavy gas, most commonly methane. The gas mixture is heated to very high temperatures in the microwave to produce a plasma ball, and inside this, the gas breaks down and the carbon atoms crystallize and accumulate on the diamond seed, causing it to grow."

"How long does it take?"

"The process can take up to ten weeks to produce a marketable diamond, but it works so well, experts reportedly need a machine to tell the lab-grown gems apart from natural ones sourced from mines or riverbeds."

"But they can still tell the difference?" Sam asked.

"Until recently they could. But now there's a third type. We suspect they're being made through a carbon seeding process, but are being planted within the thousands of recent growing craters in Siberia."

A wry smile of understanding formed on Sam's lips. "The melting permafrost releases enormous amounts of carbon in the form of methane and someone with a high-powered microwave is turning them into high quality diamonds?"

"Exactly." The Secretary of Defense sighed. "And in the process, the diamonds formed become indistinguishable with flawless diamonds mined from the Earth."

He still didn't understand how any of this was related to him, but the mystery had aroused his curiosity. "Then how do you know this is happening?"

"Because more than a hundred of these have hit the market in the past two weeks."

"I thought the diamond trade was massive?" Sam said. "How does a hundred or so of these stones have the power to collapse the market?"

"These aren't every day diamonds being released into the world for a tiny fraction of their usual value. Think of the Kohinoor—the most precious gem in the British Crown Jewels, stored in the London Tower. It's one of a kind. No one has ever come close to finding such a perfect diamond of its size. Now imagine a hundred of them flooding the market. The diamond trade is about to crash irrevocably."

"What do you want me to do about it?" Sam asked.

"I need you to find out who's making the diamonds. We know that whoever he or she is, has been working in Siberia, where the craters are popping up daily."

"You're telling me that the Secretary of Defense of the United States has an interest in the overly inflated price of diamonds in the New York diamond district remaining inflated. And I'm to do the job of the police, or Customs, or the CIA—whoever is responsible for stopping international criminal activity." Sam stated it in a flat tone that expressed his disapproval.

"I don't care. The country cares."

"Why?"

She looked at him, as though unsure how much to tell. "There's a man named Leo Botkin. He owns a number of diamond mines throughout the world. He has the most to lose here."

"So? I mean, it's not very nice, but since when has the government concerned itself with how companies like this do their business? If the market's changed and the general public are happy for it, why not let it happen?"

"You misunderstand me, Reilly." She smiled. "I don't care if

Leo Botkin and the entire diamond cartel goes bankrupt."

"Then why look for this diamond-smith?"

She sighed. "Because the enemy of my enemy might just be the ally I need right now."

Sam thought about it for a moment. "Why do you think this person is targeting Botkin specifically? He or she could just as easily be out to get the entire diamond industry. Maybe their relative or family were killed over blood diamonds in Africa, who knows?"

"No. Whoever it was has the means and know-how to target Leo Botkin specifically. More importantly, he or she is willing to overcome mountains and move oceans just to destroy the man."

"What do you know?" Sam asked, suddenly intensely curious about what he was missing.

"Hurricane Hilda came straight toward Manhattan last week. It was reported to nearly hit the city, and then at the last minute, turned ninety degrees and headed north toward the Hamptons where it was responsible for the destruction of just one house — Leo Botkin's 23,000 square-foot mansion."

Sam grinned, and his eyes filled with incredulity. "Next you're going to tell me this mysterious person was using old HAARP technology to manipulate the weather."

The Secretary of Defense set her jaw firm, and fixed her steely green eyes at him. "That's exactly what I'm telling you."

CHAPTER THIRTY-ONE

SAM BREATHED IN deeply. He could taste the tension in the air. It wasn't like the Secretary of Defense to ever reveal state secrets. He glanced at her face. A gentle crack seemed to form in her once impenetrable resolve.

"Are we safe to speak here?" he asked.

"Yes. This place is more secure than any office at the Pentagon."

"Okay." He exhaled slowly and waited.

She met his eye, and said, "The High Frequency Active Auroral Research Program, known as HAARP, was initiated as an ionospheric research program jointly funded by the U.S. Air Force, the U.S. Navy, the University of Alaska Fairbanks, and the Defense Advanced Research Projects Agency. Its original purpose was to analyze the ionosphere and investigate the potential for developing ionospheric enhancement technology for radio communications and surveillance. It has not, and never will be used for anything related to weather control."

"HAARP controlling the weather was a whole bunch of conspiracy theorist propaganda, nothing more." Sam shook his head. "So, what was controlling the weather?"

"When the conspiracy theorists argued that HAARP was artificially producing differential heating areas of the atmosphere, which could induce local weather conditions such as floods or droughts to militarize the weather, the onus of proof landed directly on the Defense Department." The Secretary of Defense grimaced. "By the time the U.N. received more than a thousand complaints regarding weather manipulation, the U.N. issued a resolution forcing DARPA to prove that such a thing by HAARP was scientifically unfounded."

"Which they did!" Sam said, "I recall hearing about the outcome of the investigation years ago. It was all over the news. Are you telling me the evidence was wrong?"

"No. That much was true."

"So, what did we lie about?" Sam asked.

She made a coy smile, entirely out of character for her. "While DARPA was putting together experiments to disprove the theory that HAARP could manipulate the weather, they discovered the potential for high powered microwaves not to create weather, but to modify the direction of existing weather systems."

Sam said, "You worked out how to direct a hurricane away from any given city?"

She nodded. "Only, we didn't implement the theory."

"Why not?"

"For starters the U.N. had only just issued a moratorium on any projects that might affect any weather system anywhere on the planet, reminding the world that only minor changes here can affect the delicate balance of the global system."

"And secondly?"

"We couldn't work out how to produce a microwave powerful enough."

"How much energy would it take?"

She smiled like the Devil. "About the same amount of energy required to emit a microwave with enough energy to produce a hundred-carat diamond."

"You think it's the same person. They're using his device to shift weather?"

"Yes."

"That's why you want to find this diamond-smith?"

She picked up the diamond and squeezed it in the palm of her hand. "No. I need to find Leo Botkin."

Sam's eyes narrowed. "Who is Botkin to you?"

"Probably the world's most dangerous man."

"I thought he hasn't made a public appearance in decades. Some think he's dead."

The Secretary studied him, with a wry smile on her face. "What do you know about Botkin?"

"Not much. Just that he went to ground twenty years ago, but stocks in his long list of companies have flourished without him." Sam smiled. "And that he owns the train that we used to escape the Aleutian Portal."

"Sam. Answer me this. Did you find the Göbekli Tepe Death Stone?'

"No ma'am."

The Secretary of Defense fixed her green eyes on him. "Sam Reilly, are you lying to me?"

"Yes ma'am."

"Why?"

Sam bit his upper lip. "For the same reason you're lying to me about what your involvement with the stone was twenty years ago — the truth is too dangerous to reveal."

CHAPTER THIRTY-TWO

———○⊰⊙———

SAM WATCHED AS the Secretary of Defense's hardened façade fell, revealing in its place a pained expression of regret.

"It was a long time ago, and I made some significant mistakes I regret to this day," she said. "I was still a junior CIA Intelligence Officer investigating large amounts of funding being siphoned through a relatively unheard-of group of archeologists working at a dig called Göbekli Tepe, in Turkey."

"What was the CIA's interest in archeology?" Sam asked. "No one had even heard of the Master Builders back then."

"At the time, we thought the archeological dig was entirely a business ruse, allowing key players from around the world to siphon money into a small and dangerous organization in the country. You have to understand that hundreds of millions of dollars had been transferred to the accounts of a small archeology firm. There was nothing extraordinary about the dig to reveal the need for such an investment. The CIA doubted that any of that money was being spent on the archeology."

"It looked like a terrorist's hotspot?" Sam asked.

"Exactly."

"So, what happened?"

"My role, like all CIA operatives, was to collect, evaluate, and disseminate foreign intelligence. I would then take it to my superiors, who would assist the president and senior U.S. government policymakers in making decisions relating to the national security. My then partner and I were assigned to infiltrate the lives of key workers at the site. By the time we'd determined it wasn't a terrorist cell, the team were already extracting extraordinary results from some of the giant T-shaped astronomy pillars."

"The Göbekli Tepe Death Stone had been discovered and was being deciphered?"

"Yes. Among other things. My superiors determined it was important for my partner and me to stay and continue our assignment."

"What did you find?" Sam asked.

"An archeologist named Emad Vernon, who uncovered the results of the Göbekli Tepe Death Stone, critically revealing the prospect of an asteroid that passes across Earth every thirteen thousand years, bringing with it species-ending changes to the weather." Her lips thinned. "The sort of prediction you found by resolving the Nostradamus Equation."

"So, what did Congress decide to do about it?"

"Nothing. It never reached Congress. The president decided, along with the advice of my boss, to keep the entire problem a secret to prevent total pandemonium and chaos, while at the same time gathering a group of international scientists and experts capable of determining the validity of the information depicted on the Göbekli Tepe Death Stone. The group was only able to narrow the return of the doomsday asteroid to a window of eighty years, and despite enormous resources being applied to the problem, the results were unanimous — efforts should focus on developing a bunker for a small colony to survive, in order to protect the human race from extinction."

"Where's the colony?"

"We don't know. A cohort of five thousand people were sent there to prepare. They've been living there ever since."

"You don't know where?"

"No. It was determined that the only way to ensure that it wasn't overrun by an entire world of refugees was to keep its location secret to all but those chosen."

"You weren't chosen?" Sam asked, without hiding his surprise.

She sighed. "I declined the offer. At worst, I might have been forty years old by the time the asteroid reached us, and potentially I might be over a hundred years old. Either way, I wouldn't have been an ideal candidate — and I had no intention of spending my life in a bunker, just in case."

"What happened to the stone?"

"It was loaded onto the *Theresa May*, one of our cargo ships at the time, and was to be transferred to Harvard, where a team of experts would verify Vernon's claims regarding an approaching cataclysmic event. As you're already aware, the *Theresa May* sank en route to Cambridge, Massachusetts."

"Vernon was then sanctioned and killed in what appeared to be a car accident, removing any verifiable claims to the cataclysmic message hidden within the stone."

She nodded. "How did you know?"

"I met his brother, a man named Dmitri Vernon, in Mount Ararat. The man was one of the remaining Four Horsemen, and a Master Builder. He told me about the stone and about the U.S. government stealing its secrets and destroying any evidence of its existence — including his brother, who appeared to have fallen asleep at the wheel and died in a car accident."

The Secretary nodded. "He was the first of many casualties."

Sam wanted to argue the morality of any of it. *Who decided to play God and pick who lived and who died?* But none of that would have helped and he needed more information from her, so he ignored the brutality and continued. "And I take it the *Theresa May* never sank?"

"No. It sank all right—it was too risky not to—but the Göbekli Tepe Death Stone was removed first and taken to a remote location in Siberia to be studied. When everything was decoded, it was determined that the stone needed to be destroyed."

"But it wasn't, was it?" Sam asked.

"No. I worried that we needed to keep the knowledge in case one-day new information would come to light, and a solution might prevail." She took a deep breath. "I tasked the only person I could trust with keeping it safe, a man named Ryan Balmain."

The name seemed familiar, but he couldn't quite place it. "You ordered the stone recalled to the U.S. after I discovered the information regarding the Nostradamus Equation and the Four Horsemen of the Apocalypse?"

She nodded.

"And the *Gordoye Dostizheniye* sunk in the Bering Strait!"

"And I lost one of the best men I'd ever known." Her eyes welled with tears, and Sam guessed that Ryan Balmain had been more to her than a colleague, but her face remained set firm with determination. "You found my shipping container, didn't you?"

"Yes."

"Why did you keep it a secret from me?"

"Ryan Balmain left a note. It said that THEY were watching you, and that if we cared about your life or those of the human race we were to remove the stone and take it to an astronomer—not associated with any government—to determine the truth."

"I dismissed the spy from my office."

"There may be more?"

"I'll deal with them, too." She turned to face him. "Have you made much progress with the stone?"

"Yes. It's still being analyzed, but it looks like we're rapidly approaching our time of reckoning. Billie has some ideas, and we're meeting up with the astronomer this afternoon to determine the next step."

"Good. Now what about the second stone?"

Sam caught his breath, and his eyes narrowed. "I only know about the Göbekli Tepe Pillar Number 44 — named the Death Stone."

"There were two — Pillars numbers 44 and 45. The Master Builders did two things when their astronomers first spotted the asteroid in the sky. The purpose of the first stone was to depict the asteroid's progress so we could work out when it was going to strike and how to manage the impact…"

"And the second stone?" Sam asked.

"Was one of last resort. It was a blueprint of an ancient bunker. A place where some of the human race may ride out the destruction and the subsequent ice age."

Sam shook his head at the enormity of the concept. They'd known for some twenty years, but had kept it a secret from the entire population of planet Earth. "Whose idea was it to keep all this a secret?"

"A long-term friend of the president and an advisor, whose council Congress had always respected. The man had a Harvard degree in geology, and specialized in deep mining. An expert in protecting subterranean structures from the constant movement of tectonic plates. A man who could put together a team who would ensure the permanent survival of the last five thousand human beings for as long as it took for the planet to become habitable again. A man who was old enough to know that he would never take up a place inside the ancient bunker. He was tough and capable, and he quickly proved that he could make the hard decisions that would enable the chosen few to stay alive."

"How?"

"By systematically cutting off every single person who knew anything about the future and might damage the safety of the colony. His ruthless tenacity has already cost the lives of three Senators, more than a dozen good men and women, including Ryan Balmain." She sighed. "At the time I thought he was doing it all for the vital, yet brutal, protection of the human race—but then you told me about the ancient covenant of the Four Horsemen of the Apocalypse, which the Master Builders had put in place. I contacted him and gave him the information—that's when more people started to die."

"He was systematically removing anyone who knew about the possible solution being stored on the Göbekli Tepe Pillar Number 44!"

"Exactly. That's when I realized, for him, it wasn't just about saving the human race—he wanted to start a new existence, a eugenics experiment filled with a colony based on superior DNA."

"But if he knew the truth about Pillar Number 44 from the beginning…"

"It means he wanted this from the start. He always knew there was a solution, but instead he kept quiet, so he could achieve his dream of producing an all new colony—a perfect race."

Sam swore. "Who?"

"His name was Leo Botkin."

CHAPTER THIRTY-THREE

SAM LEFT THE diamond merchant's tawdry office and hailed a taxi cab. He'd finished bringing the Secretary of Defense up to date with what they'd discovered about the stone tablet, and what their plan was to locate the four hidden temples that related to the Covenant of the Four Horsemen of the Apocalypse.

He sat quietly, vacantly watching the stream of cars drive by, as his mind crunched the enormity of their betrayal, as well as the task that was set before him. The taxi pulled into LaGuardia Airport and he got out, leaving a decent tip. It might just be the end of days, might as well make the hardworking driver happy.

His cell phone rang. The caller ID said *Elise*. "What have you got for me?" he said without a preamble.

She was used to it, and immediately said, "I've got some answers about the guy who attacked you, but not all, unfortunately."

"Who is he?"

"That's the part I don't know yet."

"What *do* you know?"

Elise answered. "The seaplane was rented by a proxy corporation. I've hacked the company's background, and it has led to three other proxies, which eventually lead to a defunct company, which was bought with fifty million in cash."

"So, your trail ran dry?"

"No. So, I dug some more, and found a withdrawal for fifty million registered from an account with the Bank of America in Manhattan. You want to know what company withdrew the money?"

"Go on."

"Prometheus Diamonds! It's a large diamond cartel that's expanded into rare commodities all around the world."

"Let me guess, the CEO is one Leo Botkin?"

"Hey, how did you know?" Elise asked.

"It's a long story. What about the employee who rented the seaplane?"

"I tracked the employee down, but it's unlikely he was using his real name."

"What was it?"

"Fred Flintstone."

"Yeah, all right, we can scratch that name off the list." Sam stepped into the airport and looked up at the flight numbers. He still had another five minutes until he'd need to go through security. "What about the photo of my attacker? You got the security footage from the bar, didn't you? Was there a usable image of him?"

"Oh, yes, a crystal-clear image of his face."

Sam grinned. It was finally something tangible. "That's great! So?"

"So, my facial recognition software can't find him on any database anywhere. He doesn't exist."

Sam deflated as quickly as he'd been encouraged. "What the hell? He must have a passport. A driver's license? Something, surely."

"Afraid not. It genuinely looks like he's a ghost."

"Yeah, well if that's so, he's the first ghost to nearly get me killed."

"There's something else about the Prometheus Diamond Corporation you're gonna want to hear about..." Elise's voice sounded excited.

"What?"

"Two days ago, the company started to sell off all its assets — at prices no sane person would even consider. Not unless they already knew that the company would be worthless in a few months..."

"Oh shit, they're getting ready for something big. Are there any other major companies following suit?"

"I already checked." Elise paused for breath.

"*And?*" This was killing him.

"More than a hundred leaders around the world are trying to surreptitiously sell everything they own. Dumping stocks at unprecedented rates. The financial markets are crashing, but no one can fathom what's driving the bear market. You know what this means, don't you?"

Sam sat back. Now the other penny had dropped, he could see where Elise had been leading him all along. His impatience vanished. "We're closer to the final date of the event. Someone out there knows what's going on. They're selling companies and buildings that will soon be under the world's oceans, concentrating their cash into gold. Preparing for the new world."

"Thought you'd be interested," she said, as though it were merely a new tip about the stock market.

"Thanks, Elise. Keep digging, and keep me in the loop."

Sam considered his next move. This was bigger than the guy trying to kill him. Forget about him. Sam wanted his boss, or bosses. If Elise couldn't find them, no one could. But he had a job to do as well. He dialed a number that only a few people had.

"What is it, Sam?" answered the Secretary of Defense.

"It's begun."

CHAPTER THIRTY-FOUR

―――――○⍟○―――――

Phoiki Hot Pond — Big Island, Hawaii

AIRLIE CHAPMAN STARED at the ancient world around her through dark brown, intelligent eyes, as she crept through the dense forest. She was tall and lissome, and moved with the decisive gait of someone much younger than her thirty-five years of age, as she made her way through the path that tracked upward and deeper into the jungle. She wore a bikini underneath a pair of denim shorts and a dark tank top. Her light brown hair was tied back in a French braid.

In the twilight before dawn, the mist from the various hot springs rose above the ancient forest, like something out of the Jurassic period. She left the coast of Isaac Hale Beach, in the Puna District, and headed further into the forest. Despite it being early, there was a warmth to the air that made everything feel comfortable.

She watched as her boyfriend, Adrian, jumped across the various volcanic rocks, trying to spur her to move faster.

"Come on," he said. "We have to reach the hot springs before sunlight."

"Why the rush?" she asked. "I'm on my first vacation in four years since I started my damned PhD. No one's going to make me hurry."

"I want to beat the crowds and be the first one in the water!"

He had a confident and engaging smile. With his good-natured attitude, and those boyish good looks typical of an athlete still moving toward his prime, he was fun and immature at the same time, but kind and generous — willing to do anything to please her. Not at all like the academics she tended to go for. When he'd asked her out, she surprised herself by saying yes. That was five weeks ago, and since then, Airlie had discovered that he'd brought a unique and pleasant aspect to her otherwise cumbersome and perfect little life.

"You go ahead. I'll meet you there soon," she said.

He made a face like a wounded puppy, and then smiled. "Okay."

She watched him disappear over the next set of volcanic rocks that formed a small ridge. Airlie increased her stride. Thirty seconds later, she passed a large rock and came face to face with him. He kissed her on her lips. She opened her mouth and met his tongue with an eagerness that few men in her life had ever instilled in her.

And then he pulled away.

She went to kiss him again, but he pulled back, farther. "What?"

He was grinning at her.

She tried to kiss him a third time, but he simply smiled and started running along the path. "You'll need to catch me if you want to kiss me."

Airlie laughed. This was the price she was going to have to pay for dating a younger man. "All right." She started to make her way quickly through the forest.

Eighty feet along the path and it opened to a large jellybean-shaped hot spring. Formed from a collapsed lava tube, its volcanic base was nearly fifteen feet deep and provided a startling green shade to the blue water. Steam rose invitingly from its surface. Airlie had never seen it before, but the sight took her breath away.

She turned to meet Adrian, as he kissed her again. When he stopped, she found herself smiling. The sight was stunning, but it was more than that. She found herself feeling a type of joy and contentment that no other man had been able to provide her.

"Beautiful isn't it?"

"Magic," she admitted.

"I thought you'd like it." He smiled with genuine joy. "I was looking forward to seeing your response when you saw it. There's something terribly endearing about the way your eyes light up in wonder. I'd like to spend a lifetime doing such simple things with you and traveling the world. What do you say, should we get married?"

"Sure," she said, assuming he was just speaking without any conviction.

Then he got down on one knee and revealed a diamond ring.

She swore. "My God! You're serious!"

He looked at her with a slightly confused and pained face. "I am."

She shook her head in disbelief and kissed him again. This time he pulled back and she stopped. She stared at him.

"Well?" he asked.

"Well what?"

"Will you marry me?"

She beamed. "Yes!"

He kissed her again and then said, "Let's jump in the water."

She glanced at the water. The steam seemed to be glowing off its surface, like some sort of bubbling primordial pool. "Shouldn't you test the water or something, first?"

Adrian shrugged his shoulders. "Why?"

"It looks pretty hot. The sign before said that the temperature can fluctuate."

"You think it's going to burn me?" he asked, with an incredulous grin.

"It might."

Adrian laughed. "There's only one way to find out."

He took a giant run and jumped into the deepest part at the center of the hot spring. His head dipped under the water and he disappeared.

Airlie stepped to the water's edge and watched. She felt her heart race. She stood up and chided herself. It was irrational. Her fiancé was just playing a trick. There was no reason he should simply disappear into a small hot spring.

But she found herself holding her breath.

Then Adrian surfaced. "Ah it burns! It burns… help! Quick, throw me a branch…"

Airlie, already taut with concern, reacted immediately. She ran to the edge of the hot spring, where a large vine dangled close to the water. She pulled on it, using all her weight, and the vine snapped fifteen odd feet above her.

She took the edge of the vine and threw it into the boiling water. Adrian caught it on her first throw. She quickly dragged him toward the edge, pulling it hand over hand, like a rope.

He screamed loudly.

"Give me your hand," she shouted.

He grabbed her right hand and pulled her into the water.

It was lukewarm and felt delicious under the rising sun. She surfaced from the water, and started to scream.

"You bastard! I should kill you myself."

Adrian was laughing uncontrollably now. He went to grab her and she shook her head. He caught his breath. "I'm sorry, but you should have seen your face."

"You bastard!" Her heart was still racing. "Don't you ever do that to me again."

He grabbed her and kissed her again. "I'm sorry."

She relaxed in the water for a few minutes and then climbed out, resting on the warm volcanic rocks that lined the edge of the hot spring.

Airlie watched her now fiancé play in the water, seemingly unable to tire of playing in the crystal-clear spring. *So, this was the man I'm going to spend the rest of my life with.* The thought made her happy. His carefree and playful life was almost a polar opposite to her lifetime of research and academia. Adrian would provide the balance that she needed.

She stood up and looked at the green radiating off the blue water. A small bubble surfaced, followed by another one. Her eyes narrowed, and she studied the slight change in the water. She tried to get Adrian's attention, but he was dipping under the water, swimming to the bottom and searching for different colored stones to show her.

The bubbles started to surface quickly — one after another — and she felt the irrational agitation of fear rising in her throat. "Adrian!"

He didn't hear her as he dived down again.

She quickly walked to the opposite side of the hot spring, carefully jumping across the volcanic stones, racing to get his attention when he surfaced.

Bubbles more than a foot wide were now surfacing with the speed of a rapid-fire machinegun. She watched Adrian's head break the surface.

"Get out of there!" she shouted.

Adrian turned to face her. "Hey, there's an opening down here! It looks like the entrance to a tunnel or something that leads even deeper!"

She screamed, "Get out! Something's not right!"

He glanced at the bubbles, making their way to the surface next to him. The last one was nearly five feet in diameter. His eyes widened. "Yeah, I think you're right!"

Adrian tried to swim, but even larger bubbles broke directly below him. The surface tension broke way to the gas filled liquid below, and he sank.

Airlie watched, helplessly, as he fought to reach the surface again.

When he did a few moments later, his face was bright red and he was screaming again. Airlie wanted to yell at him and tell him not to make any more jokes, but even after the first glance, she knew that he wasn't joking. His skin was blistering over. His face aghast with horror.

Airlie's dark brown eyes fixed on him and she wanted to scream. His eyes stared vacantly back at her, and she knew there was nothing more she could do — Adrian was already dead.

CHAPTER THIRTY-FIVE

――――○⊰⊙⊱○――――

University of Arizona — Tucson, Arizona

SAM WALKED ALONG the northwest corner of Mountain Avenue and Speedway Boulevard. He glanced at the large building on the right. It appeared to have been designed to look more like an oversized aircraft hangar than a university building. Over the main door, were the words, *Aerospace and Mechanical Engineering.*

He stepped inside and gave his name to a receptionist.

The receptionist, a twenty-something-year-old man with a poorly grown blond beard, glanced at him with recognition and said, "Professor Capel is waiting for you inside the metallurgy labs on level E. I believe your associate is already with him."

"Thank you." Sam ran his eyes across a map of the building.

The receptionist noticed, and said, "If you take the stairs down three flights, the metallurgy labs are the first on the right."

"They're underground?" Sam asked.

"Yeah, it's a precaution. Some of the experiments performed here can be dangerous."

Sam nodded. "Thanks."

He found the metallurgy labs a couple of minutes later and tried to open the door. It was locked. He glanced at the obvious security camera fixed on him and then knocked loudly at the door. Another minute later, the door opened.

Professor Douglas Capel greeted him. He was tall for his generation, standing eye to eye with Sam. Wiry gray hair sprouted from his head, and made his eyebrows look like those of a mad scientist. The same hair sprung from his ears like coiled antennae. His skin was surprisingly smooth in contrast. His blue eyes twinkled with good-humor. A ready smile, somewhat crooked, gave him the appearance of smirking below a large, well-shaped nose.

"Ah, Mr. Reilly, I'm so glad you could make it." The professor offered his hand.

Sam took it. The man had a firm handshake. "Thank you for your hard work, Professor Capel."

"Not a problem. Come with me. There's a lot for us to get through with, and your associate, Dr. Billie Swan, tells me that time is… how did she put it?" He sighed. "Of the essence."

Sam followed the man through a series of long, empty passageways. The professor carried his head at a slight tilt, as if questioning everything about the world around him. At the end of the third corridor, the professor put his ID card to yet another security barcode reader, and a heavy steel door—the sort you might find onboard a space-shuttle—opened.

Inside, the room was a perfect sphere. Stainless steel metal shined from every end of the room like the inside of a giant globe. A thin sheet of see-through cargo nets—made of cotton rope that appeared like a direct anachronism in the otherwise space-aged lab—cut the sphere in half, providing a means of reaching the center of the room. There, the Göbekli Tepe Pillar Number 44 stood, suspended by a series of ropes, like an island at the center of the Earth. Next to it, Sam spotted Billie already examining the markings.

Sam turned to the professor. "What's the story with the stone's new storage facility?"

Capel grinned. "Ah, you'll see."

They walked across the cotton-mesh rope to the tiny island at the center.

Sam looked at Billie. "Find anything new?"

She shook her head. "No. It's amazing, but I haven't seen anything I couldn't get out of the multiple photographs I've seen of it. But professor Capel tells me he's been waiting until you get here to reveal the most amazing thing about it."

He turned to the professor. "What did you find?"

Professor Capel grinned. "I can't tell you. This, you have to experience for yourself."

"What's that supposed to mean?" Sam asked.

"You'll see." The professor squatted down, behind the large T-shaped astronomy stone. Four openings had been meticulously cut into the back of the Mesolithic stone. "Here, Mr. Reilly, slide one of these out, and place it on the scale."

Sam glanced at the digital, scientific scale. "Okay. Can I examine the four stones, themselves?"

The professor nodded. "In due time. You won't find anything extraordinary by looking at them. You already have the photos I sent you, and so you know of the pictographs depicted on them. Just go weigh it for me, will you?"

Sam nodded. Older people in general were rewarded with the respect of a greater amount of his patience, but once-in-a-generation experts like Professor Capel were granted an infinite amount of his tolerance. Instead, he turned to Billie. "You know what he's getting at?"

"No."

"All right. Here goes."

Sam carefully reached into the opening. A hollow section, like a handle, had been cut into the stone inside. He slowly pulled it out. The image depicted on the outside was that of the Horseman of the Apocalypse known as Famine, below which was the Greek letter, Theta. He braced for the weight of the stone, but found it surprisingly light in his hands, as though it was made out of some sort of porous material. It was lighter than that. More like a feather. Certainly, no more than a few grams, at best.

"What is this made of?" Sam asked, staring at the strange material.

The stone itself was an intense shade of darkness, as though without the direct light shining on it, Sam wouldn't have been able to see anything at all.

Capel ignored the comment, and urged him onward. "Okay, put it on the scale, quickly now."

Sam carried the dark stone the three or four feet required, and then waited while the professor zeroed the scientific scale. A slight nod from Capel indicated that the machine was ready, and Sam placed the dark stone gently inside.

"Good!" The professor was grinning now. "How do you feel?"

Sam was slightly taken aback by the question. He merely carried something light across a few feet. He was even going to say so, and then he noticed the strange feeling in his fingers. They were tingling. The sensation ran right up each arm, kind of like that time you fell asleep on your arm or leg for too long, and when you woke up or tried to move them the entire thing felt like it was full of pins and needles. He wondered if he should have been wearing gloves when he handled the strange stone. It could be toxic for all he knew, emitting some sort of radiation.

The professor glanced at both of them as though they were his students. "Come closer, so you can get a good look."

Sam and Billie both stepped right up to the scale and looked at the reading. It was set to metric, the universal measurements of science, and read less than ten grams.

"Woah, that's amazing!" Sam shook his head in surprise, and turned to Capel. "How can it weigh so little?"

The professor ignored the comment. "Just watch."

The scale hadn't quite balanced, yet. The number was going up already. *Eleven, Twelve, Thirteen grams.* It increased slowly at first, but as it gained mass, the counter started to take-off.

Twenty-five grams.

Fifty grams

It was a parabolic curve — getting faster and faster.

Sam was holding his breath in disbelief. Next to him, he noticed the examination light flicker. It was so subtle, it wasn't until it did it the fourth time that the sight caught his eye. The light was bending, only slightly, but it was being pulled toward the dark stone.

He glanced at the scales.

500 grams.

"That's quite enough," the professor said. "Let's put it back inside the Göbekli Tepe pillar before we can no longer lift it!"

Sam reached in and grabbed the stone. It instantly felt much heavier, like carrying a brick instead of a feather. He worked quickly, and slid it back inside the ancient astronomer's stone.

"Are we safe?" Sam asked.

The professor, now grinning like a mad scientist, nodded. "Quite safe. The Göbekli Tepe pillar appears to neutralize the stone, allowing it to return to its nominal weight of less than a single gram."

Billie shook her head in awe. "I've never seen anything like it."

Sam eyes narrowed. "What the hell is it?"

The professor stared at them both, wonder filling his intelligent blue eyes. "This, my friends, is the first physical evidence of the theoretical particles named *Blackbody*."

CHAPTER THIRTY-SIX

———○☾☽○———

SAM TURNED TO the professor. "What the hell is *Blackbody*?"

"It was first theorized in 1860 by a man named Kirchhoff, who predicted what he called then as perfect *black bodies*." Capel took on his lecturing voice. "Basically, a *blackbody* is an idealized physical body that absorbs all incident electromagnetic radiation, regardless of frequency or angle of incidence."

Sam and Billie stared at him, without speaking.

"Does that clear it up for you?" Professor Capel asked.

"Not really," they both replied.

The professor sighed. "All right. Imagine there is a single hole in the wall of a large enclosure."

"Okay."

"Any light entering that hole is reflected indefinitely or absorbed inside and is unlikely to re-emerge, making the hole a nearly perfect absorber. The radiation confined in such an enclosure may or may not be in thermal equilibrium, depending upon the nature of the walls. In this case, the dark stone holds everything. Think of a sponge. Bereft of water, it is light. Leave it next to water and it absorbs as much water until its full."

Sam asked, "What's the dark stone absorbing?"

The professor smiled. It was cheerful and entirely indifferent to any real concerns they may have for destroying the planet with such a bizarre and alien material. "Why everything of course."

"Everything?" Billie asked.

Capel nodded. "Yes, yes. Everything that has any mass."

"It was stripping the electrons straight out of my hands, wasn't it?" Sam asked, in awe. "And bending the light from the examination beam?"

"Yes, and yes."

Billie took a deep breath and said, "It's a little alien black hole, isn't it?"

"I like that," the professor said. "It's a little dramatic, but mostly accurate."

"When would it have stopped?" Sam asked.

The professor answered without hesitation. "When the sponge was filled, I suppose."

"How long?" Sam persisted.

"It's hard to guess, but each of these stones could conceivably end up weighing a hundred thousand tons or more."

Sam let that concept sink in. "There are more of these stones hidden out there in space. One of them is heading toward us right now. That's why it's going to flip the magnetic poles."

"What?" Billie asked.

"Think about it," Sam said. "The asteroid has been following the same trajectory around the sun for the past thirteen thousand years… and yet no one has been able to see it with modern technology."

"What are you getting at?" The professor asked.

"I'm saying the stones have been out there all along, plain as today, yet no one's seen it because the damned thing absorbs all light around it."

"Exactly."

"Then how do we locate it?" Sam asked.

The astronomer sighed. "We don't."

"We can't?"

The professor nodded as though it were obvious. "No. We have to look for signs of light being taken away."

"Can you do that?"

"Yes, and I already have." The professor's blue eyes glistened with his own grandiose vision of his greater intelligence and discovery. "Using a database of astronomy charts with a new search input, specifically looking for light being distorted, I was able to track our devastating asteroid."

"And?" Sam asked, excited.

"It was there, plain as daylight for us all to see."

"How close is it?" Sam and Billie asked.

"It's close. It should enter our orbit before the end of the week."

Sam swallowed hard. "The question is, now that we know that it exists, is it too late to do something about it?"

CHAPTER THIRTY-SEVEN

THE SECRETARY OF Defense listened as Sam Reilly relayed all the new-found information regarding the asteroid, the strange material named *blackbody,* and their theory that the four dark stones could be used to somehow re-establish the correct position of the magnetic poles.

She offered him any resources he required and then hung up.

A moment later, she dialed a new number by heart, and relayed the information to one of her leading scientists.

The man had listened intently, letting her speak without asking any questions.

When she was finished, she said, "Well, what do you think?"

"If the original meteorite is still out there, we'll find it, ma'am."

"And if you do. Then what?" she persisted.

"Assuming your man, Mr. Reilly manages to correct the magnetic poles, and there's still a U.S. government left to protect, we'll be able to use the material."

"But, will it be enough?" she asked.

The scientist thought about it for a moment. "We won't need much. If it's as powerful as Reilly told you, a small collection of the material should be enough to complete it."

"Good."

"One more thing, ma'am."

"Yes?"

The man paused and then said, "Given what we now know about what is rapidly approaching, should we really be focusing on the Omega Project?"

The Secretary of Defense's response was immediate. "Even if Sam Reilly can decipher the code to extinction in time, it will change nothing of the fact that the Master Builders are still preparing for war—and if we don't intend to become extinct, we're going to need a secret weapon."

CHAPTER THIRTY-EIGHT
───────○⊱3○───────

SAM STARED AT the professor's world globe.

It was six feet high and constructed using accurate proportions based on recent satellite imaging. Shaped much like a sphere, but with flattened poles and bulges at the equator, it depicted a more realistic image of Earth as an oblate spheroid. Throughout the globe, the locations of known Master Builder temples had been set using orange flags.

The current location of the two magnetic poles had been marked using a red flag, and purple flags were used to represent their daily positions for the past six months. Contrary to what people might assume, the magnetic poles were far from static. Instead, their position was dynamic — shifting upward of fifty miles daily, in fifty-plus mile oval shaped loops. The center of those loops indicated the real magnetic poles, but even that position was known to move roughly twenty-five miles a year.

He glanced at the data from the past week, which was marked with yellow flags. They showed that the south pole had shifted nearly five hundred miles north and the north pole had drifted six hundred miles south.

Sam looked at Billie and the Professor. "Okay, we know that the four sacred stones need to be placed inside four hidden temples, in order to reset the position of the magnetic poles. That part seems simple enough."

"What makes you certain that the dark stones will even have enough weight to shift the magnetic poles?" Billie paused, and then looked at the Professor. "You said that once each stone has absorbed as much as they could, their maximum weight would still only be a matter of a hundred thousand tons. That weight seems trivial compared with the mass of Earth."

"It is trivial," Sam agreed.

"Then how can it work?"

"I've been thinking about this for some time now. What if we're overthinking the process? We're thinking that we need equal weight to move equal mass, right?"

"It's called kinetic energy."

"Sure. So, how do you overcome a weight that is heavier than you?"

Billie answered immediately. "You need to exert additional effort."

"And how do we do that, when the weight is so much larger than our weight?"

She sighed, and understanding dawned on her. "You need a mechanical advantage or leverage."

"Exactly. I'm thinking that these magnetic poles are balancing on a fulcrum. We don't need to shift the weight of the Earth, we just need to tip the scales so that they return to their rightful places."

The professor looked at the globe. "Based on that, your hidden temples must be somewhere closer to the equator where their mass can exert the most effect over the movement of the poles."

Sam thought about that for a moment. "Wouldn't they have more leverage toward the poles themselves?"

"No." The professor was defiant. "The widest point on Earth is at the equator. That's where you want to move the most amount of energy."

"All right," Sam said. "Let's bring this back to basics, and go from there. Maybe something obvious will be staring right at us."

Billie smiled. "You start."

Sam said, "The Earth spins on its axis. The inner core spins as well, and it spins at a different rate than the outer core. This creates a dynamo effect, or convections and currents within the core. This is what creates the Earth's magnetic field — the same way a giant electromagnet works."

"So then why do the poles shift?" Billie asked.

"No one really knows. It's thought that the poles move because the internal core's rate of spin and the currents within the molten material move, causing the convection in the core changes. Irregularities where the core and mantle meet make changes to the Earth's crust, which can also change the magnetic field."

The Professor said, "There's a strong correlation between earthquakes and the movement of the magnetic field."

"And there has been a tenfold increase in the number and severity of earthquakes around the world in the past two weeks," Billie said.

Sam thought about the reports of recent earthquakes and knew she was right.

"So, what makes up the physical structure of the Earth?" Sam asked, rhetorically. "The planet's inner core is made of solid iron. Surrounding the inner core is a molten outer core. The next layer known as the mantle is solid but malleable, like plastic. Finally, the layer we see every day is called the crust."

He pointed toward the poles. "The magnetic poles can naturally switch places. By examining rocks on the ocean floor, scientists have been able to determine when this has happened because those stones retain traces of the magnetic field, similar to a recording on a magnetic tape."

"When was the last switch?" Billie asked.

"About 780,000 years ago, give or take about ten millennia." Sam glanced at his notes on his computer tablet. "It's happened roughly 400 times in 330 million years. Each reversal takes a little over a thousand years to complete, and it's known to take much longer for the shift to take effect at the equator than at the poles."

Billie said, "So, based on that note, are we searching for the hidden temples at the poles or the equator?"

"I don't know…"

Sam's cell phone rang. He picked it up and talked for a few minutes. When he ended the call, Sam had a curious and wry grin. To the professor, he said, "Thank you for all of your assistance. You've been incredibly helpful. Can you gather any of your colleagues who you think might be helpful and keep trying to crunch the numbers to find the most likely position of the fulcrum? Also, I need you to work out a safe way to move the sacred stones. I don't think moving the Göbekli Tepe pillar around to each of the hidden temples is really an option."

"Yes, of course," the Professor replied. "Where are you going?"

Sam said, "Billie and I are off to the Big Island, Hawaii."

Billie said, "The same place where one of the blue sapphires from the stone tablet indicated the location of one of the hidden temples?"

"The very same place," Sam confirmed.

"I thought Elise searched Big Island using satellite and recent bathymetric images. It all came back with nothing."

"She did."

"Then what's changed?"

"There's been some volcanic activity. A young man was killed bathing in a hot spring."

Billie shrugged. "There are five active volcanoes on the island. Kohala, Mauna Kea, Hualalai, Mauna Loa, and Kilauea—and Loihi, which is a submarine volcano located twenty-two miles south of Big Island and nearly three thousand feet below the surface. There's nothing extraordinary about a tourist getting burned in a hot spring."

Sam's voice was calm and emphatic. "This one's connected to the four temples related to the four dark stones."

"What's your interest in the case?" Billie asked.

Sam took a deep breath "After the hot spring burned a tourist to death, it froze solid. At the center of the previously hot pool, a subterranean tunnel now stands. No one's been willing to enter the ancient tunnel, but someone shined a flashlight inside, and it has ice lining its walls as far as the light could penetrate."

CHAPTER THIRTY-NINE

Big Island, Hawaii

It was a stifling ninety degrees Fahrenheit on the island, with humidity approaching eighty percent. A guide informed Sam Reilly that both of these were on the extreme ends of Hawaii's average in terms of weather. He made his way along the short journey through the dense forest, feeling every bit of the lethargy that such weather extracted. Even Billie, who was generally more accustomed to the warmer climate, looked drenched in perspiration. He followed the guide past a set of large volcanic rocks, and stopped.

In front of him, what remained of the Phoiki Hot Pond appeared inviting.

Sam sucked in a deep breath of air. It was icy cold and deliciously refreshing as it breezed across his hot skin. The humidity dropped alongside the new temperature, as though he'd walked into an industrial freezer.

At a glance, his eyes raked the bizarre sight in front of him.

The jellybean-shaped Phoiki Hot Spring was frozen. Any moisture that had previously dripped from the leaves of the rainforest that lined the spring was now frozen in ice. The ground surrounding the pool was hard, as though permafrost had penetrated deep into the once warm and fertile soil. At the center of the spring, the ice tapered inward, like a giant frozen funnel.

He stepped to the edge of the opening and saw that the tunnel — just large enough for an adult to walk standing upright inside — seemed to descend farther than his line of sight.

Billie swallowed. "So, this is a vision of what's to come?"

Sam nodded. "If we don't find the remaining four hidden temples to deposit the sacred stones, it appears we're all going to need to find some much warmer clothing."

"Let's find those temples." Billie crossed her shivering arms. "I hate the cold."

There were already more than thirty people working around the icy pond, taking samples, and trying to make sense of the unexplainable.

Sam turned to face his guide. "Who's in charge here?"

The guide smiled. "That would be Demyan Yezhov — our resident Volcanologist on the island."

He glanced at the man the guide pointed to. He was a big guy. Tall and heavily overweight, but also full of muscle. To Sam, it looked as though the guy had once been into heavy weightlifting at some stage, but then his lifestyle had changed, and as he became more focused on his work, his once muscular physique was now filled with adipose tissue after years of gluttony.

Sam approached the man. "Demyan Yezhov?"

"Yes?" The man answered with the deep resonance of an American accent, and no trace of a Russian heritage. "Who are you?"

"Sam Reilly." He offered his hand. "And this is my associate, Billie Swan."

Demyan took it and met his eye with an engaging smile and recognition. "It's good to meet you both. I was meaning to contact you earlier, and then this happened."

"Contact me?" Sam asked. "Have we met before?"

"No. I read about your exploits in the Aleutian Portal. Interesting stuff. It defies most logic regarding volcanic eruptions and their subsequent lava tubes."

"I'm afraid I can't help explain any of the science behind how the damned thing formed. I'm just glad it did, and we got out alive."

"No. That's not what I wanted to talk to you about."

"Really, what then?" Sam asked.

"After I heard about the Aleutian Portal I read up about you. You've led an interesting life, and that brings with it some unique perspectives." Demyan smiled. It was an engaging smile, and Sam guessed the man would have been considered quite attractive before gluttony and his work took over his life. "I needed to talk to you about your dissertation on climate change and the movement of the magnetic poles."

Sam felt the icy wind sucked out of his chest. The last person who was interested in his dissertation had tried to kill him. "What did you want to know?"

Demyan swallowed hard. "How you predicted what was going to happen this week."

CHAPTER FORTY
―――○⛉○―――

SAM PAUSED FOR a moment, waiting for Demyan's statement to really sink in.

His mind returned to the dissertation that he and Billie had written in an attempt to draw out those who really knew the truth. It focused on the correlation of any sudden shift in magnetic poles and a disruption of the thermohaline circulation that regulated the entire global temperatures. In the paper, he'd discussed that such an event would lead to widespread natural disasters, ranging from a series of progressively worsening earthquakes through to absurd weather patterns as the poles shifted.

Sam looked at the frozen hot spring. "I didn't predict this."

Demyan grinned. "No. I don't think anyone could have predicted this. But the rest of your dissertation has come true."

"Really?" Sam knew that there had been a number of signs that the cataclysmic prophecy had come into effect, but wasn't aware it had become obvious to the mainstream media or scientists. "What, exactly, has happened?"

"Globally, there have been more earthquakes in the past seven days than last year. Volcanoes across the globe that were considered dormant or extinct have started to become active. More than a hundred wild fires rage between North and South America, Europe has indicated both the hottest days on record and the coldest." Demyan turned to look at the frozen hot spring. "And now, a stream previously fed by a volcano has become frozen in ice."

"I'll admit it's been a pretty bad week." Sam squatted down and touched the edge of the pond, even putting his hand near the ground sucked the warmth out of his hand. "Any idea what caused it?"

"None whatsoever. I was hoping you two might shed some light on it?"

"I'm a marine biologist and Billie's an archaeologist. What assistance do you think the two of us could provide?"

"I have no idea, but you tend to know about some sort of impending cataclysmic event. I have no idea what's causing it, but whatever it is, I'm telling you now — it has begun."

Sam listened to the words. If Demyan only knew how right he was. "All right, what about this ice tunnel. Has anyone been down it yet?"

"Down it?" Demyan shook his head. "Why would anyone want to do that? A young man was burned to death in the pond. You can still see his bones, frozen in the ice. His fiancé told me he'd brought her here to propose just this morning."

Sam looked at his watch. It was 3 p.m. and somehow in that short time the pond had gone from boiling to freezing. Something about the thought stuck with him. "Why is the pond still freezing? Why hasn't it thawed?"

"I know. It's nearly ninety degrees Fahrenheit outside, so why hasn't the pond started to thaw?" Demyan took a deep breath. "The temperature coming out of the tunnel is nearly thirty degrees below freezing."

"You got any explanation for that?"

"No."

Sam looked around, the area was riddled with scientists. "Where's the girl, now?"

"Who?"

"The unlucky fiancé."

"She's over there." Demyan pointed to the other end of the pond.

Sam glanced at the woman. She was tall and athletic, with pale white skin that looked like it was rarely exposed to the sun. She was reading something. Apart from the slight reddening around her eyes where she had no doubt been crying earlier, she appeared well composed. She had a strong face with a well-defined jawline. If he'd met her in any other circumstance, his first impression would have been that she was pretty. Instead, all he saw was the tremendous burden of fatigue and guilt now etched on her face, as though she should have somehow foreseen the danger. He wished someone had contacted one of her friends or family, someone she knew well, who could take care of her.

He asked, "Why is she still here?"

Demyan shrugged. "Says she wants answers. Adamant she's not leaving here until someone can find a scientific explanation for the impossible."

"What did you tell her?"

"The truth. I have no idea."

Sam glanced at the deep funnel of ice. "Any guess how deep that thing goes?"

Demyan smiled. "Look. I've seen a lot of things happen that I never thought would be possible. But none compare to this. I mean, this entire island is full of hot magma. There are five active volcanoes on the island and one submarine volcano to the south. Whatever opening ripped through the Earth, it's deeper than the roots to this island. Heck, the closest climate cold enough to cause this sort of thing would be above the Arctic Circle — but it beats me how this tunnel should reach there. If you'll excuse me, I want to take another set of samples from the ice. We're measuring the gasses inside—it might give us some indication of where this tunnel originates."

"All right." Sam looked at Billie. "You got any ideas what we're doing here?"

She shook her head. "Beats me. The coincidence between this location and the one we spotted on the stone tablet we retrieved from the Tepui Mountains is too much to be just that. But I can't see how there could be a temple anywhere near here. Unless you want to go walking down that tunnel to the frozen center of the Earth."

Sam looked up at the sky through the filtered canopy of the jungle. It was a light blue, without any signs of an afternoon rain. It was going to be a nice afternoon, despite their icy location. "From what Demyan tells us, that tunnel might well be as long as the Aleutian Portal and defy the logic of science just as much."

"So, what are we supposed to be doing here, while the sands of time are running out?" Billie asked.

"I don't know. There must be something. I'm going to go talk to the girl."

"Who?" Billie asked.

"The tourist. The one who just got engaged."

Billie bit her bottom lip. "I believe her fiancé got boiled alive and then frozen today."

"Even so. With the exception of her fiancé, she's the only person who was here when this happened. If there is anything to be learned from being here, she might be the only one to tell us."

"You think that's wise?" Billie asked.

"No. But I'm not leaving here until we're certain this event isn't connected to the missing temples."

"Suit yourself."

"You coming with me?" he asked.

Billie shook her head. "To speak to the woman who just lost her fiancé? Hell no."

Sam shrugged and walked around the frozen spring. He noticed that the unlucky tourist was rapidly scanning a book on the history of volcanoes in the region. She was transfixed in its pages, as though within them, answers might be revealed.

She spotted him glancing at her, and looked up. Her dark brown eyes examined him like a scientist dissecting her specimen. She smiled — without attempting to hide the fact that it was forced — but he guessed it would have been usually quite stunning. "May I help you?" she asked.

He offered his hand. "I'm sorry. My name's Sam Reilly. I was told you were here when this happened."

She took it without hesitation. Her handshake was firm. "I watched my fiancé burn to death."

"I'm sorry," Sam said, hopelessly. "I understand nothing I, or anyone else is going to say to you will ever make that any better."

She asked directly, "What can I do for you, sir?"

"I realize you've already told your story to a dozen or more people, but I'd like to ask you some questions about when this happened."

"Why?"

"Same reason you're still waiting here. I want answers." He sighed. "And right now, I can't even guess where they might come from."

"Okay." She smiled at his honesty. It looked genuine. "What's your role here?"

"I was asked to come here for my unique insight into the highly unusual phenomenon."

"You're a volcanologist?" she asked.

"No. A marine biologist."

"Really?" Her face scrunched up in a gesture of surprise. "What's a marine biologist know about seismic activity?"

"Nothing."

"So why are you here?"

He answered her question with one of his own. "Have you ever heard of thermohaline circulation?"

"Sure. It's a system of currents throughout the Earth's oceans, trying to achieve temperature equilibrium. Warm water to cold areas and vice-versa."

"Exactly." Sam was surprised by the confidence of her response, and instantly wondered about her background, but thought better of asking her—it wasn't directly related to their problem. "In the past two weeks, the magnetic poles have moved farther away from their respective positions and closer to the equator. This has effectively altered the course of the thermohaline system."

"You think the direction of the current's changed, meaning that instead of warm volcanic water running beneath the Phoiki spring, it's drawing its water from the Arctic?" she asked.

The question was astute, one that Sam himself had considered. "The thought's crossed my mind, but it's pretty farfetched. But I don't have any other theories."

Her dark brown eyes fixed on his with defiance. "Why are you really here, and why did you bring an archaeologist?"

"Who said I brought an archaeologist?"

"You did, while you were talking to Demyan Yezhov, the volcanologist."

"You have good hearing." Sam looked down and then met her piercing eyes. "You really want to hear my story?"

"Look. I'm not blaming anyone for Adrian's death. It was a freak accident, nothing more. I just want to know how it happened. You're not the first person to lie to me today. But I have a feeling you might just be the first to tell me the truth."

"Okay. The truth is, I have no idea what caused this bizarre event." Sam sighed, heavily. "Yesterday my friend and I were examining an ancient stone tablet we believed to be a map of four very important temples. It depicted a set of stars that matched a constellation. Another friend of mine is a mathematical genius. She superimposed the map, the constellation, and an image of the world. Only one of the locations was over land — which isn't all that surprising, given that seventy percent of the globe is covered in ocean."

"You came here because an ancient map told you to come?"

Sam's lips curled in an incredulous and wry smile. "Yeah, well you can imagine our surprise when we found out what happened today."

"Okay."

"Okay, what?" Sam asked.

"Thanks for telling me the truth."

Sam shook his head. "You wouldn't accept that I'd come here to help because I was a marine biologist, but you're willing to take my insane story at face value?"

"Sure. You're a terrible liar. You tend to hold your breath more when you're lying."

"I don't!"

"It's all right. It doesn't matter." Airlie laughed. "I'm sorry you didn't find your temple. Was it important?"

"Right now, it's probably the most important place on Earth."

"What was the constellation?"

"Aquila."

"Do you have a picture?"

"Sure. Do you know anything about astronomy?"

"As a matter of fact, I just completed my PhD in astrophysics."

"Get out of here!" Sam unlocked his cell phone and showed her a picture of the stone tablet, under a black light, where the four unmarked sapphires depicted the hidden temples that made up the constellation of Aquila."

"It's beautiful. I've never seen anything like it. But the constellation isn't Aquila."

"Are you sure?"

"Certain. See this bright star here?"

Sam nodded. "Altair?"

She nodded. "It looks like Altair, but it isn't. See how it's to the left, where it should be to the right of this triangle of stars. It's easy to confuse because it's so bright."

Sam swallowed hard. "Any idea what it is then?"

"Sure. That's the constellation of Contrarian, because it's a mirror image of the constellation of Aquila. Although I don't think your stone actually refers to the same body of stars."

"Why not?"

"Because Contrarian was only recently discovered using the Keck Telescope on Mauna Kea."

"Any chance an ancient race, highly advanced in astronomy could have spotted the constellation first?"

Airlie laughed. "Not a hope in the world."

"Are you certain? From what I've seen, the world had some extraordinary astronomers ten thousand years ago."

"I agree, but seeing Contrarian would have been impossible by the human eye without very powerful assistance."

Sam sighed. He was grasping at straws. "Just out of interest, I don't suppose you know what Contrarian means in English?"

"I sure do. It means opposite."

"If this map were made today, do you think its cartographers would have wanted us to know that the locations identified mean the opposite?"

"Maybe. That's more your expertise. I deal with the stars rather than the Earth's antipodes."

"What did you say?" Sam asked.

"I deal more with the stars than the Earth's antipodes... why?"

Sam called out to Billie. "Get your laptop out."

Billie stepped toward them, removed her backpack and started her computer. "What's up?"

Sam said, "Dr. Swan, this is Dr. Chapman. She just pointed out that we were wrong about Aquila. It's actually the constellation of Contrarian, meaning opposite..."

"Or antipode!" Billie beat him to it.

"Exactly."

Billie put her laptop on the volcanic rock in front of the three of them. An antipode was the direct opposite mark on the planet. Like the old concept that if you keep digging a hole through the Earth's crust, you'll reach China, an antipode is a mathematical opposite to any given coordinate on Earth.

She typed the current coordinates into her world map software. Mathematically, the geographical coordinates of an antipodal point can be calculated by converting each coordinate to the opposite latitude. For example, 45 degrees North becomes 45 degrees South. Then the longitude needs to be subtracted from 180 degrees. For example, 25 degrees West will be 180 degrees minus 25 degrees, making the antipode 155 degrees East.

Billie clicked enter and the program gave the answer immediately.

She shook her head. "I don't believe it."

"What is it?" Sam asked.

"The antipode to the Phoiki Hot Pond is somewhere in the southern half of Africa."

Sam's eyes widened and his lips curled into a grin. "Let me guess — the buried pyramid of the Kalahari Desert."

Billie nodded, "Exactly."

CHAPTER FORTY-ONE

WITHIN FIVE MINUTES Billie had the exact locations of the four hidden temples.

Sam stared at the list of locations. The computer had automatically identified the closest known town or spot to the location. The sight took his breath away.

Orvieto — Italy.

Kalahari Desert — Namibia

Sigiriya — Indonesia

Lord Howe Island — Australia

Airlie glanced at the list. "Nice list for a vacation."

Sam nodded. "If the extinction of the human race weren't riding on it."

"That bad, hey?"

"That bad."

Sam grabbed his cell phone again and dialed a number. "Tom! We found something. I need you and Genevieve to head over to Arizona University. The Professor there will give you one of the sacred stones. I need you to take it somewhere."

"Sure, where?" Tom asked.

"Orvieto, Italy."

"Anywhere in particular. Or just the walled city?"

"I have no idea. Just get there as soon as you can. I'll get Billie to email you with the information we found. Good luck."

He hung up and then pressed the contact number for Professor Douglas Capel. The phone rang. Twice.

On the third attempt, the Professor answered. "What?"

"We found the location of the hidden temples. Tell me you worked out how to move the sacred stones!"

"I'm still putting it all together, but the stones should be transferable within the next couple hours."

"That's great. Tom will be by to pick one of them up. Billie will send you an email with the locations where we need to send the other three stones. How would you like an all-expense paid trip around the world?"

"At my age, I'd just as happily stay at home. But, why not?"

"Good. Just out of interest, how did you resolve the problem of transporting the sacred stones of blackbody?"

"I constructed a vacuum. No air meant no electrons to steal. The stone remains a constant weight inside."

"That's great. Well done."

Sam hung up. He glanced at Airlie. "Dr. Chapman, I can't tell you how much you've helped us. Your information might just have saved the entire human race from extinction."

Airlie stood up and started to pack her small travel bag. "I'm coming with you."

Sam grinned. "Where?"

"Wherever it is you're going. To the antipode of this place. Where that constellation is directing you."

"Shouldn't you wait here?"

"My fiancé's dead. There's nothing I can do here to bring him back. But if I come with you, I might just find a way to make it so that he didn't die in vain."

Sam remained silent. The last thing he needed right now was a tag-a-long.

"I won't slow you down. But I might be able to help. If you've told the truth about anything today, we both know you're going to need all the help you can get."

He knew the importance of having something to concentrate your efforts on after a terrible event like losing someone close to you. Sam didn't know what she could do, but he wasn't going to turn her help away, either. "Look. I need to check something out. I'll be back in a few days. Give me your number and I'll contact you."

She took a deep breath and sighed. "You're right. I should probably tell his family. Call me if there's anything I can do."

"Of course."

Demyan greeted him as he was leaving. "You found something?"

"Yes. Not here though."

"That's great news." Demyan swapped cell numbers. "If I find anything I think you might need, I'll call you. You'll let me know if there's anything I can do to help, right?"

"Of course," Sam promised.

CHAPTER FORTY-TWO

─────○⛀○─────

Orvieto — Italy

THE HISTORIC RED and white funicular lurched forward with a jolt.

Tom Bower gripped Genevieve's hand affectionately as they traveled beneath a thick forest of Italian pine, which formed a natural arbor through which their carriage ascended. The medieval walled city of *Piazza Cahen* rose majestically out of a great volcanic plug that extended more than five hundred feet above.

The single line carriageway used two cars and a central pivot point to allow simultaneous uphill and downhill routes along the constant sixteen-degree slope for the entire duration of the nearly two-thousand-foot route.

Tom glanced at the approaching carriage. It traveled downward and toward them, at a combined speed of forty feet per second. He watched, half-waiting for the two to crash into one another. At the last moment, the approaching carriage shifted to the right as theirs shifted to the left and the two passed with no more than a few inches to spare on either side.

He followed its descent toward the station below, taking in the rolling hills toward the village of Umbria, where rows upon rows of olive orchards were left behind. Tom's gaze returned upward, and he watched as the line passed through the rampart, which surrounded the entire city, in a tunnel, where Tom took advantage of the darkness to kiss Genevieve.

As the light rose, she pushed him away with a mischievous smile and a reprimand. "There's work to be done."

"No reason we shouldn't enjoy ourselves in the process." Tom squeezed her hand. "Besides, how often do you think Sam's going to ask us to go to a romantic Italian village and pretend we're on our honeymoon?"

She kissed him on the lips and then smiled lasciviously. "For the sake of keeping up our cover."

They waited as the masses of tourists disembarked, and then followed.

Dominating their vision of Orvieto was the 14th century cathedral. Soaring skyward the glittering, golden-faced Duomo's walls were made of long rungs of greenish-black basalt and white travertine. Tom casually followed the crowed through one of the three large bronze doors that remained permanently open.

He stepped through the doors.

Tom swept the interior of the cathedral with his eyes, devouring its rich history dating back to the renaissance. The apse was commanded by a large stained-glass quadrifore window. Made between 1328 and 1334 by Giovanni di Bonino — a glass master from Assisi — it draped sunlight onto the golden mosaics, giant frescoes, and rows of pews. Cylindrical columns also consisting of alternate rows of travertine and basalt, led to the trussed wooden ceiling. Above which, the transept was roofed with quadripartite, or four-celled stone vaults.

He walked silently down the aisle.

Above the altar, a large polychrome wooden crucifix hung and behind that, a series of damaged Gothic frescoes dedicated to the life of the Virgin Mary. He followed the wave of tourists and pilgrims who flocked to the two large frescoes that lined the

San Brizio chapel to the right of the cathedral. They depicted a vision of an awe-inspiring Last Judgement and Apocalypse, below which were fiery scenes from Dante's journey into Hell.

Genevieve glanced at the image and then back at Tom. "Do you think it's some sort of sign?"

"What?" Tom studied the image in greater detail. "You think it's a reference to Apocalypse we're trying to avoid?"

She shrugged. "The thought crossed my mind."

"It seems unlikely that Luca Signorelli, the master who'd been commissioned to paint the frescoes, had any idea about an asteroid that was set to return to Earth every thirteen thousand years. Do you?"

Genevieve handed him the visitor's guide to the cathedral. "Maybe he did?

Tom read the note out loud. *"At the close of the 15th century, Orvieto experienced a series of events which presaged evidence of divine displeasure. Terrible rainstorms, plague, civil strife, the threat of invasion, and appalling apparitions in the sky were seen as apocalyptic warnings."*

"Any guesses what that means?"

"None. I'm a helicopter pilot, not an archeologist or historian." Tom looked around. He'd seen enough of the historic cathedral. "Sam told me to look for a receptacle for the sacred stone. His guess is that it will be underground. He has a theory that because the stone is made of *blackbody*, which draws in all mass around it, the most powerful way for the stone to be set up would be to have it imbedded in rock."

"Like a five hundred feet high volcanic plug that Orvieto rests upon?" she asked.

"Exactly! We'll search the catacombs first."

She smiled at his simplicity. "All right."

The five bells started to ring in E-flat.

Tom looked at his watch. "What do you know? It's midday, shall we find some lunch?"

Genevieve nodded. "Sure."

"Great. I'm starving. Then let's find the receptacle for the sacred stone."

They walked down *Via Ripa Serancia,* a narrow cobblestone street, which made its way toward the south-eastern edge of Orvieto. He glanced at a sign for a restaurant called, *Le Grotte del Funaro,* and then back at Genevieve. "What do you think?"

"Everything looks good in Italy."

Tom opened the door, and they entered the small restaurant. Built into the mountain, the walls were a mixture of tunneled tuff and golden sandstone.

A waiter brought them a menu. Tom glanced at it, and then ordered the special of the day.

A new patron entered the restaurant. He had dark olive skin, and his face wore the dark unshaven stubble of two day's growth. He was impeccably dressed in an Italian made suit. A slight bulge beneath his left breast pocket suggested the possibility he was carrying a holstered weapon. The man took a seat at the table farthest away and ordered something in fluent Italian. Tom noticed that he refused the complimentary glass of local Tuscany wine, opting for a glass of water instead. Tom couldn't be sure, but the man appeared distracted, constantly glancing up in their directions.

Tom unfolded the tourist map. Inside he wrote, *is the big Italian guy trailing us?* He handed the note to Genevieve and said, "Where do you want to go next, beautiful?"

Genevieve ran her eyes across the tourist map. She casually glanced at the stranger and wrote a new message. "How about here?"

Tom looked at the message. *He's not interested in the food.*

"We'll keep our eye on him and try and lose him when we're

finished."

She nodded.

A moment later, a solidly-built man as white as a ghost walked in and ordered a drink. He was wearing dark sunglasses, and took a seat four rows back from them.

The man removed his sunglasses, revealing somber blue-gray eyes.

CHAPTER FORTY-THREE

―――――○⧏⧐○―――――

Kalahari Desert

THE CESSNA 172'S altimeter read 8,000 feet. It was a STOL — short take-off and landing — taildragger with an oversized propeller. One of the last models that still used two large wheels up front and a single one at the back, making it much more capable when it came to landing off the beaten track — or in this case, in the sand.

Through the windshield, Sam stared at the seemingly endless vista of sand dunes. From the air, it was easy to see how the Kalahari Pyramid had remained buried for so long. Next to him, Billie sat silently watching the landscape go by, her face a unique mix between wide-eyed wonder and truculence. For two people who'd spent most of their lives searching for the same ancient race, they struggled to spend more than a few hours together in the confined space of a small cockpit.

His eyes swept the flight instruments before darting across to the GPS. It showed them approaching the coordinates. He reduced the single engine back to an idle, dipped the nose, and commenced his descent.

Billie turned to face him.

She smiled, but her voice was belligerent. "Tell me again, why you sent Tom and Genevieve to a romantic medieval village in Italy to search for answers, while you and I get to take the deserted pyramid in the middle of a very hot nowhere."

"What?" Sam asked. "I thought it would be nice for them. Besides, they've been working pretty hard without much of a break lately — in case you forgot, they spent most of last year trying to find and rescue you."

"Sure. How long are you going to keep reminding me that I owe you one for getting me out of the Amazon jungle where I was being kept prisoner?"

"As long as I can." He pushed the yoke forward, away from his chest, and the aircraft's attitude dipped into a steeper rate of descent. "How long do you think I can get away with it?"

"Not long."

He searched the area for a sign of the buried pyramid. It had only been eight weeks since they'd left the temple, but already any sign of the buried pyramid had been completely lost from the air. Sam glanced at the GPS marker and the large sand dune. He circled around, banking to the left in a continuous circle, until he'd reduced his altitude and was ready to set up for a final approach. He picked a spot at the nearly flat base, between two sand dune crests.

The wind was nonexistent, and he carefully took the Cessna down, easing it into the sand. He idled the Cessna to the end of the relatively flat area, and then spun the tail, setting it up for when he needed to take off later.

He shut down the engine and climbed out of the cockpit.

Billie followed him. Slipping her arms through her small backpack, she glanced across the two sand dunes that dominated the landscape. "Where's the entrance?"

Sam placed a plastic cover on the engine's air intake manifold to protect it from the sand. Then looked up at the largest sand dune to the east. "Over there, somewhere…"

She followed his gaze. "It's buried under that sand dune?"

"No."

"Then where is it?"

He switched on his hand-held GPS and waited for it to pick up enough satellites to locate the marker at the entrance of the buried Kalahari Desert temple. "It's about half a mile past that sand dune."

Billie looked at him and swore. "You're serious, aren't you?"

"Afraid so."

"Why didn't you just land over there?"

"Because over there was full of thick sand, steep slopes, and we would have never gotten to take off again—assuming I didn't kill us in the landing." Sam shrugged. "If you want, I can give it a try?"

Billie clipped the strap on her backpack. "Come on, let's get it over with."

CHAPTER FORTY-FOUR

———○ℰ℈○———

IT TOOK NEARLY two hours to reach the entrance to the buried temple of the Kalahari Desert. Billie had let Sam set the pace. Once it was established, she matched him with a constant speed until the third dune, when his endurance wavered, and she passed him, setting a new pace. She was tall and lissome, climbing the huge sand dunes with the assertive gait of an athlete. Even wearing the shapeless, loose flowing Indigo blue Alasho and traditional robes worn by the Saharan Tuareg Nomads, she had a willowy elegance about her as she climbed.

Billie glanced at her own hand-held GPS, which indicated they were right upon the entrance. Her eyes scanned the rolling hills of sand around them. She cursed, and then waited for Sam to catch up. As he slowly made his way down the sand dune, she said, "The GPS says we're here. Any idea where the entrance is?"

Sam pulled out his GPS and placed it next to hers. They were identical, and showed the entrance about five feet into the sand dune.

He removed a black folding shovel, the sort of thing soldiers used to dig trenches and latrines. "It looks like we have some digging ahead of us."

"You knew it would be buried?"

"Of course. Nothing stays out in the open for very long in the

Kalahari Desert."

It took three hours of digging to clear away enough sand to reach the opening to the buried temple.

Billie stepped back and looked at the entrance.

It looked more like a mine shaft than a pyramid buried in sand. Three old railway sleepers formed the framework for the adit. It ran at a gradual decline. Inside, the makeshift timber set—used to support the roof—mingled with a series of posts, jacks and roof bolts used to prop up the sandy ceiling. They had been placed haphazardly, giving her the impression of an old gold mine built during the American gold rush era.

She glanced at Sam. "You think the tunnel's still safe?"

"It doesn't really matter if it's not. We don't have time to strengthen its foundations."

"That's the best you've got?"

Sam shrugged, and ducked under the crude adit, into the main tunnel. "Come on."

Thirty feet inside, the angle of the tunnel changed from nearly horizontal to a steep decline. Another four hundred feet, and the tunnel separated into two directions. The original tunnel continued to descend at the same angle, while the second tunnel ran at the exact same angle, only at an incline instead.

Sam said, "It's the same anatomy as the Pyramid of Giza."

"Aren't they all?"

"No. The Atlantis pyramid was different."

"Good point. Come to think of it, so was Tunguska." Sam brushed the beam of his flashlight down and up the main passages. "So where do you want to go?"

"Take the ascending passage. Let's head to the king's chamber."

They moved quickly, climbing for another four hundred feet before the tunnel split in two again. This time the main tunnel remained at the constant thirty-degree angle toward the grand gallery, while the second one turned horizontally deeper into the pyramid's core.

Billie shined her flashlight into the horizontal tunnel. "The queen's chamber. Let's keep heading upward."

"Okay."

At the top of the grand gallery, the passageway leveled out and they stepped into the king's chamber.

The room was rectangular with a ceiling just short of twenty feet. It was nearly identical to the king's chamber inside the rest of the temples, but with one exception — at the center of the room where Billie would have expected the sarcophagus to be, a single limestone pedestal stood.

She stared at the pedestal. "What's that?"

"That's where they stored the Death Mask — the strange golden skull through which the ancient Master Builders burned their black hallucinogen to control their laborers."

The comment reminded Billie of her time spent as a captive under the same drug. "So, where's the sarcophagus?"

"There isn't one."

"You're kidding. I assumed the sacred stones would be positioned inside the sarcophagus or something."

"Guess we're going to have to find a new location."

Billie shined his flashlight around the rest of the room, in slow, focused swaths. Two pictograms lined the east and west walls. One was a series of calculations in ancient Egyptian, and the other depicted the twin volcanic peaks of Mount Ararat.

She searched specifically for any indents or openings in the stonework where the sacred stone may be placed. After twenty minutes, she found nothing.

"You see anything?" Sam asked.

"Nothing."

"Have you got another plan?"

She opened her backpack and removed the black light wand. "Yeah, let's try this."

CHAPTER FORTY-FIVE

BILLIE RAN THE black light across the eastern wall. It showed nothing but darkness. She then tried the northern side. This time, it revealed a series of texts, written in the script of the ancient Master Builders.

There was a lot about their history. Many of the words regarding time were indecipherable to her, but the last sentence struck her.

She read it out loud. *"The great kings may strive to maintain power with far reaching eyes. Ultimately it is only the queens who hold the key to salvation."*

"What the hell does that mean?" Sam asked.

"I have no idea."

Sam repeated the words. "Okay, *the great kings may strive to maintain power with far reaching eyes...* must refer to the looking glasses found inside the king's chamber of every temple we've been in."

Billie thought about it for a second and agreed. "Using such devices to see over great distances and communicate with neighboring and far away temples must have given the ancient kings tremendous power."

"But what about the queens?"

"We never found anything inside the queen's sarcophagi.

They were always empty, most likely waiting for the death of the kings."

"Sure. But what if they were never intended to house the remains of ancient queens?"

Billie grinned. "I don't believe it!"

"What?"

Billie cursed loudly. "I don't believe it. The answer's been staring us in the face all this time."

"Are you just going to keep celebrating your intelligence or are you going to tell me what you think's happened."

She smiled. "*The great kings may strive to maintain power with far reaching eyes. Ultimately it is only the queens who hold the key to salvation.*"

"I'm reading the same thing you are…" Sam said. "But I'm not getting anything."

"What about the queen's chambers?"

"What about them? They were always empty."

"That's it!"

"What the hell are you talking about? We've been through the queen's chambers. There's nothing inside. The sarcophagi are empty, awaiting the king's death for the queen to follow."

"The queen's sarcophagi. They're empty. But they're not waiting for the queen. They're waiting for the stones."

Sam swore. "You're right, let's go."

They raced down the grand gallery.

Billie stared at the queen's sarcophagus. Compared to the king's, which was covered in pictographs and intricate stone carvings, this one appeared insipid and mundane.

Sam asked, "What do you think?"

She removed her backpack and took out the small iron pry bar. "There's only one way to find out."

Together they pried the stone lid off, sliding it only a few inches to the side. Billie flashed her light inside. The final resting place was empty. If she'd uncovered it previously she would have assumed it was nothing more than an empty sarcophagus, waiting for a king or queen to die. But at its center was a single indent, slightly smaller than a typical house brick.

Sam passed her the black light wand. Billie took it and shined it into the narrow recess. It revealed the image of the Greek letter Theta and a single horse.

"Got you!" Her eyes widened. "Now what?"

"Insert the stone and see what happens."

Billie looked at the small metallic casing that housed the sacred stone in a complete vacuum. She ran her fingers along the airtight latches.

Her eyes met Sam's. "Are you ready?"

"Go for it."

Billie removed the safety latches. A small gush of air rushed into the casing. She quickly removed the stone. It felt lighter than air. She carefully placed it into the recess at the bottom of the queen's sarcophagus.

The sacred stone seemed to lock in place.

She tried to jiggle the stone and make sure it fit properly, but it was now locked permanently. Sam had a try at removing it afterward, and agreed the stone had now become permanently fixed to the recess at the base of the sarcophagus.

"Now what?" she asked.

Sam shrugged. "Nothing."

"Nothing happens?"

"It's like Professor Capel suspected. Something needs to trigger the stones to start gaining mass."

She considered what she saw when she watched Sam pick up the stone back inside the lab at Arizona University. It started to immediately gain mass the second it was removed from the Death Stone.

"You think they're aligned, don't you?"

"I'm hoping so."

"Once all four of the sacred stones are joined, it will trigger the response—and all the stones will start gaining mass?"

"Yes."

Billie looked at the sacred stone one last time and then heaved the sarcophagus lid back into place. "Come on, let's not waste any more time. One down, three to go."

They moved with determined and purposeful strides, racing to reach the outside of the temple. Once there, they quickly climbed the first sand dune. From the crest, Billie spotted the little Cessna 172 still parked where they'd left it. On the horizon, a strange cloud formation approached. It was like a heavy rain, but darker—and completely out of place for a region that normally receives less than ten inches of rain annually.

"What is that?" she asked.

Sam stared at it for a minute. "That looks to me like icy sleet!"

"In the Kalahari Desert?" she asked, incredulously.

Sam swallowed, hard. "Looks like it, and that means we're going to have to pick up our pace if we want the human race to survive."

CHAPTER FORTY-SIX

ILYA YEZHOV PICKED up his cell phone and made the call he was dreading.

"What have you found?" came the response from Leo Botkin on the other end.

"We just got a hit on our traveler's database. Sam Reilly's passport was just used to leave Hosea Kutako International Airport in Namibia."

"Leaving?" Botkin's voice took a dark tone. "When did he arrive? Why didn't you inform me when he arrived?"

"It has to do with their reporting system. They're an older airport, and sometimes their internet connections go down. When that happens, all documents relating to incoming and outgoing passengers are entered into the database afterward."

"Then how long has he been there, for Christ's sake!"

"Twelve hours and fifteen minutes. He hired a light aircraft. Took it for a short flight and then returned."

Botkin swore again.

Ilya said, "I don't understand. He knows the world's about to go to hell, so what's he doing hiring a light aircraft from an out of the way airport?"

"He's gone to visit an ancient ruin in the Kalahari Desert," Leo said without hesitation.

"Really? Why would he possibly do that?"

Botkin paused. "I have no idea. Find someone to locate him, and work out where he's going."

Ilya was certain his boss knew a lot more than he was letting on, but he'd learned long ago not to try questioning Botkin about anything he hadn't revealed. If Leo was going to let him know something, he would have already done so. If not, there was nothing Ilya could do to pry the information out of him.

Instead, he said, "There's something else."

"Yes?"

"Sam Reilly's friend, Tom Bower, and his girlfriend are in Orvieto, Italy. I'm overseeing a team who's shadowing them both now."

"Good. Do you know what they're doing there?"

"Right now, it appears they're doing nothing more than having a romantic vacation in a medieval city."

"That seems unlikely, given what they know is coming."

"Maybe they're making the most of their last few days together?"

Botkin didn't laugh. "Whatever you do, don't fucking lose them."

"Okay. Do you want me to bring them in and see if we can get some answers?"

"No. Just watch them. If they try to leave before you have those answers, bring them in."

"Very well, sir. Anything else I can do for you?"

"Yes. See if you can track down where the rest of his crew are currently."

"Reilly keeps his business on board the *Maria Helena* highly secure. His overshadowing company, Global Salvages, doesn't even keep records of his staff."

"I know. Lucky for me I happen to have a secret list of those who are under his regular employ. There's just two names on it that are almost certainly fake. One is named Elise. She used to work for the CIA as a child prodigy, before she apparently lost interest, set up a new passport and name for herself, and disappeared. I have a fair idea who she really is and why the Secretary of Defense lets her hide in plain sight, despite never using the same passport twice."

"And the second name on the list?"

"Genevieve — no surname — she's the brunette hanging out with Tom currently in Orvieto."

"Her passport says her name's..."

"It's fake. Trust me. She's been living a lie since she arrived onboard the *Maria Helena* two years ago."

Ilya stared at the photo of Tom and Genevieve. "She's cute. Tom's a lucky guy. Maybe I should personally pay her a visit?"

"Forget it. There's something familiar about this girl. I recognize something about her face from somewhere, but I can't place it. From what my sources at the Office of the Secretary of Defense tell me, she's dangerous — an ex-assassin or something — very professional. Trained overseas for covert sanctions. Don't confuse her soft smile, blue eyes and coquettish good looks for vulnerability — fuck with her, and she'll chew you up and spit you out before you know what hit you."

"So, what do you want me to do with them?"

"Nothing. Have your man observe and report back. Nothing more — and find out what the hell Sam Reilly's searching for."

CHAPTER FORTY-SEVEN

―――――○⛬○―――――

Orvieto

Tom paid for the meal and stepped out the door.

They walked three hundred feet up *Via Ripa Serancia* and into a ceramicarte—or what appeared to Tom as a boutique pottery shop. There, they waited. But no one came.

"Are you sure it was him?" Genevieve asked.

"I'm telling you, it was the man from the Great Blue Hole in Belize. I'm not sure about the rest of him. I didn't really get a good look at him before, but his eyes were definitely the same. Gray-blue eyes, almost silvery. I've seen plenty of blue eyes over the years, but never like that. It would be pretty unusual to find a second person with the same color."

"But not impossible."

"No," Tom agreed.

He stared out the window. No one left the restaurant.

Genevieve stepped back from the window. "They're not following, and there's no one else on the street. Maybe you're wrong?"

"I don't know. I was sure it was him. Even so, no reason to wait around here all day. Let's make a start.

They cut through *Malcorini Ripa Serancia* and onto *Via Del*

Caccia, before heading north-east to the *Necropoli del Crocifisso del Tufo.* The path took them along the top of the fortified defensive walls built above the dramatic near-vertical cliff-face of volcanic tuff. From there, they descended into the necropolis through an impressive pedestrian path that dropped down from *Porta Maggiore.*

The *Necropolis del Crocefisso del Tufo* was an Etruscan necropolis located at the base of the cliff of Orvieto. Tom and Genevieve casually studied the tombs. There were about seventy, all made of tuff bricks to form individual chambers. They were arranged orthogonally, with small trenches in between.

Fifteen minutes later, Tom's cell phone rang. He picked it up and spoke to Sam for a couple minutes, before hanging up.

"What did he say?" Genevieve asked.

"He said that he and Billie placed the first of the sacred stones and not to bother with the necropolis. We need to find a specific tomb."

She smiled. "There's plenty of tombs here."

"I know, but Sam says the one we're after is going to be buried underground. He recommends the Orvieto Underground."

"Sure, that makes sense."

It was a forty-minute walk, climbing the steep stairs up into Orvieto. At the main entrance to the Orvieto Underground, Tom met many guides offering their services. He found one, an older man who'd been guiding the tunnel system for more than a quarter of a century, and agreed upon a price for a private tour.

"Is there something that you'd particularly like to see?" the guide asked.

Tom said, "Yes. We're looking for a particular tomb or sarcophagus."

The guide thought about it. "There aren't any sarcophagi

down there. Lot of interesting stuff, but none of those."

"We're looking for a particular monument where one might bury an Egyptian treasure," Tom persisted.

It was an unusual request, given that the tunnels were carved by Etruscans, who had spent more than two and a half thousand years carving out the tunnels using hand tools.

The guide smiled. "I know what you're after."

"You do?" Genevieve and Tom replied in unison.

"Sure. You want me to take you to see that strange pyramid shaped hypogeum."

Tom had never heard of it, but it sounded like the closest thing they were going to get to a tomb. He smiled. "That would be perfect."

CHAPTER FORTY-EIGHT
———O&3O———

I T TOOK THEM fifteen minutes to reach the pyramid shaped hypogeum. As they descended the series of ladders carved out of the stone walls, their guide informed them that the Orvieto Underground had more than twelve hundred tunnels in total.

As Tom descended, all he could think about was how similar the place felt to the subterranean city of Derinkuyu in Turkey, with a series of interwoven tunnels and giant round stones capable of blocking off individual levels or tunnels from others.

Inside the hypogeum Tom studied the walls. It wasn't a quarry—its walls were fixed at purposeful angles. Nor could it have been a cistern, because its walls showed no evidence of previous exposure to water.

The guide said, "It's interesting to wonder what its purpose was, isn't it?"

Genevieve removed the black light wand from her backpack. "I have high hopes you might get to see the answer to that question, shortly."

The guide glanced at the wand. "What are you looking for with that?"

"I don't know yet. But I'm hoping I recognize it when I see it. Do you mind switching of your flashlight, please?"

"Hey, you're paying. If you want to play archaeologist, you

go right ahead."

The hypogeum went dark. For a moment, nothing seemed to appear, but then they spotted it. Along the southern wall, a rectangular stone—roughly four feet in height—lit up with the image of a horse.

Tom's eyes widened as he touched it. "The stone's fixed solid."

The guide laughed. "Did you think you might move it?"

"I kind of hoped so," Tom admitted.

Genevieve said, "Hang on, look at that."

Tom followed her gaze. Toward the northern wall, a series of smaller stone tiles were lit up in the blue luminescence. There were several of them and when you joined them all together, it formed the image of the Greek letter of Sigma.

He sighed. "Well, at least we know we're in the right place."

"Sure, but now what do we do with it?" Genevieve asked.

Tom pressed his weight on the first of the luminescent stones. It depressed half an inch into the ground behind. It was a small enough movement that he needed to test the other non-radiant stones nearby to see if he could achieve the same effect with them. When he discovered he couldn't, Tom carefully went around to the rest of the stones that joined to make Sigma.

When the last one was depressed, Tom heard the distinct sound of machinery. His eyes turned to the luminescent horse. Nothing changed. Genevieve went up to the stone wall and pushed. The entire stone block slid along an ancient set of rails into a hidden recess, revealing a set of stone stairs leading farther down.

"What the hell did you do?" the guide asked.

"What has to be done," Tom replied, stepping into the opening.

The guide said, "I don't think you should be going down

there."

Tom ignored him.

At the bottom of the stairs was an intricate sarcophagus. It was almost identical to the one found inside the queen's chamber.

He ran his hand across the engravings, trying to find a gap in its seal.

"Hey, don't touch that. It's an ancient artifact. The archaeologists wouldn't want you…"

Tom removed the prybar from his backpack and started prying the lid off the sarcophagus.

"Hey, hey… what about the respect for the dead?" the guide asked.

"Don't worry about it. There's no one inside." Tom slid the lid to the side.

The guide tentatively leaned over Tom's shoulder to see for himself. Inside was a completely vacant sarcophagus. At the base of it, a single rectangular recess matched what they were looking for.

Genevieve opened the vacuum sealed, metallic casing and removed the sacred stone. She gripped it in her hand in wonder, before placing it carefully in its recess. Instantly, the stone developed an affinity for its new surroundings, latching on with such ferocity that it would be impossible for anyone to remove the stone by hand.

"Who are you guys?" the guide asked.

Genevieve fixed a hardened stare onto the guide. "Not the sort of people to be crossed."

"Okay, okay." The man opened his palms outward in a placating gesture. "What do you want me to do?"

Tom said, "Give me a hand. We need to slide this lid back and seal the sarcophagus."

It took all three of them to seal the vault once more, and the stone wall leading to the hidden chamber replaced. By the time they were done, the strange hypogeum had returned to its original appearance.

Another hour later, the three of them climbed the series of stone ladders and finally reached the surface. They thanked their guide, tipping him well. The man, only too eager to leave, disappeared without a goodbye.

Tom picked up his cell phone and made a call. "Sam, it's done."

Two sacred stones down, two to go. Life was looking up for the survival of the human race. Tom then took a deep breath, because opposite the main entrance to the Orvieto's Underground, watching him, was the Italian stranger from the restaurant.

CHAPTER FORTY-NINE

―――――○⳽○―――――

TOM WALKED QUICKLY. He'd left Genevieve to double back and see if the stranger followed him. They were still in the heart of the main tourist parts of Orvieto. He headed north. It took about ten minutes, before he turned yet another corner and into *Via Magalotti*.

Away from the main tourist center near the *Duomo del Orvieto* and the entrances to the Orvieto Underground, the narrow streets were no longer filled with tourists. Tom walked slowly, seemingly as though he was taking an interest in the unique gothic architecture. He would walk a dozen yards and then pause to study a shopfront or a private residence. The sound of his feet on the cobblestones was amplified by the narrow laneway, surrounded by medieval stone buildings.

His pursuer tried to soften the sound, but there was no hiding it.

Tom meandered in a northeastern direction through the labyrinth of slender laneways, alleys, footbridges and pedestrian tunnels. He'd checked twice, and both times the same man was following him. The stranger was heavyset, but not overweight. His muscular arms and broad chest were emphatic in his seamlessly fitted Italian suit. There was no doubt in Tom's mind that if he tried to outrun him, the man would probably move like an NFL running back. Likewise, he had no doubt the slight bulge in the suit was a holstered weapon.

The thought made him move quicker. He turned into *Via dell'Olmo*. It was a slender one-way street, with no shopfronts in sight. Toward the other end, the deep guttural sound of the powerful engine of a sports car resonated and echoed. Otherwise, the street was completely empty. Tom quickened his pace. About a hundred feet ahead, he turned left into a small alcove. It stretched approximately twenty feet into the carved-out volcanic tuff, and then, like a garage, stopped in a dead end.

Fear rose in his throat like bile.

He was trapped. Tom looked for a door, a window, or anything through which he could escape. There were none. He wasn't carrying anything that could even be used as a weapon. He turned to confront his pursuer head on.

The stranger followed into the stony alcove.

Tom looked directly at him. Their eyes locked together for a moment, before the stranger broke it by darting around the rest of the alley. The man's jaw was rigid, and his face was set with determination. There was something else there, too. Tom thought he saw hesitation and doubt, as though he wasn't sure what he was supposed to do next.

But Tom knew what he had to do.

He was about to take his chance, by pushing through the man and making a run for. Someone revved an engine from across the road. The vibrations ran across the cobblestones beneath his feet.

The stranger reached into his jacket.

He's going for the gun!

The lethal realization surged him on with reckless abandon. The stranger was big, but Tom was bigger and just as fast. Mentally, he imagined himself knocking into the side of the man's right shoulder. If he hit him hard enough he could dislocate the shoulder on his shooting arm. If the man was a professional, he would probably still try and shoot, but it would be highly unlikely the man could aim. It was a long shot, but it was the only one Tom had left.

He held his breath and then stopped.

Because Genevieve came around the corner behind the stranger. She moved quickly and silently. Before the man had fully gripped the handle of his weapon, she had slid the razor-sharp end of her butterfly knife into the soft tissues of his throat, inches away from his carotid artery.

The man's arm went limp. "Okay… I'm not moving."

"Why are you following us?" she asked, her voice a dangerous whisper.

The stranger swallowed. "Not you. I have no idea who you are!"

"Then why have you been following me?" Tom asked.

The guy shrugged. "I haven't."

She put more pressure on the tip of the knife. "Yes, you have."

The man spoke in a calm, reserved voice. "No. I've been following Liu Bianchi."

"Who's he?"

"Not he. She. And she's a notorious assassin. The *Agenzia Informazioni e Sicurezza Esterna* have been hunting her across Europe for years. Her face was captured just yesterday, when she pursued you into the country."

"You work for the AISE?" Tom asked. He'd heard of the Agency. They were basically the Italian equivalent of their CIA, Britain's M16, or Germany's Bundesnachrichtendienst.

The man nodded. "If you will permit me, I'll show you my credentials."

Genevieve increased the pressure in the knife until the blade was just under the skin. "Nice and slow."

"Mr. Rigozzi. Luca Rigozzi." The man removed his ID badge

and threw it on the floor. "And you are?"

Tom picked it up and read the details. It looked legitimate, but who knew? He ignored the question and called Elise on his cell phone. He explained the situation and gave the man's details. She checked with the database, and confirmed Luca Rigozzi did work for the AISE.

Tom turned to Genevieve. "He checks out." Then, to Rigozzi, he said, "I'm Tom Bower and this is Genevieve."

Genevieve released him.

Rigozzi took a handkerchief and dabbed the fine blood from his neck. "Thank you."

Tom asked, "Someone's been following us since we got here?"

"Yes. Her name's Liu Bianchi and she's one of the deadliest assassins the world has ever seen. We thought she might have been killed a few years ago. She went to ground and didn't come back, until yesterday."

Genevieve said, "You know she's been following us since we got here?"

"Yes."

"Then why haven't you arrested her?"

He sighed heavily. "I was going to."

"But?"

"She's not alone. Whatever's happening here, it's big. We might just get to take down a lot of bad people if we get lucky. Whatever it is you're involved in, someone's paid big money to bring some of the deadliest assassins out of the woodwork. It must be pretty important stuff."

Tom nodded. "You have no idea."

"Now what?" Genevieve asked.

Rigozzi's eyes narrowed. "You can follow me back to my hotel. We're not safe here."

The raspy engine of the idling sports car finally went silent.

The three of them stepped into *Via del'Olmo,* where an older woman met them. Luca Rigozzi was the first to respond. He got off the first shot. But she fired the next two.

Tom dived to the ground next to Genevieve.

His eyes darted toward Rigozzi. Two bullets were planted right between his eyes. Professional kill shots. Genevieve grabbed the man's handgun — a Beretta 92 — and started firing.

CHAPTER FIFTY
———O&3O———

TOM LOOKED UP and spotted their attacker as she kicked in a glass window about thirty feet back along *Via del'Olmo*. She stepped inside, using it as a partial barrier, and continued to shoot. The shots went wide, and he and Genevieve retreated back into the stone alcove.

The question was, now where could they go?

Tom swept the narrow street with his eyes, searching for a way out. Like many of the laneways throughout the medieval city, this one was filled with the back-end of several small stone buildings, revealing almost no doors or windows — and no other nearby streets by which to escape.

In the alcove across the road, a man was taking some mostly ineffective cover to the side of his little red sports car. Like the garage-like alcove they were already in, the one across the road was a dead end with no rear access.

He looked at Genevieve. "What do you think?"

"About stealing the car?" she asked.

"Yeah."

"I don't like the plan." She fumbled through the dead man's coat pockets and retrieved a spare magazine for the Berretta. She pocketed the magazine, taking her total ammo count to fourteen rounds. Five in the this one and nine in the spare magazine.

"You got another idea?" Tom asked.

"No."

"Okay. I guess that settles it. I'll go first. Cover me and then follow."

"Okay, go."

Tom launched himself running across *Via del'Olmo* at a sprint some professional athletes would have been proud of. He heard a single shot fire from their attacker, followed by another two by Genevieve. The street then went quiet as their attacker was forced to take cover.

Behind him, Genevieve didn't wait. Instead, she ran straight after him, while their attacker was taking cover. They approached the car together. The owner of the sports car spotted Genevieve's handgun.

He raised his out turned hands. "I'm unarmed!"

Tom ducked down next to him. "Where are the keys?"

"What?" the driver asked.

Genevieve pointed the Berretta at him. "The keys. Give him your car keys."

"I just bought…"

Their attacker stepped out into the street and fired another three rounds. The shots skimmed the leading edge of the alcove. Genevieve aimed and fired the remaining three shots in the magazine. She removed the magazine, loaded a new one, and fired again.

Their attacker turned and started running down the street toward *Via Magalotti*.

Genevieve returned to the owner of the car, pointing the Berretta at him.

"Take the car. It's yours!" The owner handed Tom the keys without further questions.

Tom grinned. "Thanks. And sorry to really mess up your

day."

He climbed inside.

It was the first time he took any real notice of the sports car — a brand new Alfa Romeo 4C Spider in *competizione* red. The two-seater, mid-engine, rear-wheel drive coupé was right out of every wealthy Italian's exotic car magazine, with Alfa Romeo technology and DNA at its core. It used a carbon fiber tub, front and rear crash box, and hybrid rear subframe out of aluminum, to maintain a curb weight under 2000 pounds.

In the driver's seat, Tom had to shift the seat all the way back just to squeeze his six foot-four frame inside its carbon fiber shell.

He inserted the key and turned the ignition.

The raspy note of its four-cylinder turbocharged engine came alive. The dashboard was all in Italian.

Genevieve jumped into the passenger seat. "Drive!"

Tom dropped the handbrake, pulled the right paddle shifter, and the car slipped into first gear. He floored the pedal and swung the wheel to the right, launching the 4C north out along *Via del'Olmo*.

Despite the narrow street, he quickly depressed the right paddle up the gears until they shot out of harm's way. Approaching a small intersection, he jammed on the brakes and squeezed the left paddle, down shifting the gears all the way down to first.

"It's clear!" Genevieve shouted.

He gunned the pedal again. Released from the confines of regular inner-city driving, the raspy four-cylinder turbo roared, and Tom was thrown back into his leather seat like a jet pilot opening the throttles to full on take-off.

The end of *Via del'Olmo* came up an instant later.

Tom braked, quickly depressing the left paddle and changing down the gears again — the exhaust grunted smoothly, challenging him to drive faster.

"Which way?" he asked.

Genevieve couldn't see any street signs. "Go left."

Tom swerved left around the blind bend onto *Via del Paradiso*.

Up ahead, a *Piaggio Ape* — one of those Italian three-wheeled light trucks — was slowly making its way down toward them. It was small, but so was the street. There was nothing Tom could do about it. He jammed on the brake and screeched to a stop.

The driver of the *Piaggio Ape* honked his horn and yelled something in Italian that Tom guessed meant, something along the lines of, *you're driving the wrong way down a one-way street, you shmuck!*

Genevieve turned around and yelled, "Reverse!"

Tom glanced at the carbon fiber center console. An aluminum toggle stood out. He pulled it downward and the dashboard changed to blue and at the base of the screen flashed the words — *All weather driving*. He flicked the toggle again, and the screen turned red — *Dynamic*. He pressed it one more time and the screen turned yellow. A lateral G-force measuring device glowed in the middle, followed by the words, *Race Mode*.

He grinned. "Hey, look I found race mode!"

Genevieve shouted, "That's great. Now, go!"

"I'm trying, but I can't find reverse!"

Genevieve glanced at the center console. A single button with the letter R sat directly opposite the number one.

She leaned over and pressed it.

The gear shifted smoothly into reverse.

"Thanks!" Tom said.

He pressed the accelerator down hard, swinging the steering wheel left and turning back onto the end of *Via del'Olmo*.

He glanced in his rear-view mirror.

An Aprilia RSV4 yellow motorcycle raced toward them. Its female rider drew a handgun. The rider fired two shots, shattering Tom's side mirror.

Genevieve shouted, "We've got company!"

CHAPTER FIFTY-ONE

———○⋅⋅⋅○———

Tom pressed the number one button at the top of the center control panel, shifted into first gear, and gunned the engine. The Alfa lurched forward, and Tom swung wide into *Via Pecorreli*. The 1.7-litre turbocharged four-cylinder petrol engine whirred in a symphony of induction noises. The turbo quickly reached 1.4 bars of boost, and Tom felt his stomach lurch as it extracted every bit of the car's potential 177kW of power and 350Nm of torque.

The narrow cobbled street raced by in a blur.

Tom quickly lost sight of the names of any street signs, not that it was a problem. Away from the main tourist section, he didn't have a clue where they were heading. It didn't matter. He was already putting distance between them and their attacker.

Unable to aim and shoot, the rider had backed off a bit. Every now and again, she would gain on them, and Genevieve would fire another shot. The Alfa 4C wasn't designed for rearward shooting. Its carbon fiber shell and mid-positioned engine made for decent protection, but a lousy shooting platform.

Four or five blocks passed by quickly. The main road separated into two smaller one-way streets. Tom glanced at Genevieve. "Which way?"

"How the hell should I know?" Genevieve asked. "There's no map. Go right."

Tom braked hard and swerved right.

The lateral G-force meter read 1.3 gravities. He felt his entire body slide to the left, and then he straightened up and it returned to zero.

The street opened into a small piazza.

"*Corso Cavour* up ahead!" Tom said, spotting a street sign.

"Go right."

Tom rounded the corner, without easing off the speed in the process. The G-force meter read 1.6 before the back-end started to slide. He worked the steering wheel and accelerated out of the slide, straightening up in an easterly direction.

"You know where we are?" Tom asked.

"No!" Genevieve smiled like she was enjoying herself. "But look what just fell on me from behind my seat."

Tom glanced at her. She looked beautiful. Her short brown hair had become tousled in the wind, and her sapphire-blue eyes sparkled as they deliberately fixed on a tourist map of Orvieto. Her lips curled in that mischievous smile that depicted everything he'd come to love and adore about her. "Look what I just found!"

"Nice. Where are we headed?"

"Stay on this one and take the left onto *Via della Cava*."

Tom turned left and sped down and under a small bridge.

At the roundabout Genevieve said, "Go left again!"

"Okay."

Tom took the left onto *Str. di Porta Romana*. He glanced in the rear-view mirror. The rider was a fair way off, but it wasn't going to take much for her to catch up once they were out in the open away from Orvieto.

A signed pointed to the entrance to Orvieto.

"Shouldn't we be heading away from here?" he asked.

"Not yet." Genevieve grinned. "There's a sharp bend coming up."

"I see it!"

"Good. I need you to put as much distance as you can between us and our pursuer. When you get around the blind side of the bend, stop the car and let me out."

"Then what?"

"Keep going, and I'll get rid of our tail."

Tom thought she was crazy, but she had the right idea. He took the sharp bend into *Via Ripa Medici* at eighty miles an hour. The G-meter went berserk, indicating a 2.1 G lateral force. Tom glanced at it and wondered at what point the little Alfa would cease to defy the laws of physics and roll.

He straightened up and jammed on the brakes.

The car skidded to a stop.

Genevieve jumped out and aimed her Beretta toward the edge of the blind corner. Tom put his foot down and took off again.

In his rear-view mirror, he spotted the Aprilia leaning heavily into the left as it rounded the tight bend. Then he heard the shots fire. Three of them in immediate procession.

The bike wobbled, and the rider threw her body into the right side trying to save it. She might have succeeded, too, if there was more room. But in the narrow bend approaching *Via Ripa Medici*, there just wasn't enough time.

The rider realized it at the last moment, but it was too late.

The Aprilia hit the guardrail. In an instant the rider and bike were flung off the edge of the fortress-like wall that surrounded the outer ring around Orvieto — falling more than a hundred feet to the ledge below.

Tom spun the car around and picked up Genevieve.

He took off again. Driving at a normal speed, he turned left at the roundabout and down the winding *Via della Segheria*.

"Now where do you want to go?" Tom asked.

"Florence airport."

Tom looked at her and smiled. "*Perguia's* closer. That much I know."

"Sure, but Sam's jet won't be here for another three hours to pick us up, and I bet you anything you want, *Perguia's* the first place our new-found friends will go to look for us."

"There's plenty of things I want." He smiled lasciviously. "And all of them are with you. But you're probably right."

"I'm always right," she said.

"And magnanimous in your victory, too."

He pulled onto the *A1 Autostrada del Sole* and floored the accelerator. The four-cylinder turbocharged engine purred in delight. "It sounds like a great day for a drive…"

CHAPTER FIFTY-TWO

———○&3○———

Lord Howe Island

THE GULFSTREAM G650 circled the picturesque island.
Sam glanced out the large window to his side at the idyllic sight of a bygone world. Positioned some 436 miles northeast of Sydney, Australia in the Pacific Ocean, the irregular, crescent-shaped volcanic remnant formed a well-protected cove to the west that appeared turquoise from the air. The island was home to a variety of endemic flora and fauna, while its reef boasted the most southern tip of the Great Barrier Reef and was filled with a plethora of marine-life.

The aircraft came in to land, using up nearly every single one of the 2,907 feet of runway. The island normally didn't accept jets, but today they were just going to have to make an exception. On board during the flight, Sam, Tom, Billie, Genevieve, and Elise were each combing through digital databases of the island for any indication of an old burial ground, or deep underground recess or cave. So far, they'd found nothing.

Sam ended his cell phone call.

Billie looked at him and asked, "Find anything?"

"Yes. We got our first lead."

"It's on the island?" she asked.

"No."

Tom entered the conversation. "Then where are we going?"

"Beneath Ball's Pyramid."

Elise was incredulous. "Not much of a hiding spot for a temple, is it?"

Sam smiled at that. "No. But I've spoken to Demyan, the volcanologist we met in Hawaii. He tells me that Ball's Pyramid is the ancient erosional remnant of a shield volcano. He's crunched the numbers, and given the natural movement of the shape of the earth over time, the location makes a better match for the antipode than Lorde Howe Island."

"That's your lead?" Billie asked.

"Think about it," Sam persisted. "The place is the perfect shape for a hidden pyramid, its set on a volcanic plug, and with a height of 1844 feet, the stone tower would have plenty of mass to fill the sacred stone."

"How did you plan to get there?" Tom fixed on the more obvious logistical problem. "There are no helicopters on the island."

Sam said, "A local dive operator's going to take us out by boat. I've explained what's going on, and he's happy to help any way he can."

Billie smiled. "You told him about the sacred stones and the extinction of the human race? How did that go?"

"He took it better than you'd think. All right, so I didn't quite put it to him that way. I explained it was imperative we reach Ball's Pyramid and that our ability to solve the problem could have a long-lasting outcome to all life on earth." Sam took a breath. "He said he knew."

Billie looked at him quizzically. "He knew?"

"Yeah. He said for the past two days, there have been a series of strange currents and the last three dives he made, the entire reef was devoid of any marine life. He said it was the strangest and scariest thing he's ever seen—making him think of an old Stephen King book."

"Great." Billie shook her head. "So, time's running out, quickly."

"It seems so," Sam agreed.

"Back to the logistics," Tom said. "Where are you planning on entering the temple?"

"According to our dive operator, there's a large square opening at the base of Ball's Pyramid at a depth of forty feet. It's made of obsidian and goes so deep, no one has ever tried to reach the end."

The Gulfstream came to a complete stop next to the small airport. A minivan covered in the words *Dive Lord Howe Island* pulled up out the front of it.

Sam said, "Here's our ride now."

CHAPTER FIFTY-THREE
––––––○⛶○––––––

IT TOOK TWO hours by boat to reach Ball's Pyramid, which jutted dramatically out of the Pacific Ocean—a giant spire rising 1844 feet into the dark, foreboding sky. It was a monument to the once active volcano that existed seven million years ago.

On board the dive boat was their skipper, Randy and dive operator, Henry. It was Henry, a blond-haired twenty-something dive instructor, with an easy-going attitude and carefree smile, who Sam was most interested in. The man had drawn a detailed map, including depth and surrounding rock formations as navigation guides, to the entrance of the tunnel into the submerged grotto.

Sam studied the drawing. It depicted a rectangular entrance, that looked remarkably similar to the descending passage inside the Great Pyramid of Giza with the one exception being that this one was totally submerged.

He made a couple notes on his dive slate and put the map down. Turning to Henry, he asked, "Will you be joining us on our reconnaissance dive?"

Henry shook his head. His response, visceral. "No way. You couldn't pay me enough to go inside. I'm happy to guide you to the main entrance, but once there, you're on your own."

"Thanks, we appreciate your help." Sam smiled, sympathetically. It was a common enough response. Even very good divers don't like the idea of being confined in a small tunnel, under water, where there's no chance of surfacing if there's a problem with their dive equipment. "I take it you don't like cave diving?"

"No. I love cave diving and shipwrecks. I instruct in both diving specialties. But there's no way I'm going inside that thing."

"Do you know of anyone who has?" Sam asked.

"No way. No one. There's been a few who have looked at it, even the occasional diver who's penetrated the first thirty or so feet, before turning around and never going back inside. But, to my knowledge, no one's dived it to the end, mapping out the length and depth of the grotto."

Sam's lips curled with curiosity at the mystery. "Why?"

"Why doesn't anyone go inside?"

"Yeah," Sam confirmed.

Henry swallowed hard. "The place is evil."

"Evil, really?" Sam grinned, and raised a curious eyebrow. "How so?"

"The fish—when we had fish—avoided the place like it was poison. Even the coral that grows throughout the region spurns the entrance, for a distance of twenty-feet. Really, you can see a defined line in the shape of a rectangle, precisely twenty-feet out from the entrance."

"That's interesting." Sam was intrigued, but without any explanation, he still needed to dive the foreboding grotto. "All right. We still need to go inside it."

"I thought you'd say that. I'm just telling you what I know."

Sam, Tom, Billie and Genevieve finished setting up for a prolonged cave dive—using *Diving Rebreathers*. Traditional SCUBA diving required the use of a tank, or multiple tanks of breathable gas, in an open-circuit system where exhaled gas was discharged directly into the environment. But a *Rebreather* used a closed-circuit system with a scrubber to absorb exhaled carbon dioxide, reusing any of the original oxygen content. Oxygen is then added to replenish the amount metabolized by the diver. The benefit being that only a small amount of oxygen is required, allowing prolonged dives, regularly up to four hours, greater bottom times, and reduced decompression times — because the dive computer can automatically adjust the gas ratios to meet your metabolic needs at varying depths.

Tom finished checking Sam's set up. "We're all checked. Good to go."

Sam glanced at the dark clouds approaching. He wasn't sure what to believe about the grotto, but the sky certainly appeared evil. Looking at the rest of his team, he said, "Remember, we're on the clock with this one."

He then pulled his full-face dive mask over his head, checked that it formed a perfect seal, and stepped into the water.

The warm water rushed over his body. According to his dive-computer, it was 78 degrees Fahrenheit. There was minimum chop on the surface, as he signaled, *all okay*.

Sam confirmed that the rest of the team was good, and then followed Henry to the entrance of the rectangular grotto. The visibility was excellent — more than a hundred feet and his line of sight reached the rocky seafloor.

It was a short dive to reach the entrance. They descended quickly and Sam made the almost imperceptible adjustment of his jaw and slight swallowing movements to equalize the pressure in his ears.

They leveled out at a depth of forty feet.

He followed Henry around two large, submerged boulders and under a ten-foot high swim through — or covered opening between two rocks deemed not-quite a cave dive — and into another calm pool of crystal clear water.

Henry pointed to the opening up ahead.

Sam's eyes followed where Henry had pointed. There, carved into the side of the submerged section of Balls Pyramid was a rectangular, descending tunnel. At a glance, there was no doubt in his mind that the opening wasn't the natural result of erosion—it had been manmade.

Henry, who was the only one in their group who wasn't wearing a full-face dive mask and therefore couldn't speak, handed Sam his dive slate.

Sam glanced at the slate.

On it, Henry had written, *THIS IS WHERE I LEAVE YOU. GOOD LUCK.*

CHAPTER FIFTY-FOUR

———○⋅⋅⋅○———

Tom led the remaining group of four divers into the descending passage. The idea was that, being the biggest and the most experienced cave-diver, he would be in the best position to determine if they reached an unpassable tunnel.

The descending passage was the same size and shape as those found in the Great Pyramid of Giza and the pyramid buried in the Kalahari Desert, which were designed to have adult men and women walk inside. So, they offered plenty of room for diving. Even so, he wasn't taking chances. Every thirty feet he stopped and drew an arrow with chalk and wrote, THIS WAY OUT.

In the descending tunnel with identical walls it was impossible to tell how far they'd traveled by the time they reached the bottom, but his depth gauge now showed a depth of 104 feet. Unlike other pyramids that they'd searched, this one didn't have any secondary passages, like the ascending tunnel found in the Egyptian pyramids. At the bottom, the tunnel opened up to a large hypogeum, very similar to the one found in the Orvieto Underground. Tom shined his flashlight across the walls. Large and small rectangular-shaped stones lined the floor, walls and ceilings.

Sam said, "It's nothing more than a dead-end!"

"It looks very similar to the hypogeum we explored in the Orvieto Underground," Genevieve said.

Tom grinned. "It's not just closely resembling, but exactly the same."

"So what are you saying we do?" Sam asked.

Tom sighed. "We need to bring the black light wand down here."

It took close to an hour to reach the dive boat.

Tom removed his fins, passing them to Henry, and then climbed the boarding ladder. He took three steps and sat down, removing his face-mask and rebreather. Billie and Genevieve were the next to climb up and Sam the last.

Henry helped remove Sam's oxygen tank. "Did you find what you were after?"

Sam smiled. "Yes. We'll need to make a second dive, using a black light to identify what we're after, but we're confident we've found the right place, thanks to you."

"That's great news." Henry said, "You just missed a message from Elise on the radio by about half an hour."

Sam wiped the saltwater from his face with a towel. "What was the message?"

"She has the fourth sacred stone and has chartered a flight to Indonesia to deliver it. Says for you to catch up with her once you're done here. Said she couldn't wait for you to complete your work here."

"Elise has left?" Tom asked, puzzled. "Did she say why?"

Henry sighed. "She said it couldn't wait any longer."

Randy joined the conversation. "Whatever the heck all of you are involved in, the world is really copping a beating now."

Tom tried to swallow the fear that rose in his throat. "What's happened?"

"A whole bunch of stuff that shouldn't have," Randy said. "I'm starting to really believe we're about to witness the end of the world, don't you think?"

Sam said, "Not if we can do anything about it. What's happened?"

"A cruise ship carrying 3,500 passengers and 1500 crew hit an iceberg and sunk. So far there's still nearly thirty passengers unaccounted for."

"That's bad luck, where was the cruise ship traveling that she didn't heed ice warnings?" Sam asked.

Randy sighed, his lips curled up in the anguish of a story that he knew no one would believe. "The Strait of Gibraltar."

"It hit an iceberg in the Mediterranean?"

Randy nodded. "I said it was bad, didn't I?"

"What else?"

"There are more than five class four hurricanes in the northern hemisphere and six class five cyclones in the southern. Each of them recording winds in excess of a hundred and eighty miles an hour, with three being the most powerful on record." Randy took a breath and then continued. "A set of tornadoes ripped through Germany, atmospheric rains flooded Las Vegas, and icebergs washed up on Venice beach, too."

"Atmospheric rains?" Billie asked.

Sam said, "Atmospheric rivers are relatively long, narrow regions in the atmosphere — like rivers in the sky — that transport water vapor from the ocean. These columns of vapor move with the weather, potentially moving as much water as the Amazon River. When they make landfall, they can release their entire contents in a very short period of time. They're pretty common, but can be deadly depending on when and where they hit."

"Back in 2011, for example," Tom said. "There was a mass die off of oysters in San Francisco Bay after an atmospheric river overnight dumped so much fresh water that it reduced the salinity of the bay."

"Sounds pretty bad," Billie said. "But then so do earthquakes, wildfires, and icebergs where they don't belong. So what are we going to do about it?"

Tom glanced at his dive computer. "We have another hour before our residual nitrogen levels are low enough to enter the water again."

Sam said, "After that, we'll return to the submerged hypogeum and place the third sacred stone—then we're off to Sigiriya to help Elise deposit the fourth stone."

CHAPTER FIFTY-FIVE

―――――○⅋○―――――

Sigiriya — Palace in the Sky

ELISE TOOK A Qantas flight from Lord Howe Island to Brisbane and then a commercial flight to Colombo Airport, Sri Lanka and from there she chartered a local single-engine aircraft into Sigiriya. All told, she'd been in the air nearly fourteen hours. She'd slept intermittently. It wasn't much, but it would have to do. She glanced at the dark clouds in the sky, they appeared to be somehow getting closer no matter where she went.

Sigiriya was an anomaly in the Sri Lankan landscape. Rising 660 feet from the surrounding land, the monolith had been chosen by King Kasyapa in the fifth century of the Christian Era for the site of a new capital after he had wrested the throne from his father and an older half-brother who was the rightful heir. It was a good choice, eminently defensible. After the king's death, it was used as a Buddhist monastery until the 14th century, and then fell into oblivion until its rediscovery in 1831 by a British army officer.

Archaeological evidence placed the earliest occupancy of the area around the rock in prehistoric times, and the hills surrounding it were filled with cave dwellings and crude rock shelters. When the rock itself had been selected as both fortress and citadel, it provided places for the uppermost palace, other palaces located behind lavish lower gardens, and a mid-level terrace into which had been carved a massive lion guarding a gate that led to the winding stairway providing the only modern access to the extensive ruins of the citadel palace.

She paid a local driver to take her to Sigiriya—which meant Lion's Rock—and was a UNESCO listed World Heritage Site. As he pulled up to the entrance to the landscaped gardens she paid him the agreed price, giving him a gold-colored 5000 Sri Lankan Rupee banknote as a tip.

The man looked at her and shook his head. He tried to pass the note back to her. "I can not take this. It is too much. Thank you."

Elise smiled at his honesty. She squeezed his hand closed on the banknote. "I have two more for you if you wait here until I get back. Can you wait for me?"

The driver's eyes widened. "Yes. Very good. I will wait here."

"Thank you."

She walked up the main path where tourists and locals were funneled by two wire fences into a single gate. A small desk and two security guards checked her passport and her payment before she was allowed entrance onto the heritage site.

Elise moved briskly, meandering through the moats, bridges and stone paths that formed the water gardens. Artificial, rectangular lakes were symmetrically aligned on an east-west axis. Each one was connected to the outer moat on the west and the large artificial lake to the south of the Sigiriya rock. All the pools were also interlinked using an underground conduit network fed by the lake, and connected to the moats. A series of circular limestone fountains, fed by an underground aqueduct system, flowed freely—and was said to have done so for nearly fifteen hundred years.

At the end of the longest rectangular lake she followed a path of stone toward Sigiriya. After a few hundred feet she reached a pair of giant boulders that leaned in against one another to form a natural arch. A signpost said the boulders had once come from high up upon the main citadel, where the king's warriors would roll them off at intruding armies. Elise smiled as she read the description and looking up at the main Lion's Rock. It must have been an impossible task to try and overtake the ancient city.

She ducked under the twin boulders and into what was described as the boulder gardens. There, several large boulders were linked by winding pathways. The gardens extended from the northern slopes to the southern slopes of the hills at the foot of Sigiris rock. The pathway took her past eight caves, the walls of which were once adorned with beautiful frescoes. She glanced in each one, but there was nothing to suggest the caves had anything to do with the sacred stone she was carrying in her backpack. She read the note outside one of the caves, which said that the remains of meditation limestone seats, used by ancient monks, were found inside.

She left the last of the big boulders, and entered the terraced gardens at the base of the Sigirya rock. A series of terraces rose from the pathways of the boulder garden to the staircases on the rock. These were created by the construction of brick walls in a concentric mold that hugged the main stone. Just before the Lion's Staircase, she passed through the Mirror Wall.

Commencing at the top of a flight of steep stairs at the terraced gardens, it traversed a distance of six hundred and fifty feet along a gallery once covered with frescoes to a small plateau on the northern side of the rock on which the Lion Staircase is located.

The Mirror Wall was a parapet wall with a seven-foot-wide inner passageway that inched its way precariously along the near-perpendicular western surface of Sigiriya Rock. The outermost section of this passageway was built up to create a protective wall. The walkway was then paved with polished marble slabs. Only about three hundred and thirty feet of the wall still existed, but brick debris and grooves on the rock face along the western side of the rock clearly show where the rest of the wall once stood.

Archeologists believed that its mirror-like sheen was once achieved by using a special plaster made of fine lime, egg whites, and honey. The surface of the wall was then buffed to a brilliant luster with beeswax. Elise stared at the Mirror Wall. It now appeared to be stained in hues of orange. It was lined with various inscriptions, written by visitors both old and new. A few security guards were protecting it, preventing any further damage. Two thirds of the way along the wall, two steel spiral steps led nearly forty feet up the main rock, so that tourists could get a better view of the remaining frescoes.

The frescoes were remarkable artistic feats for their time. They depicted the upper half of bare-breasted women, who were believed to be Sinhalese maidens in the posture of performing various tasks. Some archeologists believed it was possible they were the King's wives or merely performing some sort of religious ritual. Elise stared at a couple of the frescoes. Despite depicting near naked women there was nothing lewd, indecent or seductive about their appearance.

She walked to the end of the Mirror Wall, where it opened up to the Lion's Staircase. That stairway now held hundreds of people slowly making their way to the top. Elise eyed the rickety-looking structure with doubt. It looked as if it might collapse with just her weight. How was it holding so many people, and when would it break loose from its moorings and send them all to their deaths?

She shuddered. She'd been documenting dozens of earthquakes and volcanic eruptions around the globe for weeks. Even a minor tremblor in this location would dash everyone on that stairway to the rocks below. She would almost prefer the shallow stone steps carved into the side of the living rock itself.

As the crowd shifted, she moved to the next step and waited again. At this rate, it would take hours to reach the summit. Careful to avoid knocking over the tourist behind her, she removed her backpack and dug in it for a bottle of water. Although the day was overcast, the temperature was already approaching 80 degrees Fahrenheit, and with high humidity it would have been suffocatingly hot but for the wind.

A monk wearing the traditional orange Kashaya robe, about fifteen feet back from her, met her eye and smiled. It was a perfectly harmless and natural thing to do. A basic form of kind communication. But something about it stirred her most primitive self-defense mechanisms. *What was it?* He seemed to recognize her. The thought was absurd. Few people outside of Sam's crew knew her. Even if the monk was connected to the people who'd attacked Sam at the Great Blue Grotto or Tom and Genevieve at Orvieto, it was impossible to think they would recognize her — let alone guess that she would be traveling to Sigiriya.

She smiled back, politely and continued up the steps. Elise was slim and athletic. She was lithe and moved with speed when there was a gap in the tourists ahead. Slowly, she outpaced the monk. The stranger seemed indifferent and made no attempt to catch up with her.

Perhaps she just was being paranoid?

Elise could hardly believe her watch when she reached the top. Granted, she'd bypassed areas where others stopped to take in the magnificent view or detoured to see the frescoes. But she'd made it to the top in only forty-five minutes, according to her watch. It had felt like two hours. Elise made her way to one end of the ruins and moved from side to side, looking for any way to enter the dig where she might access the passages she knew must be inside.

The top of Sigiriya were the remains of a unique masterpiece of architecture. A city based on a precise square module. The tiered layers reminded her of Machu Picchu, as she purposely climbed the series of graded levels toward the palace complex at the summit. From there, she could see that the layout extended outward from the coordinates at the center and the palace complex at the summit, with the eastern and western axis directly aligned to it. A combination of symmetry and asymmetry worked to interlock the man-made geometrical and natural formations.

To the west of Sigiriya rock was a park for the royals, laid out on a symmetrical plan. The park contained water-retaining structures, including sophisticated surface and subsurface hydraulic systems, some of which still worked today. To the south was a large rectangular reservoir. She turned toward the east, looking for any other spot where an opening to an underground area or tomb could have been hidden. There were none.

Instead, she spotted the same monk again. Out of a crowd of more than two hundred tourists, she immediately spied him. Her defensive nerves stirred again. The monk was staring right at her. His dark brown eyes, fixed in a mysterious and indeterminable gaze. He smiled at her again. This time she turned her head without smiling back.

She moved quickly, searching the rest of Sigiriya's architectural remains. At the end of two hours, she'd exhausted every potential hiding place, with the exception of the large water reservoir to the south. There was always the possibility a hidden tunnel formed beneath the bottom of the murky water, but that would have to be Sam's problem when he got there, not hers. Without dive equipment any attempt to reach the bottom would be futile.

Elise moved to the stairs. There were two sets running parallel. One for those going up and another for those going down. There was less traffic going down. About half the way down three older tourists slowed her pace to a very slow crawl. It didn't bother her. There was no rush, she'd exhausted all locations she could think of to find the receptacle for the sacred stone and there was nothing she could do but wait until Sam and the rest of the team arrived.

She took the time to enjoy the view of the Sri Lankan

landscape. She turned around, studying the upper reaches of the rock and then stopped. Her hart leapt into a gallop. Moving down the stairs above, was the monk she saw spying on her earlier. He wasn't going fast and if it wasn't for the older tourists who were slowing her down, she would have easily reached the bottom before him. She glanced at him and he smiled. She had never known that a smile could evoke such terror.

Elise jumped the railing between the up and the downward stairs and quickly passed the three tourists who were slowing her down. She moved quickly down a dozen or so steps, before stealing another glance at the monk, just to satiate her fears that he was going to catch up to her.

She swore. The monk was now moving quickly, darting across the railing where required to pass any tourists between them. It was the first proof that she wasn't crazy or paranoid, he really was stalking her.

Elise raced down to the base of the Lion's Stairs. At the bottom, she looked up to see how much of a lead she'd made. The steep stairs were still crammed full of tourists. Elise frantically scoured the rows of people meandering along the face of the giant stone, trying to find the monk.

She swore.

Because she'd lost sight of the monk.

CHAPTER FIFTY-SIX

―――――○ღ○―――――

IT'S ONE THING to see your enemy, but another, much worse beast, when you can't see him anymore. Elise looked toward the base of the stairs, half expecting to see him there, but instead she simply saw the throng of tourists.

She turned and started to run. She passed the Mirror Wall and kept running, as she descended each of the terraces that made up the terraced garden. On the last tier, just before she descended through the boulder garden, her eyes swept up toward the highest terrace — there, she spotted a monk, but he appeared much younger and more athletic than the one who was following her.

Even so, the sight spurred her into greater action. She turned and ran. This time increasing her pace to a sprint. There were few tourists to hinder her progress within the boulder garden. She breathed deeply and her lungs burned. Determined to reach her waiting driver before the monk caught her, she just hoped her driver was still waiting.

Taking three steps at a time, she ran through the first set of natural caves formed by giant boulders that leaned in on each other and then across a gentle slope, into a small tunnel. Where something caught her left leg.

She stumbled forward, without seeing what she'd tripped on and braced for the hard impact with the stone ground below —

but it didn't come. Instead, she fell into another tourist, who helped brace her, and stopped her falling.

Elise caught her breath and stood up again. "I'm sorry. Are you okay?"

"That's quite all right," he said, his low voice accented but his English perfect. "Next time, you must walk slowly and be careful."

"I'm sorry..." She was about to protest that someone was after her, when she felt the hard steel — of what she could only assume was the barrel of a handgun — digging into her spine just below her backpack.

"Walk this way, will you please?" he told her in a whisper.

Elise's eyes darted across the tunnel, taking in the innocent group of people from a new tourist bus approaching. Her ears picked out the polyglot sounds of the crowd, and homed in on the higher voices of children. She might have been able to take escape if she was on her own. But here, it was too dangerous. He might shoot, and with others so close, someone else might be injured by the bullet that would rip through her. A struggle could start a chain reaction. Besides, she needed to survive if the fourth sacred stone was to be placed. Better to wait for another chance. She made her decision in a split second.

"All right. Take it easy," she answered, her head turned down and her voice as soft as his had been. She began moving forward, careful to keep her pace steady, watching her feet. If she stumbled, he could take it as a deliberate move to escape. It might be her head that the bullet ripped through, rather than her spine. She felt his hard body crowding close, no doubt to conceal the weapon at her back. He was probably of average height, fit.

She kept walking.

Once outside the cave, he said to her, "Turn left here."

She glanced to her left. There was no path in that direction. Only the gradually undulating slope with a thick forest of ancient Sri Lankan jungle.

She felt the pressure of the gun barrel increase, as her attacker tried to dissuade her from attempting to flee.

"Okay, okay… I'm going."

"Good. Don't be stupid. I can make this a lot more painful if you force me to."

She kept walking. At the same time, she was searching for an escape, somewhere. The gradient increased and she wondered if she twisted, could she bring him rolling down with her? *Not if she didn't want to get shot first.* She would need to keep going and hope something would come up. She could hear the thump of her pounding heart in the back of her head and she knew her options were getting slim.

She would need to take a chance. The first one she got.

"What do you want?" she asked.

"The same thing you want."

"Really?" she smiled at that. "You want to save the human race from extinction, too?"

"Yes. Only, unlike you, I'm interested in saving those worthy of life." He laughed. "All right. This is far enough. You can turn around now."

She turned to face him. He had a strong face, big boned and fierce, with deep-set and somber blue-gray eyes. In the cover of tempestuous clouds that were slowly shrouding Sigiriya in darkness, his eyes appeared silver.

It was the same ghost who'd tried to kill Sam in the Great Blue Grotto.

"So, what do you want from me?" she asked.

"The sacred stone, of course."

She paused. A sardonic grin formed on her lips. "Then you're going to be disappointed. You're a little early. Sam Reilly has it. My job was to scout out the fourth receptacle for the stone. He'll be here by tonight if you'd like to wait around."

"I'm afraid I don't take disappointment very well. Never have. Even as a kid I had a nasty habit of erupting into violence when the other kids took a toy off me." He matched her grin. "How about this instead. I shoot you now. Then I have a look in that backpack to see if you're lying. Or, you could just hand it over."

Elise slowly unshouldered the strap of her backpack. "It was worth a try."

"No, it wasn't. Now hand it over." Her attacker pointed his handgun straight at her. He was close enough that it was impossible for him to miss.

Elise stepped closer. Her last chance was to use the metallic casing that stored the vacuum sealed sacred stone to somehow knock the gun out of his hand. It was a massive longshot, but it was all she had and she knew that the instant he received the backpack he would kill her.

She spotted something behind her attacker, up on the hill above them. It was the monk who'd been following her from before. He was moving at a sprint, silently. He placed a finger to his lips to say, shush.

Elise stopped. She needed to buy time. "There's just one last thing before you kill me."

"Yeah, what's that?" he asked, with little curiosity.

"I thought you might like to know the electronic code for the sacred stone's casing. It might take you some time to solve it, otherwise."

"Okay. What's the code?"

"Why would I tell you?" Elise asked. "You're going to kill me anyway?"

He aimed the gun at her head. "Because I can kill you quickly. Or I could kill you slowly and trust me, no one willingly chooses the slow option."

"All right." Elise said, handing him the backpack. "The code is… go to hell!"

His lips curled upward into a cruel grin. "So you want to die slow?"

He lowered the gun toward her knee.

She held her breath.

The gun fired.

And the monk swung the small tree branch like a club.

The club connected the back of her attacker's head with the crippling sound of a crunch. She had flinched and the shot went wide, scraping the side of her knee. She dropped to the ground.

Her attacker fell, rolling more than fifty feet to the bottom of the steep hill. Elise stood up, ready to run after him, but the monk gripped her shoulder to stop her.

She swung her arm forcefully, freeing herself.

The attacker stood up. He looked dazed and Elise thought she might still have a chance of reaching him. But then he took a couple steps back up the hill, retrieved his handgun and started shooting at her.

The monk threw himself onto her for protection.

Several shots went over their heads. When they stopped, Elise shuffled forward and spotted her attacker running away, wearing her backpack — taking with him the fourth sacred stone and the last hope for humanity.

She tried to chase after him, but the monk stopped her. "It is not worth it. He has the gun. All you will do is get yourself killed, and I can't allow that."

She shrugged, realizing he was right. "You have no idea how important the contents of that backpack were."

The monk smiled. It was an ascetic face, old and withered, but full of kindness. "You think all is lost without the sacred stone?"

"All is lost without... hey, what do you know about the sacred stone?"

"I know that it is meaningless if you die."

"What do you know about me?" she asked.

"We know lots about you. We've been expecting you for nearly a thousand years." He smiled. "And we are so glad you've finally arrived, Elise."

The monk started to walk toward the north. He moved with the speed and determined purpose of a much younger man. She had to work to keep up with him.

"Hey, where are you going?"

The monk didn't slow down or give her an answer. If anything, he seemed to increase his pace.

"Hey, where are we going?" she persisted.

The monk stopped to face her. "To the Pidurangala Rock, of course — to complete the prophecy."

CHAPTER FIFTY-SEVEN

―――――○୧३○―――――

Lorde Howe Island

THE GULFSTREAM G650 used every single one of its combined 33,800 pounds of thrust, produced by its two Rolls-Royce BR725 A1-12 engines in order to get off the island's meager 2,907 feet of runway. Once free of the blacktop, it climbed steadily, before banking to the northeast for a direct route to Sri Lanka. Sam took one last glance at the green and azure waters of its tranquil lagoon and then picked up his satellite phone.

He pressed the call button.

It rang twice, before Elise picked up. "Sam?"

He breathed a long sigh of relief. "Elise! You're all right. I've been trying to reach you for two hours!"

"Yeah, I've had some problems."

"What happened?"

"I was attacked by the same man who tried to kill you at the Great Blue Hole in Belize."

Sam expelled his breath silently. "You're lucky to be alive."

"Yeah, but I lost the fourth sacred stone. The man who took it said something about using it to save the human race — only he specified only the worthy few would be saved. Any idea what he meant or where he's taking the stone?"

"Yes. The Secretary of Defense said there was a second stolen Göbekli Tepe stone. It was a map to a natural subterranean cavern, or ancient bunker, where a small colony of survivors may keep the human race alive. Apparently, a man named Leo Botkin, who was chosen to lead the colony, decided to turn it into a eugenics experiment, by filling the colony with people who have superior DNA."

"So what do they care if we have one of the sacred stones?" Elise asked.

"The Secretary of Defense said that the material used in the construction of the stones appears to be identical to the asteroid that's approaching. Her advisers believe that part of the asteroid broke off thirteen thousand years ago, landing as a meteorite somewhere on earth."

"Go on?" Elise didn't try to hide her confusion.

"There weren't enough fragments of *blackbody* to construct the four sacred stones and protect the colony. The idea was if the four stones couldn't be used to avoid the disaster completely, then one of them would be used to add an additional barrier of protection to the colony."

"So we find the colony, we find the fourth stone?"

"Yeah."

"Does anyone have any ideas?" she asked.

"No. But the Secretary of Defense must have some ideas." He sighed, heavily. "Did you find the receptacle in Sigiriya?"

"Not yet. But a monk is leading me to where he believes the stone belongs."

"Really? How would he know?"

"How, indeed?" Elise's tone softened with curiosity. "He says that the local Buddhist monks have been expecting me for the past thousand years."

Sam thought about what she said. They both knew she descended from one of the Master Builders, but other than that, her genetic past was a mystery. "Okay. You go see if you can locate the receptacle. I'm going to contact the Secretary of Defense and do my best to retrieve the remaining stone."

CHAPTER FIFTY-EIGHT

———O☙O———

Sam contacted the Secretary of Defense and explained where they were at.

When he was finished, she asked, "What's your next plan?"

"I need to get the stone back. Everything depends on it, which means you're going to have to help me find the colony."

"It will be difficult. The entire system was designed so those who remained couldn't ever find it."

"But?"

"I have my ways. I've been trying to narrow its location down and I'm getting close."

"How?"

"In the past twenty-four hours a number of members of Congress and Defense Staff have taken a sudden leave of absence. Most had innocuous enough excuses. They had a cold, their children were sick. It wouldn't have even been brought to my attention, except that so many had done so on the same day."

"They were escaping to the colony?" Sam asked, incredulous.

"Yes."

"What did you do?"

"We brought them in of course. They were all catching flights, along with their families, to Moscow. Nearly a hundred people in total. All experts in their fields. Perfect citizens for the new world."

"Did they reveal the location of the colony?" Sam asked.

"Not yet. They're being interrogated right now, but they won't say."

"No one can hold out indefinitely," Sam persisted.

"They can if they don't know anything. They would have told me the truth if they had known it. You have to remember, these people know the world is ending, and right now they're about to be on the wrong side of an ancient bunker when it does."

"So they'll talk?"

"If they knew anything they would. Apparently, they were supposed to fly into Moscow where a private jet would take them to the colony."

"Had any of them been there before?"

"Yes." She sighed, heavily. "But that didn't help much. They didn't have maps or anything to tell where they had been flown."

Sam persisted. "What did they know?"

"The colony was four hours away from Moscow by jet. The ground near the colony was always frozen. There was a lake. From the sky, the lake was shaped like a big boot. In the middle of the lake was an island and what looked like the cooling tower of a nuclear power station. But other members of the party have since rejected this statement, saying that the colony was powered by an enormous geothermic generator."

"So we're looking for a Russian lake, shaped like a boot and a geothermic cooling tower?" he asked.

"Beneath which, an enormous volcanic cavern provides an ancient bunker," she added.

"I take it no one's located such a place by entering those details into the Geographic Information System?"

"No. We've tried. It didn't work. There's nothing even close to those descriptions that use geothermic power."

Sam said, "It sounds like it might be the opposite end of the Aleutian Portal."

"That's what I was thinking," the Secretary of Defense replied.

"But it would take at least four days to reach and cross the Aleutian Portal." Sam glanced out the window. It was almost permanently dark now, despite being the middle of the day. "And we don't have four days."

"So what do you want to do?"

"Keep working on it. We'll head toward Moscow in the meantime. I know someone who might be able to help."

Sam hung up and called a second number.

Demyan Yezhov picked up on the first ring. "Sam Reilly! If this strange darkness that's shrouding the world is anything to go by, it appears you haven't found what you were after yet."

"We found it, but someone took it from us."

"Really? That's bad luck."

Sam didn't have time for the chat. "Listen. I need your help. It's going to take some time to explain why I need this, and I don't have that time, but I need your expertise as a geologist who grew up in Siberia."

"Go on."

"This is what we know. There's a colony inside an ancient volcanic cave. It's roughly four hours by jet from Moscow. The ground near the colony was always frozen. There was a lake. From the sky, the lake was shaped like a big boot. In the middle of the lake was an island and what looked like the cooling tower of a geothermic generator."

"Okay, what do you need?" Demyan asked.

"I need to find the colony. I need a list of known geothermic springs throughout Russia that would be powerful enough to support a population of five thousand people. Also, if you could narrow down any place where large volcanic caves are known to form."

There was only silence on the phone and for a moment Sam thought he'd been cut off. "Are you still there, Demyan?"

Demyan expelled a large breath of air. "I can do better for that. I can tell you where it is and how to get inside."

"How?"

"Because that's Oymyakon where I was born, where I lost my entire family, and where I've spent my life vowing I would never return."

"But you'll guide us where we need to go?" Sam held his breath.

"To save the human race?" Demyan said. "I'll go to hell and back."

Sam unclipped his seatbelt, walked up to the cockpit and said to the pilots, "Change of plan. We're going to Big Island, Hawaii to pick up someone and then we're off to Russia."

CHAPTER FIFTY-NINE

―――○₷○―――

ELISE FOLLOWED THE monk as he negotiated the undulating terrain, heading north toward Pidurangala Rock. Monkeys played in the thick foliage of the jungle overhead. They crossed over a series of aqueducts and then, joining a path of stones, began their climb up to Pidurangala Rock.

"Do you know much about the history of my people?" the monk asked.

Elise shook her head. "I'm sorry. I'm sure its fascinating, but I hadn't even heard of Sigiriya until a couple of days ago. I believe you're Buddhist monks?"

"Yes." He nodded politely. "It's okay. We know a lot about you."

"Why is that?" she asked.

"It is not something we can explain. It does not make sense."

"But you must be able to tell me something?"

"No. Telling will not do. We must show you. Sometimes only our eyes will accept what our heart knows to be true."

"You think I need to see the physical proof to accept the spiritual?" she asked.

"That is exactly what I mean. Come, we are not far, now."

Elise found herself working hard to keep up with the old monk. "Tell me about your people. How long have you been here?"

"The monastery dates back to the arrival of King Kassapa."

"Your people followed the migration of the king?"

He shook his head and smiled. It was warm and ingratiating. "For many centuries, the monks lived at Sigiriya. When the king commenced construction of the citadel of Sigiriya, the monks were relocated to make room for the king's palace. To make amends, Kassapa constructed new dwellings and a temple here to recompense them.

"You were kicked out of your own place of worship?"

"Yes. But that did not matter. Our purpose was not obstructed."

Elise waited for him to elaborate, but instead he remained silent. She felt her calves ache and her thighs burn as she climbed more than a thousand stone steps leading up a steep hillside behind the Pidurangala to a terrace just below the summit of the rock. The monk pointed out the Royal Cave Temple itself as they walked by. Despite the name, there was little to see apart from a long reclining Buddha under a large rock overhang. The statue was accompanied by figures, which the monk pointed out, were of Vishnu and Saman and decorated with very faded murals.

The monk led her down the next terrace and stopped, where an old brick Dagoba—the Sinhalese name for the Buddhist stupa—stood proudly.

Elise waited for the monk to tell her about it, but instead the man remained silent. She ran her eyes across the ancient building. The dark clouds had fully set in on the world and it was getting harder to see much of anything, but she could still make out the shapes of the ancient ruin. She'd read briefly about them previously, but had never been inside one. It was basically a mound-like structure with buried relics, used by Buddhist monks to meditate. This one would be considered quite modest, approximately thirty feet high at most.

The construction of Dagobas were considered acts of great

merit. Their purpose being to enshrine relics of Buddha. The entrances were designed to be laid out so that the center lines pointed directly toward the relic chamber. Although little of the cover still remained, the guidebook she'd read on the flight, said that the outer layer was normally coated with lime plaster, white of egg, coconut water, plant resin, drying oil, glues and saliva of white ants.

"Well?" the monk asked.

Elise reciprocated the monk's monosyllabic response. "Well."

The monk smiled. It was old and well-practiced, with large creases gave evidence of years of the muscles of his face holding just such a pose. "Would you like to see where you come from?"

Elise smiled. It was more patronizing than she meant it to be. "You think I came from in here?"

The monk wasn't offended, or if he was, he certainly didn't show it. His eyes were wide, as though many generations of waiting were finally up. "Let's go inside and see. Like I said, some things, one must see to accept."

"It's getting dark."

"Good. That will help," the monk replied, mysteriously.

Elise followed the monk inside. She didn't believe for a minute that the monk was right and she had come from this region, but then, no one had ever been able to tell her where she had come from. She felt her stomach churn with a strange anticipation. All children, no matter what age they are, want to discover that they came from somewhere and belong to something.

As an orphan, she had grown up in Washington, D.C. When she was eleven years old she won a cryptic mathematics test. It has been surreptitiously added to all public and private schools standard end of year exams for that year. It had been a test, set by the CIA, in search of child prodigies, mathematically geniuses, people with a certain type of analytical mind who could be groomed into perfect code-breakers for the next generation — where the internet was the front-line of some of the greatest intelligence wars ever fought.

The CIA became her family. In her early twenties, that family had betrayed her, and after setting up a digital trail for a new identity, she disappeared. Since then she'd been working with Sam Reilly, who recognized her unique skill set. The crew of the *Maria Helena* were her new family and she was happy. Eight weeks ago, in the Amazon jungle, some truths she had often wondered about, came to surface, and she knew what she'd always known — she was genetically different. She had purple eyes, inhuman reflexes, and shared an active posterior lobe in her cerebellum that was dormant in others, and was capable of receiving high frequency radio waves in the form of images.

Sam Reilly had informed her that the Secretary of Defense said that she was found as a baby, inside an ancient temple discovered in the Khyber Pass in Afghanistan. The temple revealed the first existence of the ancient race of Master Builders. Many questions had haunted her since that day. Who were her parents and where were they? She recalled the most disturbing question being the one the Secretary of Defense had asked Sam.

The Master Builders plan everything precisely. If they intentionally left Elise to be found by the elite specialist military team I sent to examine the temple, it begs the question, why? More importantly, if there is a war with Master Builders, what side of it will Elise be on?

With her heart in her mouth, she prayed that the answer to the question wasn't written inside the temple. She followed the monk up the stairs and inside the main domed section of the Dagoba. It was dark inside and she struggled to follow the monk who appeared to walk with the familiarity of the blind.

She switched on her pen-flashlight and used its dim light to follow the monk into a deeper chamber, where the ancient relics of Buddha were theoretically stored. The path descended more than thirty flights of stairs, before opening into a small domed chamber.

Elise flicked the beam of her flashlight across the dome-shaped ceiling. It was made with a foundation of bricks, the same as the main outer dome. There were no frescoes or murals and not even any references to Buddha.

Her eyes darted toward the monk, who was grinning peacefully. "What is it you expect me to see here?"

"You will need to turn off the light if you want to see it."

Elise stared at him. Beneath his shaved head he was still smiling. He wore an orange kashaya robe wrapped around under the right arm and back over the left shoulder. There were not a lot of places for him to conceal a weapon, but it was possible. For a moment she had to swallow the fear that rose in her throat like bile. *Could she have misjudged him? Was it all a ruse? Had he taken her here to hurt her?* It seemed unlikely, but so was the thought that the truth about her past was written on the walls of the dilapidating monument to Buddha.

"Why?" she asked.

"Only you can answer that. I can only take you here. If you want to go further, you will need to open your heart."

Conflict twisted her face into a grimace of indecision. It was unlike her, but these were unlikely times. Elise took a deep breath in, took a leap of faith, and switched off her flashlight.

The darkness enveloped the room instantly

She glanced above and expelled the breath audibly, certain she'd made the right decision. A series of bricks glowed with purple fluorescence. There were eight in total and when you drew an imaginary line between them, they formed the Greek letter Phi. Her eyes darted to the base, where a large stone depicted a horse in the same purple glow.

Elise recalled Tom and Genevieve's description of the hypogeum in the Orvieto Underground. They had used a black light wand to reveal the hidden keys of phosphorescent markings, leading to the queen's sarcophagus.

"I don't understand," she said to the monk. "We don't have a black light, so why do the markings phosphoresce?"

She couldn't see the monk, but she could hear him laugh. "Markings? I see no markings."

"You don't?"

"No. The final chamber is only to be revealed to you."

"I can see ultraviolet light?"

The monk was still laughing. "How would I know what you can see?"

Elise thought about it. Reindeer relied on ultraviolet light to spot lichens that they could eat. Some scorpions released a purple ultraviolet glow to distinguish between their family and predators. Butterflies are able to see and emit ultraviolet light as a hidden means of communicating with other butterflies. To this effect, many flowers have evolved to display ultraviolet patterns that help butterflies directly land on their nectaries, resulting in pollination of the flower. And now, she too, had been given the gift of vision within the ultraviolet spectrum.

"Now what?" she asked.

"Do you want to find out more, or have you had enough of the truth?"

"I want answers."

"Good. Then only you can lead the way."

Elise stared at the ultraviolet markers in the brickwork above. She felt the first brick. It had a little movement. It could be potentially put down to age and dilapidation, but she knew better. She pressed it hard, and the brick appeared to move inward. She repeated the process on the other seven glowing bricks. She then gently put her weight on the glowing horse on the floor.

She grinned.

And the stone on which the horse had been secretly painted now moved down and forward—revealing a set of hidden stairs, leading deeper into the Dagoba.

CHAPTER SIXTY

Ese-Khayya, Siberia

THE RUSSIAN BUILT Ka-32A11BC helicopter seemed unnatural to Sam as it whirred its way across the eastern Siberian landscape. With its dual rotor blades that spun in alternative directions, negating the need for a tail rotor to counteract the torque generated by the single blade on a traditional helicopter, the helicopter appeared more like the shape of a strange toy than a functional aircraft. The helicopter had been chartered at the last minute with great expense. In addition to the two pilots, on board were Sam, Tom, Genevieve, Billie and Demyan.

The Gulfstream G650 had been left in Zhigansk Airport, roughly three hundred miles to the west, where it was being refueled. If their mission was a success, the jet would need to be ready to race back to Sigiriya with the final sacred stone. Sam looked at the dark clouds that seemed to encapsulate every end of the world, slowly suffocating the light. He made a silent prayer that there was still time.

He glanced across at Demyan. "You're sure you dad still has the blueprints for the tunnels?"

"Certain," Demyan replied, but his grimace appeared less than certain.

"But what?"

"My dad has some cognitive impairment. It might be difficult trying to find them."

"He has dementia?" Sam asked.

"No. Profound guilt."

"What?"

"When I was still a kid my mother died. A week later, my father took a new job working for Leo Botkin, to put in place a secret tunnel to an enormous underground cavern. At the time, he thought he was doing the right thing. He was trading his own happiness for the survival of my brother and I. When the project was nearing completion, Botkin betrayed my father by trying to kill him and all his men in order to maintain the secret of the tunnels."

"How did he escape?"

"My father climbed out through a ventilation shaft. Then, when he came home to find out what became of my brother and I, we were both gone and one of our neighbors told my father that my brother and I drowned in Boot Lake."

"Under which the colony exists?"

"Exactly."

"Why did your neighbors think you were dead?" Sam asked.

"My brother did drown in Boot Lake."

"I'm sorry."

"Yeah, me too. He was an angry kid and we never really got along, but after my mother died I was determined to be a better brother to him."

"It must have been hard."

"You have no idea. When I got home Leo Botkin was there. He told me my father had died in a mining accident and gave me the Russian equivalent of a hundred thousand US dollars at the time, for compensation. I knew the story was all crap and that Botkin was lying to me, but what could I do?"

"What did you do?" Sam asked.

"I took the money and fled to Moscow. I hid most of the money, but spent enough to get an education. As it turned out, I had a strong ability in mathematics and the sciences. I studied geology and that led to my interest in volcanoes."

Sam smiled at the revelation. "Why did you study geology of all things?"

"Because I was angry at Botkin. I was certain he'd lied to me about how my father had died, and that the money was his way of offloading some guilt — although at the time I had no idea about what."

"So, you studied geology?"

"I was angry. In the course of a single week I'd lost my entire family. We weren't local to Oymyakon. My father had moved us there only the year before to be closer to work, but we were outsiders and never really belonged within the close-knit community."

"And you wanted revenge?"

"Yes. Stupidly, I assumed that if I became a leading geologist I could ruin Botkin."

"You planned your revenge nearly a lifetime ago?"

"Sure. It was a crazy idea and by the time I finished my first degree and then moved to the U.S. to study my doctorate at Harvard I'd lost all interest in revenge and turned my efforts toward volcanology."

The helicopter banked to the left, dipped its nose and ran along the Yana River. "What changed?"

Demyan sighed, as though serendipity was hard to swallow. "I watched the BBC."

"Come again?"

"About ten years ago the BBC did a program on the Batagaika Crater, a tadpole shaped thermokarsk of melting permafrost in eastern Siberia, for the Discovery Channel. In the recording there were a few people from one of the local villages, searching the base of the crater searching for ice-age fossils to sell to interested archeologists. It was extremely dangerous work because of the constantly shifting and collapsing nature of the landscape. As it was, I happened to spot my father among the scavenges."

Sam's lips curled in an upward and incredulous smile. "You recognized him from a nature show?"

"Yeah. I had to contact the network and buy a copy just to get a better look, but it was definitely my father."

"What did you do?"

"I flew out meet him straight away."

"How did that go?" Sam asked, intrigued.

"He was in complete denial. He didn't recognize me. Told me his sons had died years ago."

"That must have been hard."

"Yeah, it was devastating. I kept coming back to the Batagaika Crater to talk to my father. Some days he would talk, other times he would ignore me completely. Sometimes he would assume I was the ghost of his lost son and he would tell me things. That's how I learned about the colony and what Leo Botkin had done."

"I bet that stirred up some old wounds."

"Yes. The desire for revenge raged like it had never done before. I thought about killing Botkin, but it was too easy. Instead, I needed him to suffer. I needed to ruin him. I needed to bankrupt him until he was destitute living on the street. Then and only then would I come to him, and let him know that I was the cause of all of his misfortune."

"How did you set about doing that?" Sam asked with genuine curiosity.

"I studied with a man who worked on high frequency microwaves for the HAARP project. Have you heard of it?"

Sam nodded. "The High Frequency Active Auroral Research

Program was initiated as an ionospheric research grant to investigate the potential for developing ionospheric enhancement technology for radio communications and surveillance." He grinned. "But the conspiracy theorists all assumed it was related to mind and weather control."

Demyan nodded. "Right. Mind control through microwaves was nothing more than science fiction, but weather control was conceivably possible — if the UN hadn't expressly sanctioned against such research."

"I was told some of the intellectual property was sold," Sam said.

"And I was the one who bought it."

"Why?"

"My friend failed because he lost funding for his specific research at HAARP. Out of a job, he approached me for another possibility. I used my knowledge of geology and high pressures alongside his microwave technologies to produce high quality, undetectable, synthetic diamonds."

The Ka-32A11BC helicopter circled a small village. Its pilot picked out a landing site, hovered, and gently set down on a small field of frozen soil. The pilots switched the engines off, and the alternating rotor blades began to slow.

"It was you that set about to crash the diamond markets?" Sam asked.

"Yes."

"And destroyed Botkin's property?"

"Yes. He's been suffering a long run of bad luck for nearly two years now. But he's always been protected. He's too big, to rich, and too well insured for me to cause any lasting damage — until now."

"Until now," Sam repeated. "If we do this, it will destroy everything Leo Botkin has worked on for more than twenty years!"

CHAPTER SIXTY-ONE
———O&3O———

Sam followed Demyan along the unsealed road into the village of Ese-Khayya and up to a log-piled house at the edge of a gently sloping hill. It was dark and both needed flashlights just to follow the road. The darkness was less unusual in this part of the world, given that it was early winter.

Demyan knocked loudly several times until a man came to the door. A combination of urine, feces and continuous rot wafted from inside. The stranger was unkept and obviously malnourished. He walked with a significant limp, due to what appeared to be a once massively crushed lower leg.

"Sam Reilly, meet my dad, Anotoly Yezhov."

Sam offered his outstretched hand. "Pleased to meet you, sir."

Yezhov rejected it. "Who are you and what do you want?"

"He's a friend and he needs your help."

"I don't have any help to give anyone." Yezhov threw his hands downward, in frustration. "Can't you see, I can't even look after myself!"

Demyan glanced at the putrid mess from inside the house. "I thought I told you to get some help?"

The old man held his palm outward in a placating gesture. "With what? I've got no money!"

"Dad!" Demyan shook his head. "I gave you one of the best

diamonds in the world what did you do with it?"

Through heavily aged creases, Yezhov studied Demyan. "That was you, was it?"

"Yes. What did you do with the diamond? That was supposed to let you live out your old age in comfort and peace. Away from all this cold and hardship."

"I gave it away."

"You gave it away?" Demyan sighed heavily. "Dad, that was a hundred-million-dollar diamond!"

"I didn't want it."

"But you can't live like this."

"Did you ever stop and question if maybe I liked the cold and all this hardship. I deserve it, you know. I might as well have killed my entire family."

"No, you didn't dad. You were just trying to do what you could to provide for your family. That was all. I'm still alive."

Yezhov studied Demyan's face. "Your eyes are the same. I'll give you that. But you're not the same man I left all those years ago. Demyan's dead. He drowned in Boot Lake along with his brother, and there's nothing I can do about that except repent. You want to help me? Let's have a drink."

Demyan nodded and followed him inside. This was where he'd gotten to a hundred times since he'd found his father still alive. He would have intermittent periods of lucidity, followed by the utter gibberish of a confused old man. But when they drank vodka, his father would treat him as a drinking buddy and no longer a stranger. His dad had always been an alcoholic. Even in Oymyakon, their family were outcasts, because of the violent way his father became when he started drinking—and he drank every day.

Yezhov poured all three of them a shot of vodka.

Sam looked at the glasses and said, "None for me…"

Yezhov handed him a shot. "Drink!"

Sam glanced at Demyan, who gestured that it was the easiest way to deal with this. Sam raised the shot up to his lips. It burned for a second and then he downed the entire thing. It tasted like something that should be used on a jet engine and for a moment he wondered if he'd done permanent damage, despite the fact that the two Yezhov men had consumed the same thing and appeared unfazed.

"Another one?" Yezhov asked, filling all three glasses.

"Dad," Demyan said. "We need to talk about the blueprints."

"What blueprints?" Yezhov drank all three glasses.

Sam said, "The ones for the secret tunnels you built to the ancient catacombs beneath Boot Lake, in Oymyakon."

Yezhov paused, carefully studying Sam's face. "Who are you? I don't know what you're talking about. Secret tunnels. I know about no such thing."

"Dad. We need the blueprints. It's important. We have to get inside."

"Inside?" Yezhov's eyes were now wide. "No one goes inside anymore. Thousands of people once entered those tunnels, but no one's ever come out again."

"All the same, we need to find those tunnels."

Yezhov poured another drink. "What tunnels."

Sam said, "Sir, we need your help to go back there. The entire world is counting on your help."

Yezhov shrugged. "And why should I help the world out? It never done nothing for me!"

Demyan downed another shot of vodka and then looked at his father directly in his eyes. "Because we want to kill Leo Botkin."

Yezhov's eyes went livid. He no longer appeared disoriented when he spoke. "That I can help you."

CHAPTER SIXTY-TWO

Pidurangala's Temple

Elise switched on her flashlight and shined its beam at the hidden stairway.

"Do you know where they lead?" she asked the monk.

"Yes."

"Are you going to tell me?"

"No."

"All right." Elise sighed, theatrically, and then commenced her descent.

The stairs descended in a large, square spiral that continued for what appeared to be hundreds of feet. The monk slowly followed her.

At the bottom, the stairs turned into a long tunnel that headed due south.

"We're going to Sigiriya?" she asked.

The monk nodded. "I told you the Lion's Rock was always our home."

The tunnel stretched a little over a mile and opened into a labyrinth of ancient catacombs. Recalling the Master Builder's proclivity toward symmetry and central power structures, Elise continued to take turns that led her to the very center.

It opened up to a large, rectangular vault.

At the center of which was a sarcophagus fit for a king, or in this case, a queen.

Overlooking the ancient queen's chamber was a beautiful fresco. The painting looked similar to the ones depicted above the Mirror Wall at Sigiriya and possibly more than a thousand years old. Away from all weather, it was in a much better condition, too.

She studied the painting.

It depicted a beautiful woman, with a high jaw-line, gentle features, silky black hair and intense purple eyes, that were fixed upon the queen's tomb. In her arms was a baby. There was something familiar about the baby.

Elise stared at it for a while. It evoked memories that were so distant that she couldn't be sure they were even hers. The baby's eyes were open.

And they were a deep purple.

Elise turned to the monk. "Is the sarcophagus…"

"Empty?" The monk replied. "Yes."

She felt her heart race. "Then my mother's still alive?"

The monk sighed, deeply. "That, I no longer know."

CHAPTER SIXTY-THREE

────○♋○────

The Ancient Catacombs of Oymyakon

SAM GLANCED OUT the windows to the left. The helicopter circled the large geothermal power station's cooling tower and the remains of a rocky outcrop at the center of Boot Lake, where the old Stalin-era prison and death camp rose out of the water. The place appeared deserted and according to Anotoly Yezhov, no one had entered or exited the building for more than twenty years.

The helicopter continued north, before dipping its nose and finally settling into a hover just above a field of ice. Anotoly's eyes were wide. In the hours since Sam had met the man, he had come alive, losing decades of age and returning to the strength and vitality of his youth. Revenge, Sam discovered, was a powerful motivator.

He met the old man's eye. "Are you certain no one's going to notice the helicopter?"

"Not at all. The volcanic vault is a quarter of a mile deep. They don't know and even if they did, they wouldn't care. I doubt any of them even realize the old ventilation shafts still reach deep into the ancient catacombs below."

Demyan entered the conversation. "What about lake?"

"You mean the colorful crystals?" Anotoly asked.

Sam asked, "The lake has colorful crystals?"

Anotoly nodded. "Yeah. They're a type of coral found at the bottom of the Maria Trench. They feed of the geothermal energy and then release UV light. Leo Botkin spent a fortune manned submarines to retrieve them from around the world."

"Why?" Demyan asked.

"Plants and animals need UV light."

"Can't they produce it with electricity?" Sam asked.

"Sure, but it draws enormous amounts. You have to remember the colony was designed to survive long after the world as you and I know it has disappeared. At best, this ice-age will last a century, but it may last millennia. Botkin wanted to set up a fully sustainable environment underground and that included producing natural UV light."

The helicopter's rotor blades came to a complete stop.

Sam looked at Anotoly. "You sure you want to come with us?"

"Are you kidding me? I'd rather die than miss it."

Sam guessed there was a good chance, the man would die today if he did come, so the severity of that statement wasn't missed on him. Even so, they needed the old man's knowledge and he certainly wasn't going to be dismissing any help he could get.

"All right. Good to have you with us."

"What about a gun?" Anotoly asked.

They were all carrying Heckler and Koch MP5 submachine guns.

Sam smiled politely. He was indebted to the old man for his blueprints of the colony and the ancient catacombs, but he would be damned before he gave a loaded submachine gun to a man with more than a bottle of vodka on board. "I think we're all out of them."

"What am I supposed to kill Botkin with?"

"When we get around to it, I lend you my knife," Demyan said. "More personal that way, don't you think?"

"Right you are, son."

Sam opened the helicopter's sliding door. Using GPS, he located the site of the main ventilation shaft that ran down to the catacombs far below. He cleared away the snow. Below it, ice was thick.

"The thing's frozen over!" Sam shouted at Antonoly.

"Yeah, I thought that might be the case."

Tom said, "What good is a ventilation shaft when its frozen shut?"

Antonoly shook his head. "No good. But it was only needed while we were working. By now Botkin will have his ecosystem balanced so an equal amount of oxygen is produced and carbon-dioxide is removed."

"Then how do we get in?" Sam asked.

"We dig." Demyan carried out a large steel pole with a sharp point on the end. "We used to do this for hours when we were ice fishing as kids."

"That's great," Sam said. "We might not have hours. How deep do you think this ice is?"

Anotoly and Demyan studied the ice, with the experience of a lifetime living with constant ice.

Demyan spoke first, "Maybe five feet."

"Probably closer to ten," Anotoly replied.

"How long will it take you to chisel your way through it?" Sam asked.

Demyan replied without hesitation. "Under twenty-four hours if we work constantly."

Sam didn't even acknowledge the statement. Instead he

walked back to the helicopter, removed a heavy backpack and returned to the ice.

He laid out several rows of dynamite. "New plan. We're going to blow it up."

CHAPTER SIXTY-FOUR

―――――O&3O―――――

THE DYNAMITE WAS imbedded into the ice before being lit. Sam watched as the explosion sent a pile of snow and ice fifty feet into the air. The surrounding ground shook violently.

"What do you think?" he asked Anotoly.

The old man shrugged. "They might have heard that."

"All right let's go then."

Harnessed to a safety line attached to the helicopter, Sam approached the new opening. The ice, including the steel grid that protected the shaft had all disappeared.

Anatoly and Demyan checked the strength of the surrounding ice and agreed it would still support the helicopter.

Demyan made a signal to the pilot and he went through the process of warming up the rotor blades and moving the hundred or so feet to land directly opposite the opening to the ventilation shaft.

Sam looked inside again. "How deep did you say this thing goes?"

"A little over fifteen hundred feet. Deep enough that it passes the main volcanic chamber where the colony exists, and enters the ancient catacombs a farther hundred and fifty feet below."

Sam looked at the rescue winch built into the side of the helicopter. "You're sure that thing will take it?"

"Certain," Anotoly said without hesitation.

"What are you basing that on?" Sam asked.

"Just a hunch."

Demyan stepped in. "It's all right. The helicopters have these winches fitted specifically for mine rescues in the deep diamond mines near Yakutsk. I had it checked out. The winch and cable will take two of us at a time."

Sam didn't trust it for a minute, but that didn't matter. The fact was, it was their last chance at survival, so they needed to take it. "All right."

CHAPTER SIXTY-FIVE

―――――○⛬○―――――

Sam and Tom were the first to make the descent.

Harnessed to the same line, the winch began to unwind. The machine was operated on board the helicopter, but the end of the cable had a camera attached, so the operator could see where they were and how close they were to the ground.

It became dark quickly and Sam switched on his flashlight. Above them, the last of the ambient light from the opening had finally disappeared.

Tom said, "You feel like this belongs on the set of *Silence of the Lambs?*"

Sam grinned. "Yeah, but I'm pretty certain the FBI Agent... what was her name again?"

"I can't remember. I just know she was played by Jodie Foster."

"All right. Either way, I don't recall Jodie Foster getting to carry submachine guns and a backpack full of C-4 explosives."

Tom cradled his Heckler and Koch MP5. "Right you are."

It took nearly ten minutes to reach the bottom, where it placed them inside a large tunnel made of granite. Without their flashlights the tunnel was pitch dark. They switched their lights back and searched the area within the immediate vicinity of the winch cable. Billie and Genevieve were the next two to come down, followed by Anotoly and Demyan. All in total, it took close an hour to shift the six of them and Sam hoped to hell they didn't need to get out in a hurry.

Sam opened the digital version of the blueprints based on the charts Demyan had given him. It depicted the lowest level, where the ancient catacombs ran like a labyrinth, constantly turning inward until it reached a large room in the middle. It was in that room, Demyan told him, that he had once seen an Egyptian sarcophagus. He said he would never forget it because it seemed so strange given their location in Siberia.

It took another hour of winding through the granite maze to reach the center. The bright lights swept from the room into the dark tunnels. Sam quickly switched off his own flashlight and the rest of the team followed suit. The echo of broken voices leaked from inside the room.

Sam, Tom and Genevieve approached, while Billie, Demyan and Anotoly guarded the exits. Sam entered the room first. There were three men working on breaking the code to the metallic vacuum casing that housed the fourth sacred stone. Two had laptop computers open and appeared to be running a program to crack it, while the third one paced back and forth.

Sam raked the entire room with his eyes. Confident there were no other occupants and with the knowledge that the only entrance was being guarded by the rest of the group, Sam aimed his Heckler and Koch at the only one who was standing.

He switched the lever to fully automatic and yelled, "Hands in the air!"

The two computer guys turned to face him and swore. The one who was standing turned and said, "What the fuck?"

Sam met the man's eye. They were the same bluish-gray as the man who'd tried to kill him inside the Great Blue Grotto. "It's you!"

"Sam Reilly?" the man studied him, his mind struggling to make sense of what just happened.

Sam nodded. "Yes, and who might you be?"

The stranger shook his head. "My name's not important. Don't you get it? Nothing's important now. The darkness has taken its grip over the planet. We're already entering a new ice age."

Sam shrugged. "Suit yourself. Billie, come grab our suitcase, please."

Sam, Tom and Genevieve moved closer to their hostages, so they could be sure of the shot if they had to take one.

Billie moved quickly and retrieved the metallic case. Toward the side of the room, Billie typed in the encrypted code and pressed enter. The case flipped open.

"The sacred stone's here," she said to Sam.

"Great. Make sure you seal it up again before the damned rock starts to take on mass and we lose our ability to move it."

Demyan and Anotoly entered the room.

"Did you find what you needed?" Demyan asked.

"We got it," Sam replied. "We're good to go."

"What about them?" Anotoly asked. "You can't leave them here. They'll alert the rest of the colonists."

He had a good point, but Sam wasn't about to go killing three people in cold blood, either. "Maybe we could guard them until the last pair are ready to make their ascent? Once on the winch, you said yourself, no one from the colony could reach us before we're back on board the helicopter and heading for home."

Anotoly swore and his eyes went wild. "Are you crazy?"

Before Sam could calm him, Anotoly grabbed Billie's gun. She tried to stop it, but he overpowered her. Before anyone could stop him, Anotoly fired a burst toward the three prisoners. The nine-millimeter rounds ripped through their bodies with ease.

Only the man Sam had recognized managed to get a shot off. The bullet missed Anotoly, but struck Demyan in his chest.

Sam, Tom and Genevieve moved quickly to secure the three prisoners. Two were dead, and the one who'd shot Demyan had multiple wounds to his chest that would prove fatal.

Genevieve aimed her submachine gun toward the only surviving prisoner.

Sam went to Demyan, who was clutching the side of his chest. A relatively small wound had blood pouring out of it. Sam tried to block it with part of his vest and direct pressure, but he had no misgivings about the outcome. The bullet must have ripped through a large blood vessel. Without already being in surgery, he would bleed to death within minutes.

Anotoly looked at his son. He grabbed his knife and ran toward the only surviving prisoner. "What have you done!"

Sam turned and watched Anotoly drive the knife into the prisoner's gut.

There was a small moan, as the knife went in. The prisoner was in agony. He sat rigid on the cold granite floor with his back hard upright against the sarcophagus. Tears of pain squeezed from his eyes and rolled down his once malevolent face.

"Father!" the prisoner said in a voice barely a whisper. "At last I've come to visit you in hell."

"Ilya?" Anotoly asked. "Is that really you?"

There was recognition in Ilya's eyes. "Father?"

"Ilya! I thought you'd drowned!" Anotoly hugged his son. "You killed your brother! What have I done!"

"Demyan was alive?" Ilya glanced toward Demyan, whose body was now still on the floor, with his unseeing eyes wide open.

"This is all my fault!" Anotoly said. "And it is all because of Leo Botkin!"

The name somehow aroused something inside Ilya. Sam watched him reach into his jacket pocket. Sam moved the barrel of the submachine gun closer as a warning.

"It's okay," Ilya said, removing his cell phone.

Sam glanced at the ceiling, where a series of wireless communication hubs were mounted on the ceiling.

Ilya quickly texted a few words and pressed send.

When Ilya dropped the cell phone, Sam picked it up and read the message out loud, "Botkin. We broken the casing. The stone is gaining weight and we don't know where it needs to be placed."

Anotoly looked at Sam. "Go! Get to the surface and do what you must with the sacred stone."

"What about you?"

"My life will be complete when Leo Botkin dies."

CHAPTER SIXTY-SIX

———O&3O———

Anotoly dragged both of his now dead sons together and cuddled them as he waited. There he lied still as the dead, waiting for their retribution. It wasn't long—ten minutes at most—before Leo Botkin walked into the room. He hoped Sam and the rest of his team were able to reach the winch okay and were already on their way to the surface.

Botkin glanced at the pile of wrecked and mangled bodies. He approached Ilya, quickly searching for the sacred stone. He stopped at Ilya and swore. "I should have let you drown you useless piece of shit!"

Anotoly stared at Botkin's brown eyes and lunged for his throat, digging his thumbs hard into the man's windpipe. Botkin reacted quickly, pulling his handgun and shooting him in the gut.

Anotoly heard the shots and felt the pain of three razorblades slicing through the soft tissues of his abdomen. He started to laugh. It was short, and intermingled with a blood-stained cough, but it was deep and profoundly satisfying none the less.

"What's so funny, old man?" Botkin asked.

Anotoly held the grenade hard against Botkin's chest. "This!"

Botkin tried to move, but Anotoly gripped him with the ferocity of a man who'd borne a hatred for nearly twenty years and was willing to undergo any amount of pain and suffering just to finally have revenge.

The grenade exploded.

Both men were torn to pieces as the grenade's fragments shredded them. Anotoly hit the ground, his face fixed in a permanent and sardonic grin. Botkin's face was ripped apart. One of his eyeballs, dislodged from its socket, rolled along the floor, losing its brown contact lens.

The purple eyeball finally came to rest, looking back upon what remained of its owner's lifetime worth of preparation.

CHAPTER SIXTY-SEVEN

THE FOURTH SACRED stone was placed inside the tomb beneath Sigiriya.

Over the course of the next two weeks, the magnetic poles returned to their normal position. The thermohaline circulation returned to its normal direction and the darkness dissipated from the clouds that had enshroud the earth. Some of the wealthiest men and women, once leaders of the world's largest multinational corporations, emerged from their place of hiding. Their fortunes having been decimated by an unusual sell-off of their property, cash and assets only a few weeks earlier, the natural distribution of wealth around the globe had never been so equal.

Sam Reilly watched as the darkness above finally gave way to crepuscular rays of sun. He picked up his cell phone and called the Secretary of Defense.

She answered on the first ring, without preamble. "What's the outcome?"

"It's finally over."

The Secretary said, "Not completely. I'm afraid some things have only just begun."

"Really?" Sam held a tight-lipped smile. "The asteroid's passed Earth and the ocean's thermohaline currents are flowing in the right direction again—as far as I see it, everything's just fine."

"I read your report on the mission to the temple in Tepui Mountains."

"And?"

"A Master Builder was found strung up on a stalagmite. Evidently killed by one of his own people."

"You think there's going to be a war between the remaining Master Builders?"

"Yes," she said. "The question is, who's side are we going to take?"

CHAPTER SIXTY-EIGHT

―――○℘○―――

THE SIKORSKY BLACKHAWK VH-60N VIP designated helicopter landed in the clearing, where more than a hundred marines had secured the forest. The surrounding land dipped into a shallow crater.

As the rotor blades began to wind down, the Secretary of Defense stepped out of the helicopter. A five-star General stepped up to greet her.

"Well." She said. "Did you find it?"

He grinned. "Yeah, we found it all right."

She closed her eyes and took a deep breath. "So, Leo Botkin was right all along. The meteorite did break in two, sending the second fragment of *blackbody* into a completely different part of the world."

She ran her eyes across a large, dark stone. Light appeared to be distorting near it. The stone was being lifted by a twin-engine tandem rotor Chinook helicopter.

Her eyes turned and fixed to the man in a white coat next to the General. "The trillion dollar question is, will there be enough of the usable material left?"

The scientist nodded. "Yes, ma'am."

Her tightlipped smile relaxed. "Good. Can you control the material?"

"It will take time. But I believe we can make it work for us."

"Good. No more setbacks. I want to see the Omega Project up and running within the year. Can you achieve that?"

The scientist smiled decisively. "Yes, ma'am."

THE END

Want more?

Join my email list and get a FREE and EXCLUSIVE Sam Reilly story that's not available anywhere else!

Join here ~ www.bit.ly/ChristopherCartwright

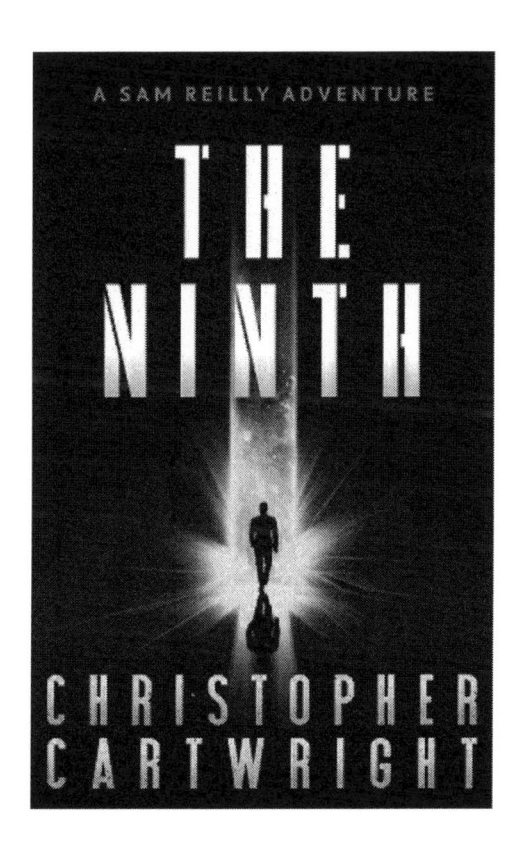

Printed in Great Britain
by Amazon